The Thing About My Uncle

PETER J. STAVROS

To Niko

The Thing About My Uncle

CHAPTER ONE

It wasn't my fault.

I told him that, more than once, a dozen times at least, but he didn't care. Mr. Smitherman didn't want to hear none of what I had to say. And I couldn't rightly blame him. After all, I did already have two strikes against me. Heck, more than that on account of "my behavior and my attitude and my shenanigans," as Mr. Smitherman called it. I would admit, I wasn't the best student at Putnam Middle School. In fact, I was probably one of the worst. Not that I was dumb. I had a vocabulary like a thesaurus on account of the crossword puzzles I worked on in class, and a keen intellect. Mama said so herself, usually when she was disappointed in me for screwing up at school, but even so.

Eighth grade just didn't hold much interest for me, like grades one through seven before it, and no doubt like the rest of the grades to follow. I didn't want to be cooped up all day in some stuffy classroom, being taught geometry or civics or whatever other nonsense they were trying to cram into our brains. I wanted to be out and about, having adventures, doing something else, anything else. I didn't have time for school. "Life's too short," Pops would preach, before he went away. There was a whole wide world waiting to experience, and I had this burning urge to get on out there and experience as much as I could. But the State said I had to stay in school until I was eighteen, and I still had four more years for that. I just had to bide my time, and do what I could, and get away with what I could until I couldn't get away with anything anymore.

I told Mr. Smitherman that it wasn't my fault, nearly pleaded with him, and that wasn't like me because it was usually much easier for me to be convincing. But I had lied to him a lot, so I could maybe understand his disinclination to believe me. Yet, this was the God's honest truth. That gun he pulled out of my backpack wasn't mine. It surely wasn't mine! It was Timbo's, of all people, my so-called best friend since kindergarten. He was showing it off to a bunch of us before class, shooting the shit out back behind the dumpster that smelled like sour milk, bragging about how he had swiped it from his old man's dresser when he was searching for his nudie mags. That son of a bitch must have slipped it into my bag when he spotted Mr. Smitherman walking in our direction, and someone must've tipped off Mr. Smitherman since everyone snitched and tattled and told on everyone at this stupid school that I didn't even want to be at anyhow. There was no honor here. But, dang, I never saw Mr. Smitherman coming. I must've had my head in the clouds, as usual. Nor did I expect what was to follow.

"Expulsion!" Mr. Smitherman shouted to me, at the top of his lungs, that one vein that ran up the side of his neck warped and crooked and purple, and I swore it was pulsing like some sort of alien earthworm. Jabbing his stubby finger in my chest—his chunky gold ring with the red ruby shimmering in the morning sun—he reeked of musty aftershave and stale cigarettes.

"How's that?" I followed, barely able to get the words out, caught completely off guard by that, convinced I had misheard him as I had a knack of doing. I didn't always listen to people when they spoke to me, especially adults, especially adults like Mr. Smitherman with his shiny bald head and that ill-fitting gray pinstripe suit and paisley bowtie he wore day in and day out: his uniform we teased behind his back. "What'd you say," I asked him, and to include some speck of respect for that asshole for once, I added, "sir?"

"You heard me, Mr. Littlefield," he answered, abrupt as if he was expecting me to say that and pounced on my words. And when he called me by my last name, I knew he was serious, that this was serious, that I was in trouble, and if I had had any doubts prior, they were long gone. "You're out of here! I'll have no more of your shenanigans!"

Shenanigans, again. That was Mr. Smitherman's favorite word. I would've laughed at him for that like I normally did—we all would've like we all normally did—but this wasn't normal. A circle of students three or four deep had formed around us the way they did whenever there was a fight or something scandalous, materializing out of nowhere with a rowdy, manic energy. A piece of me, deep inside, broke off and fell heavy into the pit of my stomach with a *kerplunk* as it finally connected: the gravity of my predicament. Mr. Smitherman's face was beet red and bloated like a balloon that was fixing to pop. The other kids "oohed" and "aahed" and whispered and murmured to one another, delighting in my demise. I just stood there, frozen. I couldn't move if I tried. It was all I could do to keep breathing. I couldn't believe this, could absolutely *not* believe this.

Perhaps I did have it coming—and for a while now—for all the other stuff I had done, all of my previous shenanigans. But not for this because this wasn't my fault—I swore it wasn't my fault! I turned to Timbo, threw my hands out palms up like, "C'mon, buddy, say something. What gives?" But he just shrugged and slinked away, disappearing into the crowd, leaving me out there empty and exposed, all alone on my own to deal with Mr. Smitherman, how he was with his entire body trembling, his hands forced stiff down at his side, both fists clenched, and that vein on the side of his neck growing bigger.

The school resource officer, Officer Smiley, who we called Cop Smiles—and he didn't seem to mind it because he did always smile and wish us a nice day and to keep out of trouble as best we could—grabbed at my arm, and it hurt. He was grim all of a sudden, which was strange to see coming from him. He had his head bowed as if to apologize for this since he couldn't verbally apologize because Mr. Smitherman was keeping a watchful eye on us, and I reckoned Mr.

Smitherman, as Vice Principal, was Cop Smiles's boss, so he had to do what he was told. And what Cop Smiles was told was to lead me off, making a hole through the circle of students who surrounded us. He took me into the building, down the empty hallway—our footsteps echoing, as class hadn't yet begun and kids waited until the very last possible moment to go inside—and into the front office where Principal Vickers was waiting with a manner that told me I was in deep. She had me sit before her in that hard, wooden chair in the front of her desk that she made all the kids who got into trouble sit in while she called Mama and broke the bad news to her, glaring at me all the while, which only added to my discomfort.

From what I could surmise from the volume of her voice that came across clear as a whistle on the other end of the receiver even while Principal Vickers held it pressed close to her ear, Mama wasn't one bit pleased about the situation either. When Principal Vickers hung up the phone, she just stared across her desk at me, wearing a smug countenance as if she had finally won. It was a long wait, the longest wait of my short life, as I sat there with Principal Vickers and Cop Smiles, straight and stiff, not even fidgeting—and I had to pee whenever I got nervous—and I waited for Mama to arrive, which she did subsequently in a huff and a panic. Principal Vickers told it to her all over again, what they claimed I had done, as if she needed to hear it again, but more likely because Principal Vickers just enjoyed saying it. And none of them still with any interest whatsoever in my version of events. Mama had to sign some official document, and Cop Smiles had to sign it too, and Principal Vickers affixed a stamp to it that she pounded into an ink pad and then pounded onto the paper with extra—and what I perceived as wholly unnecessary—vigor. Mama took me home without talking to me, not one word, without so much as a glimpse in my direction.

The next morning, I was on a Greyhound bus on my way to my uncle's house somewhere deep in the hollers of Eastern Kentucky.

The thing about my uncle was that I hardly knew him. Uncle

Theo kept to himself, some would say he was a recluse, and by all accounts, that was how he preferred it. I couldn't precisely recall when I had seen him last in the flesh. I just had a foggy recollection from when I was little, like a grainy home movie with cracks and skips and frames missing, of him being around a bunch and doing just fine and all right one moment, and then being sick, deathly ill, the next. Mama visited him in the hospital, and Grammy and Gramps came in to see him too when they were still alive. It wasn't so much a memory as it was this feeling of denseness in the atmosphere, choking and suffocating, with a heavy sense of dread, seriousness draped over everything. The sun didn't even shine as far as anyone in our family was concerned, sour and dour expressions on everyone. That was also around when Pops left, just up and out unexpectedly, never to return. There was a lot going on, and none of it any fun. It wasn't a pleasant time at our house back then.

There came a point though, when Uncle Theo got better, and he up and left too. And I never saw him since—I didn't know of anyone who had—though he kept in touch with me, here and there, now and again. I would get cards and gifts from him in the mail on occasion, for my birthday or Christmas or whatever, sometimes with a crisp twenty-dollar bill folded inside. Once, he sent a card to congratulate me for making the Little League All-Star team. I remembered that one because the front of the card had a cartoon of a dog spinning a basketball, which struck me as peculiar, and it didn't make a lick of sense given that I had made the baseball team, not the basketball team. But it could've been that Uncle Theo wasn't able to find a card that had a cartoon of a dog with a baseball bat, and so maybe that card had to do.

Regardless, it was always a treat to get cards in the mail from Uncle Theo, just him taking the effort to reach out, his way of saying hello I supposed. He must have had some inkling of what I was up to, yet I hadn't a clue how. Mama never mentioned him, and he never came back around, and since I wasn't allowed on the Internet, I couldn't hunt for him myself. It was as if Uncle Theo had just disappeared, except that he obviously hadn't, not completely, since here I was on my way to see him, on what felt like an endless bus ride with a multitude of stops in-between, from Louisville across I-64 and then over the Mountain Parkway to Prestonsburg. The plan was for Uncle Theo to meet me at the bus station there and then drive me to his house to stay, as Mama explained, until I "straightened the hell out, however goddamned long it took."

Although I didn't properly know a whole lot about my uncle, I did venture to guess that he was a millionaire and that he lived in a mansion with tall white columns and a porch that stretched clear around the house that had rocking chairs and swings, an in-ground marble swimming pool out back with two diving boards, a high dive and a low dive, and a fizzy, bubbly Jacuzzi. And his lawn was the size of a football field and expertly manicured like a putting green, and you could lie down on it and sleep like a baby on a feather bed if you desired. Off to the side, there was a two-story garage chock-full of expensive automobiles—a Rolls, a few Bentleys, Jaguars and Porsches and Maseratis—and a speed boat that he would take out on his private lake to water-ski if he wasn't in the mood to ride one of his fleet of Jet Skis. Uncle Theo ate steak every night, medium rare, with a loaded baked potato and a glass of red wine.

At least that was how I pictured him. I recalled Mama saying how Uncle Theo didn't work anymore, so I just figured he was rich like some type of millionaire, that he had to be because everyone had to work if they weren't rich. Sometimes, Mama worked three jobs, and I had a paper route until I got fired for tossing the Sunday edition onto Mr. Williams's porch and knocking over his statue of a pig that I asked him, to be a wiseass, if it was a relative. So, with Uncle Theo not having to work even one job, it stood to logical reasoning that he had to have been a millionaire who lived in a mansion and ate steak every night. And that made me feel a little bit better about where I was going, that this trip would be somewhat worthwhile for me since, if nothing else, I would be staying in a mansion. Yet, I still didn't altogether understand why I had to go and live with Uncle Theo to begin with. But as I pondered it—and I had nothing to do but ponder on this endless bus ride with a multitude of stops in-between—I couldn't fully assert that it was a surprise either. Not with the way I had been, the way I had acted toward people, and to Mama specifically.

Mama and I had been having it out a lot lately, and we really had it out last night. Although, to be clear, Mama had it out with me, and I kept quiet as a church mouse to not give her any more reason to take the wooden spatula from the kitchen drawer and beat me along the backside with it. Mama was angry all right, the angriest I'd seen her. And sorry to say that I've made her plenty angry in the past. She yelled that she was "fed up, Rhett!" with her voice sharp and shrill and that liked to rattle the windows. "Fed up to *here!*" She motioned high above her head to indicate exactly how fed up she was, which was the most fed up I've ever made her as far as I was aware and was apparently more than she could take. Mama carried on such that she made Ella Mae, my four-years-younger little sister, cry, and Mama had to take a break from yelling at me to tend to her. But then once Ella Mae had settled down, Mama came right back at it with me.

At the end of her tirade—though I would have never dared to tell it to Mama that I considered she was having a tirade—Mama proclaimed, as she pulled herself together, breathing in through her nose and out through her mouth and pushing her hair from her face and resuming to using her inside voice, that she had arrived at the conclusion that the best solution was to get me out of the house after my "latest stunt." She called Uncle Theo—and that was the first ever I'd heard her call Uncle Theo—and went on and on and on with him about how fed up she was with me and how badly I'd been behaving, and a whole host of other stuff as Mama was quite the talker. She said something to Uncle Theo about how "you need to see what you caused" which seemed like an odd thing to tell him, but I wasn't about to question Mama about it, not with how she was. Then, she sent me straight off to my room without dinner—and it was tuna mac night, my favorite—and instructed me to pack a bag, changes of clothes, clean underwear and such, my toothbrush and comb, and the Bible because she said it was high time I commenced to reading that. And the next morning, here I was on a Greyhound bus on my way to my uncle's house somewhere deep in the hollers of Eastern Kentucky.

The bus was nearly full, nary an empty seat, which surprised me, as I wouldn't have guessed there would be many folks inclined to travel to these parts. Across the aisle sat an elderly woman flipping through a worn copy of *The Saturday Evening Post*, her hair in tight curls with a pale-bluish tint and letting off a fragrance of flowery perfume and mothballs. I caught her looking at me, and she said I had sad eyes. When we were just outside of Frankfort, she reached over with a greasy paper bag of home-baked chocolate chip cookies. She shook the bag in my direction and whispered with a reassuring smile—and one of her teeth, on the top row toward the back, was silver—for me to take one cookie for now and one to save for later, which I gladly did. Although when she dozed and began to snore, I ate them both on account of, aside from missing dinner, I hadn't had breakfast this morning either and I was fairly hungry.

The bus ride was tedious and boring, with not a lot to see, only anonymous stretches of highway under an overcast sky. When we got past Winchester and veered onto the Mountain Parkway, the view was slightly more scenic, with dense emerald foliage and a gradually building mountain landscape, like pine-covered walls in the horizon. I spotted a fawn gingerly traipsing through the brush on spindly legs to catch up with its family, as the foothills of the Appalachians began to rise on all sides. I felt my eyelids grow heavy, having not gotten much sleep last night from tossing and turning and being concerned for my quandary. But whenever I was just about to drift off, a coal truck would rumble by, belching out billows of black dust. I finally managed to nod off to the vibration of the bus and the monotonous humming of its engine, my head resting against the window, my jacket balled up as a pillow.

I had a weird dream where I was playing ball out in the backyard with Pops, and I hardly ever dreamed about Pops anymore. It was just him and me, tossing a baseball back and forth, Pops telling me to zing it in to him, to not hold back, to really let it fly. And I did, and I did, with the ball landing with a *smack,* flush into his mitt, and Pops grabbing it and lobbing it back to me. He kept yelling at me to go harder, to let him have it. The dream was so real that it was as if I was living it. My heartbeat increased and beads of perspiration gathered on my forehead as I threw the baseball at Pops as hard as I could, but not as hard as Pops wanted me to. I was giving it everything I had, but it was never good enough for Pops, no matter how I tried. This went on for what seemed like forever, tossing the ball back and forth like that, when off in the horizon, right beyond Pops, a storm cloud formed, dark and menacing with jagged streaks of electric lightning. It rolled in, but Pops told me to pay it no mind, to keep throwing the baseball at him as hard as I could, which I did—or at least I tried to—while the storm cloud got closer and closer and the wind picked up. It started to rain, blinding sheets of rain that drenched us and made it so that I could hardly make out anything in front of my face. But I kept throwing the ball all the same, with every ounce of my effort, an exertion I hadn't known, until a clap of thunder like a shotgun blast rang out in my dream and jolted me back to consciousness with the bus grinding to a halt at our destination—the bus station in Prestonsburg—an exhale from the exhaust like a last gasp.

I gathered myself and my belongings, and I joined the other passengers as we patiently filed off. I let that elderly lady with the blue hair from across the aisle go ahead since Mama had taught me that stuff like that—being polite and whatnot—was the gentlemanly thing to do, and I was a gentleman after all, despite my shenanigans. I followed her out and then stepped to the side to wait for the bus driver to pull everyone's suitcases from the luggage compartment at the bottom. My bag was the last to be freed, and when the bus driver tossed it to me, it had been scrunched and smooshed, but it was none the worse for wear, sort of like me. I slung it over my shoulder, thanked that elderly lady again for the chocolate chip cookies, not revealing that I had eaten them both at once contrary to her wishes, and wandered around to the other side of the bus with no inclination where I needed to go or what I needed to do.

That was when I saw him, standing over yonder in the parking lot, leaned against this beaten up and dented and rusted-out green-and-white pickup truck, yet the tires appeared to be brand new, for some odd reason, which didn't seem to fit in with the rest of the vehicle. It was my uncle. It had to be him, looking mostly the same as he did in the photograph Mama had given me this morning, which I pulled out of my pocket, now crinkled and creased, to compare it nonetheless to the person I was gawking at. He was older, and somewhat haggard, and heavier. Not so much a fat-heavy but a muscular-heavy, with an extra-large torso and a thickset waist. It was him. It had to be him. Even so, just to be certain, I called out, "Uncle Theo?"

"Come on, boy." He flung his hand out like he was disgusted with something. "Don't just stand there, deer in the headlights. We gotta get a move on." Then he got into his truck.

That was him, all right. I nodded and hurried across the street as quickly as I could, almost tripping over my feet. My uncle had this presence—some attitude he conveyed, this air about him—that told me I had best do what he said, and posthaste. I hustled over to where he was and yanked open the weighty front door, the hinges screeching as if in mortal pain and they might snap, and climbed up into the truck cab, my bag on my lap. Uncle Theo turned the ignition, and the motor shuttered to life with a cough and a sputter, and we drove off with a jerk and a spurt. I was both excited and nervous, my belly overrun by a swarm of agitated butterflies. But I was also eager to get this adventure underway.

Uncle Theo wasn't much of a talker. In fact, he barely spoke. He just drove, eyes forward, his left hand high on the steering wheel, and his right hand nursing something out of an insulated travel mug that he would put to his mouth and take a swig from, going about his business as if I wasn't even sitting next to him. He could've been driving by his lonesome for how he was. I could've been invisible, nonexistent. I stared straight ahead, as well, while the truck bounced along on these uneven, potholed backcountry roads. Every so often, I'd sneak a peek over at him whenever I had the chance, whenever I could do it such that he wouldn't notice, so as not to make it obvious, to see what I could gather about this man.

My initial impression of Uncle Theo was that he was hairy, a very hairy individual with wild sprigs of hair flipping out from under his sweat-stained ball cap and a bushy, unkempt beard, gray around his mouth and on his chin and brownish everywhere else. He had broad shoulders and solid arms like he might've played football in high school, maybe even college. He wore a red-and-black checkered flannel shirt with the sleeves rolled up to his elbows to expose a veritable cornucopia of tattoos covering both his forearms. Every sort of tattoo imaginable it seemed: nothing continuous, just random designs and lettering. I could make out a feather and a cross and something written in cursive but couldn't tell what all else during my sporadic glances. His jeans were worn with ragged holes in the knees, like he had actually torn them and not like the trendy torn jeans the popular girls at school wore that were already torn when they bought them, and his hiking boots were coated in dried mud. He smelled like a campfire.

"What'd exactly you do again to make your mother so mad at you?" Uncle Theo ultimately broke the silence I had gotten used to so much that the sound of his voice, which was deep and firm as if emitting directly from his gut, caused me to flinch in surprise.

"Got kicked out of school," I answered, sheepish, still staring straight ahead as the road grew narrower.

"That'll do it." He snorted a laugh, and under his breath, I heard him say, "My sister."

We didn't interact any more after that on our drive. I just sat there and looked out the window, attempting to figure out where we were. We passed through a few small towns that the signs on the sides of the road said were called Gross Sandy Creek and Birchmont Village and Cole's Landing, and we took some turns and some twists. After a while, there was hardly anything around resembling civilization: some trailers, and cars on blocks, and barns in the distance, crumbling into various stages of disrepair. Sometimes, we would come to a blinking red light at an empty intersection that seemed to have cropped up out in the middle of nowhere without any rhyme or reason.

We drove like that, it being otherwise silent except for the rattling of the truck, for roughly forty-five minutes in my estimation before Uncle Theo pulled onto a dirt path through a rusty gate, lazily swinging open in the breeze. He drove right smack dab into what seemed like the heart of the woods, the trees full and spread, curving up above us to create a canopy as if we were traveling through a tunnel, blocking out what light there was. I thought to myself how if this old truck broke down now, we'd be trapped out here, and no one would ever be able to find us. That caused my body to tense up, and I just held my breath and clenched tight to my bag, hoping that we would get to where we were going in one piece. And sure enough, after a ways, we did. The woods miraculously parted, and we came upon a holler sunken into this little gap between the hills. Up ahead, I could make out a house, and not a very big house at that. Certainly no mansion. But it was the only house around. I glanced over at Uncle Theo, concerned that we might be lost, but he acted like he knew what he was doing as we continued on in the direction of that house and onto a lengthy gravel driveway that ran beside it. He eased the truck into park with a squeal and cut the engine.

"This it?" I asked, gaping out at the house and then turning to my uncle.

"Mm-hmm," he replied as he exited the truck.

"Thought you lived in a mansion," I said.

Uncle Theo stopped and peered back inside at me.

"A mansion?" He snickered. "Yeah, bud. Welcome to my mansion."

Uncle Theo slammed the door shut and ambled on up to the house. I waited a second, just to make sure, about anything. Then I jumped out of the truck and ran to catch up with him.

ও

Uncle Theo's house wasn't a bad house. Not completely, I reckoned, as far as houses went. Four walls and a roof, and that was about that. It just wasn't what I had grown to expect, not if Uncle Theo was so rich that he didn't have to work, my imagination getting the better of me yet again. It was a plain, ordinary, average house: square for the most part, a smidge off-kilter on the foundation, one floor from what I could ascertain from the outside, wood painted white that was chipped and peeling and could use a decent pressure washing to remove the crusty sage mold, a couple of the black shutters just clinging on, a red brick chimney missing some of its red bricks. There were no tall columns, no wrap around porch, but it had a stoop with a broken flowerpot absent any flowers, not unless dandelions were considered flowers. I didn't need to peruse any further to assume there wasn't a swimming pool out back nor a garage chock-full of expensive cars. The yard, however, was big, though not well-maintained, and the grass probably hadn't been cut in weeks, with stray clumps of weeds throughout and meandering splotches of brown patches and divots. Most definitely not putting-green quality.

Uncle Theo's house wasn't much bigger than the house we had in Louisville. And actually, as I continued to scrutinize it, I'd venture that it was smaller than our house. That was when it dawned on me, as I tried to accept what was to be my new home for the foreseeable future, that when Mama said she was sending me here until I "straightened the hell out," she had really just sent me here to punish me, forcing me to live in Uncle Theo's sad house to get back at me for my "latest stunt" and the rest of my shenanigans. If that were true, then Mama was more shrewd than I gave her credit for being, because it was certainly working. I was already feeling terrible for everything I had done—and for a few things I hadn't—and for all that I had put Mama through, and I was missing home something awful. I sighed, and I gulped, and I surrendered myself to the disheartening notion that this was the hand I was dealt. I had no other option than to do what I could to get through this as I plodded up the cracked concrete sidewalk.

No sooner was I about to take one foot onto the stoop as Uncle Theo pushed opened the front door with a jiggle of his key, when this beastly creature, a blur of teeth and fur, came charging out of the house, its eyes wild, its fangs exposed and dripping with saliva. It was a dog, I presumed, but it wouldn't have surprised me if it was a wolf, and it most assuredly had to have had some percentage of wolf in its DNA. This dog was like one of those hounds of hell from the comic books I read in class—jet black, with pointy ears and sharpened claws—and weighing well over one-hundred pounds, it had to be. It was causing quite a ruckus, barking and snarling and all that, and it was headed forthwith at me!

I dropped my bag, pivoted, and hightailed it back to Uncle Theo's truck. I was never the fastest kid in my grade, usually ended up somewhere in the middle of the pack whenever we had to run laps for PE class, but I became an Olympic sprinter at that moment. I ran like my life depended on it, and sadly, it probably did. I ran like there was no tomorrow, and if I didn't make it to Uncle Theo's truck before that dog got to me, there surely wasn't. I didn't bother trying to pull open the door to the cab. I just jumped headfirst into the truck bed, landing with a thud and a crash onto what felt like gardening tools, which pained me, but not nearly as bad as what that dog might do.

I lay there like that, on my back, shivering I was so afraid, staring up at the early evening sky as the sun—a burnt orange poking through the stubborn gunmetal clouds—was fixing to set and close out this day that still wasn't anywhere close to ending for me, waiting for that dog to leave me be, praying that it would, that maybe it would get bored or just give up. But no chance for that as it growled and roared, its meaty paws hitting and scraping against the rear fenders. I could hear my pulse pounding in my ears, could feel it in my fingertips. I was convinced that I was a goner, that that was it for me, that I was done for and it was over. I would never see Mama again. I would never even make it inside Uncle Theo's sad house to find out how truly sad it was. The only thing I knew to do was to lie there like that and pray for this to pass. I closed my eyes tight, and I prayed.

"What are you doing?" asked a voice from above.

I opened my eyes, thinking that for once it might be God, to find instead Uncle Theo staring down at me, hunched over the truck bed, his arms leaned up against it, and I noticed some more tattoos on him: a typewriter and a shark and some scribbled words.

"Huh?" was all I could muster.

"What are you doing in the back of my truck?" Uncle Theo repeated. "Aren't you coming into the house?"

"Yeah, but…" I didn't know what to say, what there was to say, how did this need any explanation with that wolf dog or whatever still behaving as if it wanted to tear me limb from limb?

"Oh," Uncle Theo said, nonchalant, as if only then did he understand my concern. "Chekhov."

"Chekhov?"

"Chekhov. My attack dog. You don't like dogs?"

"I like dogs just fine," I answered, "but this one…this dog's gonna kill me."

"She's not gonna kill you," he dismissed. "She just needs to get to know you. Now, c'mon. We don't have all day."

I thought Uncle Theo was kidding. He had to be kidding. Either that or he was as plumb-crazy as his devil dog. But as I lay there, with him looking at me incredulously, I had a sinking feeling that he meant it. And when he slammed his hand against the side of the truck, the dull metallic thud reverberating inside the bed, there was no doubting that he meant it. So carefully, cautiously, highly reluctantly, such that I had to practically force my body to move, I sat up as the dog was unrelenting in her woofing, not letting up one iota and, if anything, she had gotten louder with a boundless intensity. I wondered how this beast was supposed to get to know me, but Uncle Theo didn't strike me as someone who was going to take no for an answer on this or on much of anything. Against my better judgment, I scooted myself over to the side of the truck bed, and I peeked down at the dog, who was crouched and ready to strike, every canine in her oversized mouth showing.

"Um…hey, girl," I offered up weakly, and it sounded pathetic as I said it. "I'm Rhett. Nice to meet ya."

My forced and stilted introduction did nothing to settle this animal, but rather seemed to further infuriate her as she leaped against the truck. Uncle Theo did nothing to stop this. He just stood by and watched this play out, a sly grin sneaking across his face for some reason.

"With more effort," he coaxed me, "like you really mean it. This dog can see right through a bullshitter."

I took a deep breath and a heavy exhale and tried not to show Uncle Theo that I was shaking like a leaf, and I said, with more effort and a smile to help convince the dog that I was okay, "Hi there, Chekhov. I'm Rhett. I'm a good boy."

That made Chekhov particularly upset, and she let loose with a wail that sent shock waves rippling throughout my body.

"You don't bare your teeth like that to an attack dog," Uncle Theo scolded me. "Don't you know anything?"

I didn't know anything, at least not when it came to attack dogs, and I shook my head to convey this to my uncle.

"I don't have time for this," Uncle Theo muttered as he went around to the back, released the tailgate, and, to my absolute horror, led that monster up into the truck bed, his hand on the dog's collar to control her, but even so.

Out of reflex, I darted in the opposite direction, slamming myself against the back of the cab. Undaunted, Uncle Theo brought the dog farther in, holding her face mere inches from mine, close enough that I could smell her hot breath, and it smelled like she had just eaten something rotten with a side of dirty socks and garbage.

"Chekhov," Uncle Theo demanded of the dog, still with a tight grip on her, "this here's Rhett. He's family, and you need to treat him as such."

Those few words, or more likely Uncle Theo's forceful tone, had a noticeably calming effect on Chekhov. She instantly ceased the barking and growling and all of that carrying on, and let out a little whimper, nothing I would have expected from a dog that fierce. Then she sniffed in my direction, her big dark eyes fixed on me.

Uncle Theo told me to "go ahead and give her your hand."

"What?" I asked, alert, certain that if I gave that dog my hand, I wouldn't get it back.

"So she can sniff you," Uncle Theo said like it was obvious.

"Um, huh?" I asked, and when Uncle Theo didn't say anything, I stuttered, "All right," as I again knew that my uncle wasn't going to take no for an answer on this either. I warily held my quivering hand in the dog's direction, diverting my eyes so as not to witness the carnage that was undoubtedly to follow. But to my surprise, and abundant relief, the dog didn't take my hand off. She just licked it, wet and sloppy, and followed with a similar lick about my face from cheek to cheek and even on my mouth, which was gross, but I had to let her do what she wanted. Her breath was still horrible, so horrible that it made me want to giggle. And without giving it a second thought, I reached out and put both of my hands around the dog's enormous head and rubbed her behind her pointy ears as she kept on licking me. I had always wanted a dog when I was growing up, and in that instant, I realized why.

"Okay," Uncle Theo said bluntly to break things up, "enough with this lovefest." And to the dog, "C'mon, girl. Let's eat."

Uncle Theo hopped out of the truck, Chekhov bounding off with him, and they returned to the house. I saw that Uncle Theo walked with a bit of a limp as his dog trotted on ahead and waited for him on the stoop, tail wagging. When Uncle Theo got to the front door, he turned around to where I was, still in the back of the truck.

"Aren't you coming in the house?" he hollered to me.

"Yeah, I'm coming," I replied, not even bothering to try and come to terms with what had just happened.

I jumped out of the truck, grabbed my bag, and ran into the house.

❧

"So why Chekhov?" I asked Uncle Theo, between bites of dinner, some kind of mystery meat, with mashed potatoes, and green beans with bacon, and yeast rolls, and a glass of milk for me even though I would have rather had a can of pop or, better yet, a cold beer like Uncle Theo was drinking.

"Huh?" Uncle Theo said like he didn't understand the question.

"Chekhov," I went on. "Why'd you name your dog Chekhov?"

"Why not Chekhov?" Uncle Theo asked me back as he stood and put a second heaping helping of everything on my plate. "It's as good a name as any, don't you think?"

"Yeah, guess so." I paused to think. "But what's it mean?"

Uncle Theo stopped, remained completely still while holding a pot of mashed potatoes, serving spoon in hand, and looked at me like I was plain nuts.

"You really don't keep up with your schoolwork, huh?" he said to me, and I just stared back at him. "Anton Pavlovich Chekhov was one of the greatest writers of all time: plays, short stories, you name it. Are you telling me you've never heard of Chekhov?"

I shook my head no, and I hadn't. I didn't even remember if we'd been taught about him in English class, and if we had, I wasn't paying any attention, as usual.

"Guess I've got my work cut out for me." Uncle Theo sighed and returned the pot to the stove, and then joined me back at the table, Chekhov—the dog and not the greatest writer of all time—at his feet begging for table scraps.

"What work?" I inquired of him as I considered what he had just said.

"To get you up to speed on your studies," he answered, "so they'll let you back into school, and you can get out of here, and I can get on with my life. So that we both can get on with our lives."

I still wasn't totally sure what Uncle Theo had in mind, until he motioned with his fork between his fingers down at the other end of the table to a large cardboard box.

"Your studies," he said. "It's all there: your books, assignments, all of it. It came in right before you did. Your mother sent it. Along with some notebooks, pencils, whatnot." He waited for my reaction, which was no reaction. "You didn't think you were here on vacation, did you? Hanging out at my *mansion* just lounging around, eating my food, taking up my time." He wagged his fork at me. "Oh no, no, no. You're here so I can straighten you out."

I waited for some indication, some sign that Uncle Theo was joking: an upturn to his mouth, a twinkle in his eyes. But nothing. And Uncle Theo didn't seem like he was one for joking anyhow. Hearing that, and grasping that, made my entire being deflate.

"It's life, buddy," he told me. "Best get used to it."

We finished our meal without saying anything else, just utensils clinking against plates, chews and swallows, Chekhov begging for table scraps, a clock on the wall steadily ticking the seconds away. It wasn't bad enough that I had to stay at Uncle Theo's sad house, with him hardly wanting to have anything to do with me, but then learning that he was going to make me keep up with my studies to boot. I didn't keep up with my studies when I was at school, and now that I'd been kicked out of school, I had to study? If this was life, then it wasn't fair, and it didn't make much sense.

"You done?" Uncle Theo asked when he noticed my empty plate.

"Uh-huh," I answered, my belly full, my spirit broken. "What was that mystery meat anyway?" I asked him.

"Venison," he replied, finishing his food, then wiping his mouth with a paper napkin and tossing it onto his empty plate.

"What's venison?"

Uncle Theo chuckled. "You really don't know much about anything."

"Never had venison," I told him, and it was true. "Mama mostly makes us spaghetti or chili or her tuna mac."

"Venison," he said, pausing to take a last gulp of his beer, "is deer meat."

"Deer meat?" I questioned as my stomach churned. "You mean like Bambi?"

Uncle Theo exhaled, and I couldn't tell if I was amusing him or aggravating him.

"*Bambi* was a cartoon," he told me, rising from the table and taking his plate and glass into the kitchen. "Venison is the lean, nutrient-rich meat of the deer. It's good for you. And judging from how scrawny you are, you're in no position to be turning down a meal."

I reckoned he had a point there, and it was tasty, just so long as I didn't think about it being deer meat, and I wished I didn't know that. But this only raised more questions for me.

"Where'd you get the deer meat?" I asked Uncle Theo at the risk of either amusing him or aggravating him further. "Do you hunt? I saw that shotgun over the mantel."

"Sure are inquisitive," he said, sort of just to himself rather than directly to me as he ran the water in the sink. When he shut the faucet off, he turned back around and pointed across the room—as this house was really just one big open room divided up by the sparse furnishings—to the opposite wall where the shotgun hung. "And don't go messing with that shotgun. It's no toy." Then he added, "I don't want to find it in your backpack."

That last comment struck me as a low blow, and it hurt. Mama must have told him about Timbo's gun, even if it wasn't my fault that it ended up in my backpack. I didn't have a response, just slumped my shoulders and lowered my head, an automatic reaction. The mood swiftly shifted to awkward, and I sensed that even Uncle Theo seemed to get that he had gone a little too far. When I looked back up over at him, he had retreated and softened as if he felt bad for saying that.

"Anyways," he picked back up, more measured, and turned around to the sink, "the venison is from one of my neighbors."

"Neighbors?" I had trouble believing that. "What neighbors? I didn't see any other houses anywhere near here when we were driving in."

"I got neighbors," Uncle Theo snapped, returning to his surly self, and that strangely put me at ease. "Don't you worry about that. You might not've seen them, but they're around. We keep an eye out for each other. They bring me what they might've gotten in a hunt, and I give them something from my garden."

"You got a garden?"

"Out back." And just as I was about to ask Uncle Theo something else, he cut me off. "Now, enough with the cross-examination. Bring your plate over. I want you to do these dishes."

"I don't do dishes," I said, and as soon as I said that, and before Uncle Theo gave me a scowl, I knew I had said the wrong thing.

"Well, here in my house, my *mansion*, you do the dishes. Capeesh?"

I didn't know what "capeesh" meant, only that it meant that I had to do the dishes.

Uncle Theo tossed a sponge at me that I caught against my chest, getting the front of my shirt wet. Under his breath, he complained, "I don't have time for this," as he walked away.

I stood at the sink, examining what I had before me, contemplating where to begin, before proceeding to do the dishes, squeezing soap out on the sponge, and moving it around the plates and the glasses and the silverware, then rinsing, and setting them on this rubber mat to dry. Chekhov was beside me, watching as if inspecting my work. I half-expected her to unleash a torrent of barks and growls and howls if I messed up. Once I was finished, I returned to the table where Uncle Theo had emptied the textbooks and composition notebooks and pens and papers and whatnot from that box.

"You're gonna have a schedule," Uncle Theo announced, "just like you were still in school." He looked at me. "What time do you normally start class?"

"First period's at, um…eight." I was hesitant, briefly considered telling Uncle Theo that it started at ten or eleven so I could sleep in, but I already knew better than to lie to him.

"All right, then," he said. "So at eight, you start studying here, at this table. And you go from subject to subject. First period, second period, and so on and so forth. How long are your classes? About an hour each I would suppose."

I just nodded slowly. I wasn't thrilled about any of this.

"An hour on math class, an hour on English, an hour on history, all of it." He ruffled through a stack of papers. "We got lesson plans, study notes, everything. No excuses."

I could've thought of a million excuses.

"You'll get breaks too, like you do in school," he continued, "for lunch, recess. And some physical fitness training, as scrawny as you are. But it's a schedule you'll have to follow. A regimen. A routine. It'll be good for you. It's good for all of us. You'll see."

I just nodded again. And I was feeling low about this, down in the dumps, and nowhere as confident as Uncle Theo seemed to be. And I guessed maybe he saw that.

"It'll be all right, bud," he adjusted his tone, an attempt to console me as best he could, as I doubted he'd had occasion to do much of that, and he put his large hand on my shoulder. "We'll get through this."

All I could do was nod and stare down at the floor, at the scuffed hardwood and Uncle Theo's muddy hiking boots. It got quiet, with Uncle Theo's gaze on me and the steady ticking of the clock on the wall. Perhaps Chekhov could tell I was let down too, for she nuzzled against my leg to let me pet her, and that kind of helped.

"All right, well…it's been a long day for you, I imagine," Uncle Theo spoke up. "I'll show you to your room, and you can unpack, get settled in, and turn in early. I'm sure you're beat."

"Yeah," I swallowed hard over the lump in my throat. "I'm beat."

Uncle Theo paused like he had something else he wanted to say. But instead, he got up from the table to walk me down the narrow hallway on the right to take me to my room. Before he could get away, however, I reached out without even thinking about it, because had I thought about it, I probably wouldn't have gone through with it, and I tugged at his shirt. He stopped.

"Thank you, Uncle Theo," I said, and I meant it.

"Oh, um…" He stammered like that caught him by surprise. "Um, yeah, sure. Sure thing, bud, um…Rhett." He patted me on the back, stilted but sincere. "It'll be all right. You'll see. We'll figure this out."

"Okay," I said, as Uncle Theo resumed walking, and I followed him to my room.

❧

That night, I had trouble sleeping. I nodded off fast enough from what an exhausting and draining day it had been, but by three in the morning, I was wide awake. I just kept thinking about everything and nothing, about how quickly our lives can change, how one little incident can send everything spinning.

I lay there in bed, wondering what Mama was doing right then, and Ella Mae. If they were both in their beds, if they were asleep—probably so—and what they had eaten for dinner: leftovers of Mama's tuna mac, no doubt, because she always made enough to feed us for a week. Uncle Theo's deer meat was okay, and he wasn't a bad cook himself, but nothing could compare to Mama's tuna mac. I wondered if Mama was still angry at me. I hoped that she wasn't, but I could understand if she was. I was going to do right by her. I was determined to. I should've never let Mama down like that.

I thought about my buddies from school, even Timbo, even though he was the one who got me into this mess. Although, as I considered it, not really. I had done this to myself, that much I could accept. But still, sneaking his dad's gun into my backpack? What a jerk move. I wondered if my buddies missed not having me at school with them. I wondered what kind of trouble they got into today, what kind of trouble they'd be getting into tomorrow and all the other days when I wasn't there. I wondered what they would do without me.

I thought about Mr. Smitherman too, if he would miss me, although unlikely, but who knew. And Principal Vickers and Cop Smiles and my teachers. Would they even notice I was gone? I ditched class so much they would probably just think I was ditching class once more. They would go on without me like they always did, I was sure of that. School would go on without me. My whole world, or what used to be my whole world, would go on without me as if I had never been there. Thinking that way, thinking about it like that, left me hollowed out and empty inside, and I didn't much care for that sort of feeling.

I wondered what would become of me, how long I would have to stay here in Uncle Theo's sad house, when I would get to go home and be back in my bedroom with my bed and my pillow and sheets and my posters on the walls and my books on the shelves and my clothes in a pile on the floor that Mama always yelled at me to pick up. I swore that if I got to go back home, I would never leave my clothes in a pile on the floor anymore. I was done letting Mama down.

I rubbed at my eyes to keep the stubborn tears from escaping, and I sniffed in, and I glanced about this room to take my mind off all the things that were bothering me. It wasn't a bad bedroom. It wasn't my bedroom, but it wasn't bad. The bed was firm enough, comfortable for the most part. I could put my clothes in the dresser, and there was a nightstand where I kept a framed picture of me and Mama and Ella Mae that I sneaked from the table in the living room on my way out this morning. And directly above me on the ceiling, there was a galaxy of star stickers that glowed in the dark like some distant constellation. I wondered if those were already there, or if Uncle Theo had put them up there just for me.

I guessed he wasn't such a bad guy. And we were family, like he told Chekhov. I just wasn't sure what his deal was, who he really was, why he didn't have to work if he wasn't rich, and he sure didn't seem like he was rich. I wondered if I really annoyed him, if I really aggravated him with me showing up here and disrupting his routine, his regimen, or if he didn't really care one way or the other, if he just thought of me as amusing. I wondered if he would care once I left and went back home, whenever it was I got to leave and go back home. Hopefully soon.

I thought about how maybe I would eventually figure Uncle Theo out, and maybe I would eventually figure all of this out. Maybe. I prayed to God that I would, because Mama always told me that if I had a problem that I couldn't do any more about on my own, that I had best just pray to God and put the problem in his hands to take care of. And that was what I did as I lay there in this strange bed, in this sad house, and thought about everything and nothing, and tried to get back to sleep.

CHAPTER TWO

The next morning, I was awoken by the light shining in my eyes and something warm and wet against my face. I sighed, or groaned, and covered my eyes and brushed aside whatever was dripping on my cheek. I wasn't ready to get up, suspended in this middle ground of consciousness, not sure where I was, what bed I was in, which bedroom, which house. It had been a rough day the day before, and a difficult night. I just wanted to stay in bed.

I went to roll over, and when I did, I hit my hand upon something solid and furry. Before I could react, a blaring yelp pierced what had been the calm and stillness. I snapped my eyes opened wide, jerked my head, and there was Chekhov, this brute of a dog, standing by the bed, practically hovering over me as tall as she was. She let loose with a second yelp, equally as disarming. I bolted upright, knocking the metal headboard against the plaster wall with a smash and a rattle.

I feared that, overnight, Chekhov had forgotten who I was, that I was family as Uncle Theo had said, and she had reverted to attack dog mode. My heart revved up, beating like a Derby contender, and I held my arms out, a feeble attempt to keep her at bay; as if that would do any good against this beast. Then, I did the only other thing I could think of. I called for help.

"Uncle Theo! Uncle Theo!" I yelled. "Come get your dog. Uncle Theo! Help me! Help!"

There was no response, no movement in any other part of this small, sad house, no urgent rushing along the hardwood to come to my rescue, no creaking of floorboards. Nothing. Dead silence. I repeated my call, but still nothing. And once more, and again, and still only dead silence, with the operative word being "dead" because I was certain to be dead if Chekhov attacked me. I slipped into a panic, this behemoth of an animal about to eat me whole if I didn't do something to defend myself. But what could I do? I looked about, searching for something, anything, any way to defend myself. But nothing. What could I do? How was I going to get out of this? What had I gotten myself into? Why had Mama sent me here? Did she hate me that much?

All these questions ran rampant through my head, with none of them of any help. Was this it for me? Was this how it was going to end? I resolved that maybe this was it for me and this was how it was going to end, when I glimpsed over at Chekhov, preparing myself for whatever she was about to do. She was just staring at me, her enormous head tilted to the side like she was as confused about this situation as I was. Then, she offered a gentle whimper and moved closer, non-threatening, and nudged against my arm, her big, dark eyes fixed on me. Chekhov just leaned up against me like that, not wanting to eat me but just wanting to be near me. My pulse gradually returned closer to normal, and my body more or less relaxed, and it dawned on me that maybe Chekhov was only here to wake me, my hundred-pound living, breathing, furry alarm clock.

"Is that it, girl?" I asked her, my voice wavering, timidly reaching for her, and when she didn't resist but seemed to welcome it, I scratched her behind her pointy ears. "Are you just here to wake me?"

Chekhov replied with one more yelp as if she understood, and she probably did because she seemed like a smart dog, and I doubted Uncle Theo would have a dumb dog. She nudged against my arm a tad more forcefully, her way, I guessed, to let me know that it was time to get moving already. Lest there be any doubt—and it seemed that Chekhov ran out of patience as quickly as my uncle—she bit down at the covers, clasped in her sharp incisors, and shook her head to yank them off me.

"Okay, Chekhov, I'm going," I said, rubbing the sleep out of my eyes without pausing to really consider how different it was to be woken up by a gigantic dog and not by Mama, but such was my life now.

I pulled myself out of bed, this leg, then that leg, and stood to acclimate to my new surroundings, fully revealed in the brilliant early morning sunlight that was streaming in because, as I was just now discovering since I hadn't paid attention to it last night, there was no curtain on the window, something I suspected Uncle Theo had intended so that I couldn't sleep in. As if a massive dog wasn't enough to get me up. I also noticed as I looked outside across the yard, fifty yards or so behind the house, a weathered wooden barn with the door slid open. I could make out Uncle Theo in there exercising with weights, an entire collection from what I could tell: barbells and dumbbells and various machines in his own home gym.

Chekhov barked to keep me from loitering at the window, as I must not have been moving fast enough for her liking.

"Okay, okay, I'm going," I told her.

Chekhov trotted off in front, glancing back every few steps to confirm that I was still with her as I followed her out of the bedroom, down the short hallway, and into the kitchen. I was instantly, and delightfully, greeted by the delectable aroma of crispy bacon and scrambled eggs and home fried potatoes. It was a wonderful surprise, and particularly good with how harshly I had been roused from bed; mostly my own making, my imagination getting the better of me, but still. The one complaint I had, as I admired this spread, was that I could have also used a steaming cup of coffee, but Uncle Theo had only brewed enough for himself. Maybe I would put in a request for coffee for tomorrow, though I wouldn't want to press my luck.

All the same, this breakfast was most appreciated. Back home, I normally only had time for an overripe banana or a cold Pop-Tart, as I was always in a rush to catch the bus. Uncle Theo had everything neatly arranged on the plate for me, rounded out with wheat toast and strawberry jam, tomato slices, and orange wedges. Chekhov barked to pull me from my food trance, and that was when I spied some extra strips of bacon wrapped in a greasy paper towel on the counter that must have been for her. When she realized that I had seen this, she barked with an urgency to confirm that that was indeed her breakfast, and perhaps also her reward for doing her job and getting me up.

"Oh, yeah, right," I said as I took the hint, and fed the bacon to her, which she gobbled down in two seconds, leaving my fingers drenched with her saliva but otherwise still attached to my hand. Chekhov barked a final time for good measure, probably her way of saying "See ya later," then spun around and charged out the partially opened kitchen door, across the backyard, and into the barn to meet up with Uncle Theo.

I grabbed my plate and the glass of milk that Uncle Theo had poured for me, and I took these inside to the table where my textbooks were lined up in the order of my classes. Atop each book was the lesson plan for the day. I shook my head. Reality had set in. I glanced over at the clock on the wall with its steady ticking, and it was eight o'clock on the dot. Uncle Theo and his schedule.

My first class was English Composition, and my assignment was to write a three-hundred word essay on something I was grateful for. I ruminated on that as I shoveled eggs and bacon and potatoes into my mouth like I hadn't eaten in days. I had to admit, Uncle Theo wasn't a bad cook, and I would dare to acknowledge that he was a pretty danged-good cook. I was grateful for that.

I took a gulp of milk, then picked up a pencil and a notebook, but as I flipped through the pages, I found that there was already something written inside. I just assumed that Uncle Theo might have been thrifty—which wouldn't have surprised me given the looks of this place—and had gotten me a used notebook, until the writing struck me as familiar. Upon closer inspection, I recognized this writing, the way the i's were dotted and the t's were crossed, and there was my name, with the swooping capital R. This was Mama's writing. Mama had written me a note!

Sorry it had to come to this, Rhett, but you'll get through. Just say your prayers and listen to Uncle Theo. Love, Mama!

I read that, and my eyes got watery. And I read it a second time, and even more tears. And another time after that, and the same. Yet I couldn't stop reading it. I couldn't stop staring at it. I pictured Mama sitting at the kitchen table, writing that note for me before putting the notebook and the rest of my school supplies into the box to send to Uncle Theo. That made me both sad and happy, seeing Mama's handwriting like that, reading that note she had taken the time to write me. It couldn't have been easy for her, I knew it couldn't, sending me off like this. And I felt that much worse for letting Mama down. But it was comforting in a way to know that maybe Mama wasn't still so angry at me, not if she had taken the time to write me. And I was glad that she still loved me, and I knew she did because she said so right there in that note.

I promised that I would do what Mama said, and then some. I would get myself straightened out. And I would get through this. And I would be back home with her and Ella Mae before long. I was certain of it. I would be back, and I would do all the things that Mama wanted me to do. Just as soon as I could get these stupid stubborn tears to stop.

Pops left us when I was four, just up and out unexpectedly one night, never to return. I had always believed it was my fault, Pops leaving, though I didn't know what it was exactly I did to cause that. I just figured that I had to have done something to make him go away suddenly, without any notice, without any warning. Just up and out. Mama took it bad. She was real broken up over it, spent days on end holed away in her bedroom, buried under the covers, crying, melancholy songs playing on the radio. She was pregnant with Ella Mae, so everyone was especially worried about her. Grammy and Gramps came over often to check on us, to bring us warm meals and such, to keep us company. They bought me toys and puzzles and comic books. Grammy baked me chocolate chip cookies. Gramps took me to see wrestling at the armory. That helped, kind of, yet it wasn't near enough. It wasn't enough to bring Pops back.

I used to wait up at night, lying in bed, staring at the ceiling, hoping to hear the front door creak open and Pops's heavy footsteps strolling in: the way it used to be when he would get home late from work. Then, he would call for me to join him downstairs like he did, not loud enough to wake Mama, but loud enough for me to hear, his raspy voice from those cigarettes he smoked. I'd sneak down in my PJ's, and we'd sit on the couch together and eat popcorn, and he'd drink a beer, and we would watch TV, one of his black-and-white movies that he enjoyed so much, but I could never fully comprehend what was happening in them—usually some kind of gangster shoot-'em-up movie—or sometimes a ball game, wrestling if it was on. Every night after Pops left, I waited for him like that.

But Pops never came back, no matter how much I stayed up waiting, and how much I hoped and prayed to hear him strolling in. I kept at it all the same, steadfast in my commitment, because what else could I do? I was hardly sleeping some nights, which caused me problems at school. I was always tired and would nod off in class, and that got me in trouble with the teachers. They made me talk to this man, a mental health counselor: a very serious person with beady eyes and a red buzz cut. His name was Colonel White, which I found unusual given he didn't wear a uniform, just a regular suit and tie.

Colonel White would come in first thing and pull me out of class, and take me to his office, cramped and tiny, no bigger than the janitor's closet, with stacks of musty, dusty books. For a half-hour, we would talk about Pops leaving—even though that wasn't a subject I wanted to discuss, particularly not with some man I didn't know—and how I thought it was my fault and that I was waiting for Pops to come back. Colonel White told me that it wasn't healthy. He said me expecting for Pops to come strolling into the house was something called "magical thinking." I didn't know about all that, but I reckoned magical thinking might not have been such a bad notion if it worked to bring Pops back, and who was Colonel White to say otherwise? It could've been that maybe I was magic, and my magical thinking would work some kind of magical spell on Pops.

But it never worked out that way. And as time passed, night after night of waiting up for Pops, I got older, and I found that nothing worked out that way. I wasn't magic after all, and magical thinking wasn't very healthy, as Colonel White said. So I gave up on waiting for Pops to come back, and I gave up on a lot of other things too, school being the primary other thing. I continued to go because the State said I had to, but I wasn't there, not in my head. Sitting in class, I was a million miles away. I hardly paid attention and pretty much did as I pleased. Sometimes, I would stick around. Other times, I would ditch and wander down to the park and sit on the swings and smoke cigarettes that I had cribbed from Mama's purse and watch the squirrels scurry about like they had things to do, places to be. I had nothing to do, nowhere to be. I just bided my time and did what I could and got away with what I could, until I couldn't get away with anything anymore.

Mid-morning, I took a break from my schoolwork since Uncle Theo said I could take breaks. After my second class, which was math—where I had to solve a whole mess of multiplication problems, but I had a calculator on my phone so it wasn't that difficult, only just took a while, and it was dull as all get out—I went into my bedroom, or that bedroom that was mine to use while I had to be here. I was going to text my buddies to see what they were up to, but I couldn't get a signal, no matter where I stood or how I angled my phone, even balanced on a stool in the kitchen, holding my phone flush against the window. What a sad house this was.

Instead, I flipped through some wrestling magazines that I found piled at the bottom of the hall closet. I didn't consider it snooping, just exploring my new surroundings, and the closet door was ajar anyway, like it was practically calling for me to have a peek inside. Most of the magazines dated back to before I was born, with wrestlers

I'd never heard of and who didn't appear to be in the best shape, not compared to how wrestlers are today. These guys were bloated and flabby and red-faced, some bleeding with cuts to their foreheads, the blood dribbling down into their eyes. Uncle Theo must have been a big-time wrestling fan to hold on to these magazines. Maybe that was why he was in the barn exercising with weights, training to become a professional wrestler. He was big enough, for sure, but way too old, though I wouldn't be willing to go toe to toe with him in the ring because I bet Uncle Theo could still bring it.

I got comfortable in the bed, flipping through these wrestling magazines, stretched out and relaxed with my feet propped such that it caused me to fall asleep, and there was really nothing wrong with a nap mid-morning. I wasn't sure how long I was out when I was startled by a shuffling and a moving about down the hall. I got up quickly, and scurried into the front room. There was Uncle Theo, sitting at the table, leaned back, legs crossed, hand on his head, reading one of my composition books. He was still wearing his workout gear—baggy, black mesh shorts that showed off more tattoos on his legs and a sweaty, sleeveless gray t-shirt, black Converse sneakers, no socks—squinting through a pair of horn-rimmed glasses.

"I see you liked your breakfast this morning," Uncle Theo said to me without interrupting his reading as I sidled in to join him. "Clean plate award. Just don't get too used to it. The first one's on the house—after that, you fix your own." He closed the notebook, tossed it on the table, and pulled his glasses off. "But no coffee," he said as if he could read my mind, pointing his finger at me, and he had little X's and O's and arrows tattooed on his fingers. "It'll stunt your growth, and you're already scrawny as it is." He waited for that to register with me, then he said, just to confirm, "You hear me?"

"Yes, sir, I hear you," I told him, unenthused and disappointed because Mama didn't mind that I drank coffee in the morning, although, she might not have known, and come to think of it, she didn't.

He lingered on me, and asked, with a curious expression,

"Where were you just now—in bed?"

"Nah," I lied. "I was just, uh, taking a break." And I was quick to add, "Like you said I could: take breaks."

Uncle Theo seemed not completely persuaded by my response. He eyed that ticking clock on the wall. "Stick to your schedule, remember?"

"I know," I said, and I went down the line of textbooks to select the one for my next class, which was history, which was ever so boring.

"All right then, I'll leave you to it." Uncle Theo got up from his chair, and motioned toward the kitchen. "There's peanut butter and bread in the pantry, and a jar of that strawberry jam you had on your toast in the fridge. Bananas on the counter. Make yourself a lunch after this next class." He hesitated. "Then get out in the yard and…run around or something, for recess."

"Yes, sir."

"And then back at it this afternoon. Right?"

"Right," I answered. "I know, the schedule."

"That's right, the schedule," he repeated. "The schedule. Routines, regimens: they're good for a boy your age. They're good for everyone, but especially for a boy your age. Capeesh?"

"Mm-hmm, capeesh," I said, still not knowing exactly what "capeesh" meant other than it meant I had to do what Uncle Theo said.

He stood there for a few seconds longer, giving me the onceover, and it seemed like he wanted to say something else, but he left whatever other thoughts he had and just said, "I'll check in with you a bit later," and he went to walk off.

"Where you going?" I blurted.

"None of your business," Uncle Theo responded, not in a rude manner, but just to convey that it was none of my business, and I didn't reckon that it was, but I had to ask all the same. Uncle Theo might have figured he owed me a better explanation though, because he added, "Just out to my garden. Gotta tend to my, um, crops."

"Tell me about this garden?" I queried, because I was interested in it and also to delay me from having to study history, and I poked my head up and around as if I could see it from inside the house. "Where's your garden at? Can I go? Can I help?"

Uncle Theo paused at the kitchen door, turned back toward me.

"It's out behind the barn," he answered. "And no, you can't help. You got your schoolwork, remember? The schedule."

"But what about after?" I persisted.

"No, nuh-uh," he said firmly. "I don't want you out there. It's not for you. You can't go traipsing about my property. Who knows what you might stumble into, and get yourself hurt, and then I'll have to answer to your mother, and I don't want that. Neither of us do."

"How would I get hurt?"

"You might…trip over something, sticks or stones—I don't know." Uncle Theo was getting frustrated. "Just…just…just do what I say, all right, Rhett? This'll go a whole lot smoother if you just do what I say. Now focus on your schoolwork. I don't need to be worried about what else you might be up to. Okay?" He waited for me to respond, but before I could, in a tone that made it clear that he was the adult in charge, he said, "Rhett."

"Yeah, sure, Uncle Theo. No problem," I told him, and just to show him that I meant it, I sat back in my chair and took out my history book and acted like I was reading the assignment for the day. I could sense Uncle Theo's gaze still on me as I focused on the words on the page, or at least trying to show Uncle Theo that I was focused on the words on the page.

After a momentary silence, Uncle Theo said, "All right," seemingly somewhat convinced. "I'll see you a little later."

With that, Uncle Theo left through the kitchen door. I waited a few seconds to make sure that Uncle Theo was really gone, that he wasn't going to come right back into the house for something, possibly as a trick to make sure that I was still seated at the table doing my studies. When I was confident enough that the coast was clear, I got up and went into the kitchen and looked out the window. I saw Uncle Theo walking off, that little limp of his, Chekhov running to catch up with him from wherever she had been in the yard, her tail wagging. They proceeded on around behind the barn and out of sight.

I got myself a glass of water from the faucet and returned to the table to my history book and my assignment for the day. But I couldn't help but think about Uncle Theo's garden, my mind wandering as it was apt to do, especially when faced with schoolwork. I wondered how big this garden was, what Uncle Theo grew, and, most importantly, why he didn't want me out there. How could I get hurt in a garden? Uncle Theo was just full of secrets. Granted, I didn't know him well to start, but being around him, I felt like I knew him even less. It was frustrating but also intriguing, and it only made me want to know more. Still, I couldn't bother with that for now, because like Uncle Theo said—and I had to agree—I needed to focus on my studies, that way I could straighten myself out so that I could leave this strange place and go home where I belonged.

I stared down at the table and set about to do my history lesson, something about the Revolutionary War. But just like how the American soldiers struggled to fight off the British soldiers, I was struggling to fight off the boredom that came with studying history, trying to concentrate, forcing my eyes to stay open and my eyelids not to droop and my head not to bob as that clock on the wall kept on with its steady ticking, only it didn't seem like time was moving one bit.

I was harshly broken out of my monotony by an ear-piercing ringing, like a vibrating tin bell. I couldn't rightly make it out, what it was, where it was coming from. I was scared that it could've been a fire alarm. But I didn't smell any smoke, and nothing seemed to be on fire—and I doubted this sad house had a fire alarm. It continued ringing and ringing all the same, and then I deduced that it was a telephone, had to be, and a landline telephone at that, considering there was apparently no cell reception here. But where was it?

I got up, moved about, and located a chunky beige phone

perched on the side table in the living room area. I reached to answer it, if for no other reason than to stop that obnoxious ringing, but I held off. I wouldn't know what to say, and I wouldn't want to get Uncle Theo angry by answering his phone. So I just let it ring and ring and ring, and after what seemed like an endless number of rings—the person on the other end must have really wanted to talk to Uncle Theo to keep on like that—there was a click, and Uncle Theo's voice come on the answering machine. It struck me as kind of hilarious that Uncle Theo had a landline *and* an answering machine. He was definitely behind the times on a lot of things.

Uncle Theo's outgoing message was, as I might have expected, short and to the point: "I'm not here, leave a message."

I waited and listened, and after the beep, a man's voice came through: "Ted, it's Hank. Just checking in. Heard there was a couple fellas in Prestonsburg asking about you. Wanna make sure you're all right. Lemme know. Okay. Bye." *Click.*

I waited for more, but there was nothing more, and that odd message immediately sent my mind into overdrive. I'd never known Uncle Theo to be called Ted. And who was Hank, and why was he checking in? And what fellas were looking for Uncle Theo in Prestonsburg, and why? I considered running out to tell Uncle Theo about this message, which would have also given me a legitimate excuse to see this garden. Yet, I thought better of it, the schedule and my schoolwork and all. Besides, it might've caused Uncle Theo to peg me as an eavesdropper, even though all I was doing was sitting here, minding my own business, studying history when the phone rang and that message came through. But what was that message about anyway?

It was difficult being the inquisitive type, as Uncle Theo had called me, but I returned to the table and to my textbooks and assignments, and I studied, or I tried to study, my imagination taking control, the way it was apt to do, playing all sorts of scenarios in my head just from that single message. My uncle was different, all right—that was a given. Just what was he up to?

❧

"You get all your studies done?" Uncle Theo asked me between bites of dinner: some other kind of mystery meat, with steamed white rice and cooked buttered carrots and yeast rolls, a cold beer for him and a glass of milk for me, even though I would have rather had a can of pop, or better yet, a cold beer like Uncle Theo was drinking.

"Mm-hmm," I answered, swallowing.

Uncle Theo peered up from his food, hunched over his plate, elbows on the table, and I could tell he wanted more from me.

"Yeah?" he said, suspicious.

"Yeah," I said back, "honest."

He kept watching me as he chewed, and he made a sucking noise with his tongue against his front teeth like he was trying to get some food unstuck from between them, before offering up a tentative "all right," which I took as meaning that Uncle Theo was satisfied enough with that response, but only barely. He resumed eating, as did I. We ate—mostly without talking—at the table that served many purposes, as I was learning, the only table in the house, really one of the few pieces of furniture. There was a sofa and an easy chair in the next room, along with a glass coffee table that had a burned-down cinnamon candle in the center and scattered newspapers, the side table with that old-fashioned telephone and answering machine, and a TV, not HD, of course not HD, but a small RCA with a wiry antenna at the far corner by the fireplace. I hadn't seen Uncle Theo turn that TV on, would have been surprised if it worked from the looks of it—a thick layer of dust coating the screen—and if it did turn on, I wondered what kind of reception it would get, probably nothing but static.

Uncle Theo had stacked my textbooks to clear off space for dinner. And he said I needed some separation between school and home, which I didn't completely understand because I wasn't in school and neither was I home, not my real home. But he had the right intention, I supposed, and I appreciated the gesture nevertheless.

"You go outside any today?" Uncle Theo questioned, taking a

swallow of his beer. "Recess?"

"Nah." I had my head down, still eating, famished since the peanut butter and jelly sandwich I had made myself for lunch left a lot to be desired, and Uncle Theo was a pretty danged good cook, whatever this was I was eating, and after our meal last evening, the deer meat, maybe I didn't want to know.

He pushed back from his plate. "You gotta go outside, it's important for a boy your age. You need to be moving, stay active. Trust me, when you get older, it's a lot harder to turn the engine."

"Okay," I said, scooping a forkful of rice into my mouth, then stabbing at a bunch of carrots and wolfing those down too. "I'll go outside tomorrow, move around. Turn the engine."

"Good," Uncle Theo said with a nod. "It's important."

We continued eating, no more talking, just utensils clinking against plates, chews and swallows, Chekhov begging for table scraps, and that clock on the wall steadily ticking the seconds away. I cleaned my plate, and when Uncle Theo noticed that, he stopped eating and went into the kitchen and came back to ladle a second heaping helping of everything onto my plate. I didn't mind it. It all tasted good, not Mama's tuna mac good, but it was all right, and Uncle Theo told me I was a scrawny kid so I needed to eat, and I was just waiting for him to say that to me again, his big thing to say to me.

"What's this mystery meat?" I asked Uncle Theo when he sat back down at the table, pointing at it on my plate with my fork and knife, hesitant to find out but curious.

"Rabbit," he answered as he took another bite of his.

I drew back, fork and knife still in my hands, poised to continue eating, but I had to pause when I heard that, cursing myself inside for having to ask what it was.

"Like Bugs Bunny?" I said.

That seemed to amuse Uncle Theo.

"Is your only frame of reference cartoons?" he asked me.

I wasn't sure if it was, though it did seem that way; I shrugged.

"This is wild rabbit that a buddy of mine got on a hunt last week. He had some extra, brought them over." Uncle Theo obviously recognized my blank stare, and it caused him to sigh before he continued. "Rabbit meat is high in protein and low in fat, and it's an excellent source of vitamins and minerals." Uncle Theo could doubtlessly tell that I still wasn't buying that, so he added, "If we weren't eating it, some hawk would be." I remained silent, which prompted another sigh from Uncle Theo. "Boy, where do you think your food comes from? Some grocery shelf? Where do you think it comes from before it gets on the grocery shelf?" He nodded at my plate. "Now, c'mon, there's nothing wrong with this food. And you're in no position to be turning down a meal, as scrawny as you are."

There it was, and it made me smile to myself to hear Uncle Theo say that, his big thing to say to me. I went back to eating because it was tasty after all, and I was starving, and Uncle Theo was a pretty danged good cook, and I tried not to picture that that was Bugs Bunny on my plate, or Peter Rabbit, or Thumper. Uncle Theo went back to eating too, and we just kept eating like that, Chekhov begging for table scraps, with no further words to exchange.

As we were finishing our meal, there was a heavy knock on the front door as if the person outside had wound up with a closed fist and really laid into it. That surprised me such that it made me jump, both by the unexpectedness and abruptness and because I didn't believe there was anyone within miles, despite that Uncle Theo claimed to have neighbors. Chekhov didn't seem to care for it much either, and she showed her disapproval by letting loose with a series of bone-chilling barks as she bolted for the door.

Uncle Theo remained unaffected. He simply rose from his chair and calmly strode over to see who it was, squinting through the peephole. I waited, apprehensive, but apparently Uncle Theo knew this person because he told Chekhov that it was okay, with a pat that quieted her. He turned around to me and said he needed to step outside for a second to talk to a buddy and for me to do the dishes. Then, Uncle Theo opened the door just wide enough for him and Chekhov to get through and pulled it shut behind them.

I sat at the table and stared at the closed door, straining to hear what was going on out there, for any clues as to who Uncle Theo's buddy was or what business he might have with him at this time of day, or night, right when we were having dinner, which Mama said was the most inconsiderate time to call on a person. I couldn't hear anything, only muffled voices that drifted off, but I resisted the urge to sneak over and put my ear to the door. I finished my milk with a gulp and gathered the plates and glasses and silverware and took them to the kitchen to commence with washing them like Uncle Theo had said.

As I stood at the sink, I saw from the window a pickup truck in about as poor a condition as Uncle Theo's, parked outside running with the headlights on since dusk fell early here in the mountains and it was already getting dark. There was a man standing in front of the truck, tall and lanky, wearing overalls and a t-shirt, a red bandana tied loosely over his head with a stringy ponytail. He was face-to-face with my uncle, Chekhov loyally at Uncle Theo's side. The man and Uncle Theo chatted, and it seemed cordial enough from what I could surmise. Uncle Theo slapped the man on the shoulder, and they went across the backyard and around behind the barn, where they disappeared, and I guessed they entered the barn through the back when I saw the lights go on inside.

I was so caught up with what was happening out there that I wasn't paying any attention to what I was doing, and the sink filled with water and was about to overflow before I snapped to and shut it off. I washed the dishes, putting them on the rubber mat next to the sink for the excess water to drain off, still keeping watch outside, when I caught sight of Uncle Theo, Chekhov, and that man reemerging from behind the barn. They were walking to the truck with that man carrying what looked to be two full trash bags of something, one in each hand, hanging low at his sides. Once they got to the truck, the man shoved both bags into the passenger seat and reached in and brought out a Styrofoam cooler that he presented to my uncle. They shook hands and exchanged a little more chitchat. Then, the man got into the

41

driver's side of the cab, kicked the truck into gear, and drove off with a backfire and a sputter of exhaust. I saw Uncle Theo walking toward the house, and I quickly recommenced my dishwashing, drying off the plates and glasses and silverware for my uncle to take note of when he and Chekhov came in through the kitchen door, acting as innocent as I could be.

"Got us some squirrel for dinner tomorrow night, bud!" Uncle Theo announced, excited, holding up that Styrofoam cooler. "And before you ask, no it's not like Rocky the Squirrel. Squirrel meat is lean, a lot like rabbit, but sweeter from the nuts the squirrels eat. I can pan fry it, with some brown gravy. You'll like it."

"Who was that man you were talking to?" I ignored the fact that I might have to eat a squirrel tomorrow.

"Huh?" he asked, taking the squirrels out of the cooler one-by-one and stacking them in the freezer. They reminded me of Rocky the Squirrel, only stiff and dead.

"Out back," I said, turning away from the sight of frozen squirrels and rubbing Chekhov behind her pointy ears.

"Oh, that was my buddy, who I got the squirrels from. He had some extra from a hunt he'd been on, brought them over."

"And what did you give him in exchange?" I followed, worried I might have been on unsteady ground, but I wanted to know, and so it just came out.

"Hmm?" Uncle Theo finished putting the squirrels away, shut the freezer, and tossed the Styrofoam cooler into the pantry.

"I saw that man carrying a couple garbage bags."

Uncle Theo breathed out a laugh, but I wouldn't exactly describe it as an amused laugh, and it could've been that I was annoying him. "Boy, you sure are inquisitive. You'd make a good lawyer someday—though I wouldn't wish that on anyone." When I didn't react to that statement—wasn't certain how—he became nonchalant about it. "Just stuff from my garden. I told you how we trade off around here. Neighbors helping neighbors. That's all."

"What kind of stuff?" I kept on, at the risk of further annoying my uncle, or worse. "Like vegetables?"

"Mm-hmm, yeah, something like that, Rhett." Uncle Theo brushed me off and moved into the other room. "Don't you worry about it, all right?"

"But I—"

"I said don't you worry about it." Uncle Theo gave me that look that told me I had gone far enough and not to push it. "Now, I'm gonna review your lessons from today, and I'll go over them with you shortly. You just…just…"

"I'll go to my room," I offered because I didn't want to get Uncle Theo angry at me for prying into his business, whatever his business was, whatever that whole thing with that man was, "and read a magazine or something."

"Yeah." Uncle Theo softened. "All right then, you do that." And to Chekhov, "Girl, you go with Rhett and keep him company."

Chekhov seemed to understand that, and she accompanied me, nearly knocking me over in her enthusiasm, as I went to my room, wondering what Uncle Theo was up to, wondering what was going on here.

&

That night, I had that dream again, the one where I was playing ball out in the backyard with Pops, and Pops was yelling at me to throw the ball harder even though I was throwing it as hard as I could. Each time, the baseball hit Pops's mitt with a smack that had to have hurt his hand, yet it still wasn't good enough for him. He would just pluck the ball out like it was nothing and toss it back to me, scolding that I could do better, that I wasn't trying.

But I was trying, throwing the ball with all my might. And I kept on, and I kept on. My shoulder was throbbing, and my elbow was aching. *Smack, smack, smack* with the baseball landing in Pops's mitt, and Pops yelling at me that I could do better, like he was disappointed in me, like I had let him down somehow. I didn't know how much harder I could throw the ball, didn't think it was physically possible for me to throw it any harder, and in fact, I was throwing it less and less hard as I was beginning to tire. Still, I kept on all the same because I couldn't quit on Pops, just up and leave on him. And I was just glad that Pops was in the backyard with me, and I didn't want him to go away.

Eventually, just like before, a storm cloud came rolling in, right beyond Pops, but Pops told me to keep throwing the baseball to him, to pay that storm cloud no mind. I tried to—I did, I tried my best—as the wind picked up, and the rain came down in blinding sheets, and I could hardly see my hand in front of my face. I kept throwing the baseball to Pops with everything I had. I was drenched—we both were—as we continued to play ball out in the backyard in the midst of this tempest. Pops wouldn't let me quit. He wouldn't let me go in the house. He said we had to stay and finish this.

I was committed to finishing this, whatever it took, because Pops said so. I kept throwing him the baseball, giving it my all, refusing to give up, until out of nowhere, a blur of teeth and fur came charging at me. It was Chekhov, at full speed, but I stood my ground because I knew she didn't mean me any harm. She just wanted me to go inside and get out of the storm, tugging at my pant leg. I pushed her back as best as I could considering how strong she was, telling her that I had to stay, that I wasn't done, that I needed to play ball with Pops. Chekhov just continued to tug at my pant leg to get me to leave.

"No!" I shouted at her. "I can't, Chekhov. I have to stay out here and play ball with Pops."

Chekhov carried on, behaving as if I hadn't said anything, unrelenting in her efforts to get me to leave. I resisted as best as I could, and I kept throwing the ball at Pops, harder and faster, the way he demanded, but still not good enough for him. And I guessed that Chekhov finally realized that she wasn't getting anywhere with me. Instead, she turned her attention to Pops, and she ran at him in attack-dog mode. Chekhov jumped at Pops and caught him square in the chest, the force of it knocking him to the ground, flat on his back. Then, Chekhov proceeded to maul him like he was some sort of rag doll, a chew toy. She would surely tear him limb from limb. I dropped the ball and my mitt, and sprinted to Pops to help him. I grabbed Chekhov around her brawny body to pull her away. But there was no way. She wasn't budging, not one inch. She just persisted in going after Pops, with Pops unable to do anything to defend himself.

"No!" I shouted to Chekhov as I yanked at her and slapped at her and did whatever I could to get her off of Pops. "No, Chekhov! No! You're going to kill him. Stop it! Stop it!"

I couldn't catch my breath, and my arms and legs were cramping, and my pulse was pounding like a drum beat in my temples. There was a stitch in my side like a white-hot sharpened stick jabbing me. The exertion was more intense than anything I had ever experienced, but I kept on because I had to, because I didn't know what else to do, what more I could do, only that I had to do something, or else Chekhov was going to kill Pops.

"No! No!" I cried out, pleaded, begged, spit flying from my mouth, my voice cracking. "Stop it, Chekhov! Stop it! You're going to kill him! Stop it, Chekhov! Please, stop it!"

I woke with a shudder, lurching in the bed, straining to breathe, wheezing and choking, sweat soaking my t-shirt and shorts and the pillow and sheets. I coughed and gagged, my heart about to explode from my chest. I desperately tried to compose myself, to convince myself that it was only a dream, only a dream, that it had to have only been a dream, focusing on the galaxy of star stickers that were shining on me. I just centered on this glowing constellation above and took in a bunch of deep breaths—in through my nose and out through my mouth—and pushed the hair out of my face until I was able to calm down. At the side of my bed, there was Chekhov, staring at me.

"Hey, girl," I said, strained a smile, thankful that she was all right, that we both were. I leaned over and reached out for her, rubbing her behind her pointy ears. She whimpered and nuzzled her head against me and licked the sweat from my face. "It's okay. We're okay. We're going to be okay." I said it as much for her as I did for me.

I just kept rubbing Chekhov like that as she nuzzled me, until I was able to fall back to sleep, hopefully with no more bad dreams.

CHAPTER THREE

Oh shit!

I overslept, woke up flummoxed, didn't know what was going on, but I could tell that something wasn't right. I blindly flung my hand out, reaching for my phone on the nightstand to see exactly how much I had overslept, though I was afraid to look, knew it had to be a lot with the sun streaming well into my room through the curtainless window. I tipped over a glass of water in the process, rescued my phone before the water could ruin it, and wiped the screen with the bottom of my t-shirt. It said it was 10:37! Oh shit, I really overslept!

Uncle Theo was going to be angry. He was going to be pissed. He was going to let me have it. I was late for my schoolwork! I flung myself out of bed and hustled from my bedroom, not bothering to change. I took a hard angle, losing my balance, my socked feet slipping on the slick floor, and charged into the front room. There was Uncle Theo in his sweaty workout gear, sitting at the table, leaned back, legs crossed, hand on his head, horn-rimmed glasses, reading the paper and drinking a cup of coffee. I stopped as soon as I saw him and approached cautiously, contrite, with my head bowed and my hands behind my back, anticipating the tongue-lashing I was certain to get, and I deserved it.

"You're a late riser," Uncle Theo said, matter of fact, concentrating on his paper with a lazy sip from his coffee cup.

"Huh?" I was taken aback by that reaction—or lack thereof.

Uncle Theo dropped his paper to look at me.

"I've already gotten my workout in, and you're only now just getting up." He sighed, shook his head like he was disappointed. "You're not old enough yet to appreciate how precious time is." Then, more to himself, "Kids these days."

"I'm sorry. I didn't sleep good last night," I said, more like pleaded, "but I'll study late today, as long as it takes. I'll get my classes in. I'll do all my work for the day. Promise. All of it."

Uncle Theo furled his brow as if I was speaking a different language.

"Do you normally go to school on Saturday?" he asked me.

Again, I was taken aback. "What's that?"

"It's Saturday, Rhett. You don't normally have class on Saturday, do you?"

"Um, well...nuh-uh," I answered. And puzzled, I asked him, "Is it Saturday?"

Uncle Theo grinned, but I couldn't tell if it was a happy grin or just more disappointment from him.

"Yeah, bud, it's Saturday. You must still be out of sorts from the change in your situation. Guess I'll cut you some slack then, won't rib you too hard about it." He shrugged. "But maybe I oughta put a calendar up in your room."

"Ah, it's Saturday," I said, at last comforted, and I let loose with a heavy exhale. "So, no studies today?"

"I'm not gonna make you study today, not if your school doesn't make you study on Saturdays." Uncle Theo paused, to sort of gauge me. "Not unless you want to."

"No, sir, I don't want to," I asserted, and it was the truth. "I'm good, Uncle Theo, trust me."

"Okay, that's what I thought." He resumed reading his paper, but kept talking to me from behind it. "So, go into the kitchen, and fix yourself some breakfast. I got cereal, hardboiled eggs, muffins, bananas, peanut butter. Whatever you want. Just fuel up. I want you to be active today. I want you to be on the move."

"On the move?"

"Yeah, on the move." He brought his paper back down, glanced over at the kitchen window. "Have a look outside there."

I hesitated, not knowing what Uncle Theo was up to, before I eased myself over to the kitchen window with no idea what I might find. I looked out, and I saw a shiny red mountain bike leaned up against a tree, tricked out with chrome shocks and thick knobby tires, a helmet hanging from the handlebars. My pulse quickened, my mood did a complete one-eighty.

I pivoted back around to Uncle Theo. "What's that?"

"You never seen a bike before?"

"Well, yeah, sure I have. But…well…is that for me?"

"You need to exercise," he said, returning to his paper. "I can't have you just lounging around all day in my *mansion* like you're on vacation."

"Wow, for real?" I still couldn't believe it. "That's awesome!"

"There are a lot of old coal trails around here, makes for good mountain biking. Thought you might wanna give it a try."

"Yes, sir, I would!" I almost couldn't contain myself.

"C'mon, now," Uncle Theo said as he neatly folded his paper and got up from the table, "make yourself some breakfast, fill up a couple water bottles, and head on out. Time's a-wasting!" To further drive his point, he clapped his hands. "Chop! Chop!"

"Yes, sir. Yes, sir. Chop, chop!" I repeated, dashing into the kitchen to do as he said. "Are you coming with me?" I asked Uncle Theo as he followed me in to put his plate and coffee cup in the sink.

"No, I need to run some errands. You'll be all right on your own." He cracked open the kitchen door and pointed off into the distance. "There's a trail that starts just beyond the barn, to the left on that little rise. Can't miss it. Take that, and it'll lead up and around. Some nice elevation, single track in spots, but nothing too technical. You can handle it. It's one big loop that'll bring you back around." He grabbed at my arm with his large hand, and I noticed some more tattoos on his forearm that I hadn't seen before—an anchor and like an old-fashioned compass and some weird symbol—as he playfully shook at me for emphasis. "Get you some exercise, boy. You're young. You gotta move." And he repeated, louder, in my face, "Move!"

"Move. For sure!"

He waited like he was sizing me up, and then, he said, satisfied, "Good." He stepped away. "Now I'm gonna change and get going. And you get going too. Don't squander the day." And he clarified, "Any more of the day."

"I won't. I'm on it! Thank you, Uncle Theo."

"Have fun, Rhett," he called back to me as he made his way to his room with that little limp of his. "You're a kid. You're supposed to have fun."

"Yes, sir!"

I was riding that mountain bike on the coal trail that took off from behind Uncle Theo's barn, and while the trail might've started out flat, or on a "little rise" as Uncle Theo said, that sure didn't last, because it was soon all uphill from there. And I was realizing just how out of shape I really was. Uncle Theo was right about a lot of things for sure, but he was definitely right about me needing to move more and to be active and to exercise. I was huffing and puffing like an old man; although, to be clear, Uncle Theo was an old man, and I had no doubt he would be able to handle this trail a lot better than I was. I guessed I was just huffing and puffing like an out-of-shape teenager.

I hadn't been on the bike for maybe all of ten minutes when it became too difficult for me to even pedal, despite how tricked out it was. I had to bail before I got my nuts crunched on the top tube, as I was hardly able to keep the bike upright. I stumbled on my dismount, nearly falling over. I glanced around out of reflex to see if anyone had seen that, but there was no one else out here. Even so, it was embarrassing just for myself. I needed to get my act together.

From there, I was forced to push the bike up a steep incline that winded such that I couldn't make out where, if ever, it crested. It just kept going up and up and up. Making this even more difficult was that the ground was mostly soft clay, with a squishy, spongy quality to it that gave under my weight such that I couldn't rightly gain purchase, and it was wet and puddled in spots, though I hadn't recalled it raining. It reminded me of the *Tarzan* movies I would watch on TV with Pops, where some poor guy—usually one of the bad guys—wound up getting stuck in quicksand and would helplessly sink, flailing his arms and screaming for help that only worsened the condition, until all that was left of him was his safari hat resting on the surface. That was how I felt, slipping and sliding as I pushed that bike up this hill.

I tried to focus ahead. As Mama always said, you had to concentrate on the direction where you were going and not where you had been. But as I did, I saw, dishearteningly, that this journey wasn't going to get any easier for me as the trail banked and curled, and in certain sections, it angled some forty-five degrees, give or take since I wasn't the best at math. All I knew was that the trail ascended such that it might as well have been vertical, nothing like riding my rickety hand-me-down bike on the streets around our neighborhood back home when the worst I had to contend with were potholes and broken glass.

I was determined, however, not to push this bike up the entire way, no matter how daunting the task of riding it would be. Pushing the bike wasn't working for me anyhow, as my thighs began to burn and my lower back ached. Once I had sufficiently caught my breath and overcame that initial onslaught from the combination of slanted, slimy ground and gravity, and I wasn't bent over gagging and about to puke, I got back on the bike where the trail smoothed out, relatively, straddling straight-legged and not sitting because I had to stand out of the saddle for the leverage to stomp down on the pedals while pulling up at the handlebars.

I labored just to get the bike to budge, grinding the gears and stretching the chain. And it worked, somewhat. Still, no sooner would I arrive to the top of one slope and it would taper off and I would have a momentary break, when the trail would stiffen into another slope, and another after that, and on and on. I exerted as much pressure as I could, with my sneakers coated in gooey mud slipping off the pedals and causing me to fumble and falter. But I hammered away all the same, and I was going to make it to the top of this trail if it was the last thing I did. And at times, it felt like it just might be.

It was, without question, my hardest physical challenge ever. Yet, even with it being strenuous and demanding and tiring, and on more than one occasion I swore I was this close to toppling to my death, it was, everything considered, fun. Loads of fun. And exhilarating. And thrilling. And it made me feel alive! There was just something special about being outside like this, in the crisp, fresh air, on what had turned into a picture-perfect spring day, with the clouds gone and the sun, as big as a yellow saucer, shining bold and bright in the pale-blue sky, streaking through the tree coverage to shine my way. This was just what I needed after a stressful week. Uncle Theo was right about a lot of things, and he was certainly right about this. At that moment, I felt I could do anything, even pedal a bike straight up some mountain deep in the hollers of Eastern Kentucky.

When I had the chance to relax, when I wasn't fighting to maintain my minimal momentum, I was able to admire the scenery, taking my mind off of how impossible this ride seemed to be. It was beautiful out here, unreal, like a postcard, like I had to convince myself that I was actually here and not watching some travel show on television. I was surrounded by lush greenery: trees and shrubberies full and broad and impenetrable, everything blossoming and blooming, clumps of wildflowers sprouting as if painted on by an artist, flashes of vivid red and orange and blue, the sweet fragrant scents of lavender and lily and honeysuckle. Heck, even the dirt had a pristine quality to it, like brown sugar, with no cigarette butts or chewed gum or hocked-up loogies, sprinkled with a dusting of dried pine needles.

And this forest could have been a grocery store for Uncle Theo, what with all the critters, some of which he'd already cooked up for us or talked of cooking up for us. There were squirrels everywhere, too numerous to count, rushing around, chasing each other, scattering up and down the trees, digging for the nuts and seeds they had buried over the winter, and rabbits hopping and stopping, and hopping and stopping, their cute cotton-ball tails, and chipmunks nervously darting in and out, some leaping through my tires. And although we hadn't eaten any chipmunks yet, as far as I knew, I wouldn't put it past Uncle Theo to pan fry one of those little rascals. Alongside a babbling creek just off a ravine, there was a timid deer enjoying a cool drink. "Best run along, little venison," I said to it, giggling, as I pedaled past, "before Uncle Theo gets ahold of you and tosses you in his pot!" This seemed like an entire world removed from Louisville. Spring had always been Mama's favorite season, and mine too for that matter, but I had never experienced a spring like this.

After nearly an hour on the bike, when I finally reached what I assumed to be the apex on a summit that plateaued before the trail continued on downhill, I stopped, with every muscle in my body strained and yanked and screaming in agony, to catch a breather and rest my legs and gulp down more water and eat a banana I had taken from Uncle Theo's kitchen. I climbed off the bike, this leg, then that leg, and set it down on its side, globs of mud caked on its tires and bits of twigs and leaves and other debris coating the frame. I arched and stretched and shook my hands to get the feeling back and massaged my neck as I moseyed over to a rocky ledge set out like a stack of granite shelves that jutted from atop a high bluff to sit for a spell.

Staring out from that height was some sight: the land extending infinitely in every direction, peaceful and serene and unblemished, no traffic or sirens or construction zones, nobody talking or fussing or fighting. Just perfect, uninterrupted silence: the silence of nature, with birds chirping, bees buzzing, and the smooth breeze blowing. As I considered it, I reckoned this place wasn't so bad, though I still missed the things and the people I no longer had, and maybe it was the solitude that put that in perspective for me. I took out my phone and held it to the heavens, and lo and behold, there were bars! And that was when I decided to call Mama.

I heard the ring, that monotone, foreboding humming, and it

made me nervous for some reason. I wasn't altogether sure what I was doing, didn't know what I would say when she answered. Nor had I considered how Mama might feel about me calling her. Would she be happy, would she be sad? Would she be angry at me? After all, she had sent me away to live with Uncle Theo. And she said my phone was only to be used for emergencies, and did this qualify as an emergency? I went through this mishmash of emotions and all of these questions. Sitting out on this rocky ledge, my phone working for once, able to get a signal—and that had to have been some kind of sign—I went through with the call, nonetheless, listening to the phone ring.

I cleared my throat in anticipation and took another gulp of water. And I smiled, wide and toothy, and I was sure I looked foolish, but I wanted to project my voice as having a pleasant disposition because Mama could always tell what was going on with me, and I didn't want to make her feel bad. I just wanted to call and say hi, to see how she was doing, Ella Mae too, and maybe my buddies. "Oh hi, Mama! Is that you?" I would say as if it were nothing. "It's me Rhett, just calling to check in and let you know that things are going great here at Uncle Theo's. Just great! Really great!"

I sat there, on this rocky ledge, and I rehearsed it, never having prepared and anguished over and fretted about a call as much as this one, as the phone rang and rang, that monotone, foreboding humming. With each ring and when Mama didn't answer, my hopes sank, and sank a little more, and a little more each time, until my call rolled over into Mama's voicemail. My anticipation was replaced with disappointment and discouragement that covered me like a wet wool blanket, made all the more worse by hearing Mama's voice on her outgoing message but not being able to talk to her.

I hung up without leaving a message and shoved the stupid phone back into my pocket. I scolded myself because it was a dumb idea. What was I thinking, anyway? What was I going to say? I would've just sounded like some dork, like some loser, like some whining baby who wanted his mommy. That wasn't me, and that surely wasn't what Mama would have wanted to hear. It was probably for the best. If

Mama wanted to talk, she would call me. And maybe she would call once she saw that I had just called her. She would, wouldn't she? I was certain she would call. Unless maybe, Mama didn't want to talk to me.

That thought sent me spinning into a mild state of panic. Could it be that Mama didn't want to talk to me, that she saw that I was calling and decided not to answer? As I stewed on that thought and many more just like it, it only made me sadder, with a suffocating melancholy to where I didn't want to go any farther on this old coal trail, didn't want to do anything, couldn't leave this rocky ledge, didn't think I could even move. I was just going to sit here forever and do nothing. Because what was the point to this, to that, to anything, if Mama wasn't ever going to talk to me? I just wanted to cry.

I was stuck, mired in my misery, and I didn't know how to free myself as I sat like that, pondering. But after a bit of wallowing in my own self-pity—and it must have been those sessions with Colonel White that were coming back to me—I recognized what was happening: that I was letting my imagination get the better of me, as it was so apt to do. I couldn't think like that, I knew that, and I told myself so. I told myself to stop it, to knock it off already, to get back to moving because moving seemed to make me feel better.

I shook my head to shake myself out of this funk, and as I did, a tiny voice surfaced to reassure me that of course Mama would have picked up the phone had she known it was me calling. She was just too busy, how she was always too busy, tending to Ella Mae or pulling an extra shift or making dinner. Mama would call me as soon as she saw that I had called her, or better yet, it would get her to consider bringing me home, and she would call Uncle Theo to make the arrangements. Thinking like that made me feel a whole lot better, like flipping a switch.

I finished off one of the water bottles and saved the other for the ride back. Uncle Theo said it was one big loop, so I would just need to follow the trail down. I got off from the rocky ledge and went over to my bike, easing it up from where it lay, and mounted it tentatively, as my legs and my lower back had tightened during this pit stop, and I really was out of shape, which I would've thought hilarious if it was someone else, but since it was me, it was just plain pathetic. I did what I could to ready for the return trip, rubbing my quads and twisting at my core and taking in some sustained inhales to sort of center myself. Being mostly downhill, I anticipated that it wouldn't be as difficult as it had been on the way up, but once I got started, I swiftly realized how wrong I was about that.

As it turned out, it was just as difficult going down as it had been going up—and then some. While I might not have had to pedal as much, or strain to get the bike to move, I had to hang on and control the bike, and as I got going, that proved to be the challenging part. I maneuvered around the switchbacks and the narrow gaps, barely squeezing between the trees where the trail tapered to a single track. There was a whole series of rolls that sent me airborne each time, and countless bumps from the exposed roots, thick and twisted, that snaked across the path, and broken limbs and fallen sticks, and jagged rocks and stones that I tried to avoid, yet still managed to hit about every one. I probably would have had a better chance of missing these obstacles if I just aimed directly for them. This was like the gnarliest of roller coasters, except that I wasn't strapped in or protected. I was totally exposed.

I was holding on for dear life, pumping at the brakes to ease my speed, but that didn't really slow me any. In a couple instances, I clasped the front brakes too hard and nearly flipped myself over the handlebars. I bounced and jounced and ricocheted, my knuckles white, my teeth gritted, every part of me vibrating. There was pressure in my wrists and in my calves and still in my lower back, this constant stress and tension, as the land rushed past beneath me and I barreled over the trail. I was at the mercy of this bike I had never ridden before today as I careened down the side of this mountain.

As if it wasn't enough that I had to keep a close eye out for the dips and pits and drop-offs and whatever other snags and surprises awaited, there were also the critters I needed to be aware of. I could sense them rustling about, with the wind whistling through the vents in my helmet. On the plus side, if I did crash into some animal and prematurely end its life, I could gather the remains to bring to Uncle Theo to cook up for dinner. That made me laugh, and I needed to laugh on this harrowing escape, and in spite of the intensity of this rapid descent and the necessity for me to concentrate lest these efforts result in my own untimely demise, I couldn't help but to smile. This was still fun—loads of fun—and I was certainly moving.

"Yee-haw!" I exclaimed, and it just came out of me like that.

I glanced up ahead and noticed a split in the road that I was approaching at a breakneck velocity. With my concentration being mainly on not crashing, I couldn't rightly recall which path I had taken on the way up, nor did I have any idea which path I needed to take down—and I didn't have the luxury to deliberate on this with as speedily as I was proceeding. Since both trails appeared to be headed in the same general direction that I needed to go, which was down off this dang mountain, and Uncle Theo said it was one big loop, I randomly picked one prong of this fork, the prong to the left, and hoped for the best.

I carried on nonstop on this frenzied, adrenaline-charged ride, grasping tight to the handlebars and shifting my bodyweight to conform to the cuts and hairpins and switches to keep my balance. Surprisingly enough, I was getting the hang of this. Somewhat. I leaned this way and that way, left and right and whatnot, and bobbed at the knees and lurched forward to better absorb the knocks and thumps, whatever I could do to keep myself on the bike and the bike on the trail, before the road widened and leveled.

In the distance, I could make out Uncle Theo's barn and, just after that, his house. I breathed a welcomed sigh of relief. I was confident enough at this point to just go for it on this final homestretch, with a broad straightaway that opened into a field, pedaling with a fervor and a resolve. It was a total rush as I went over this one last ridge, and then it was a sharp line to the bottom with a whip and a whoosh. I just grinned from ear to ear, I couldn't help it. I was alive. I was experiencing life. And it was fun. Loads and loads of fun!

"Yee-haw, haw, haw!"

I came zooming off the mountain like a bat out of hell and swooped through this gathering of plants, tall and willowy weeds with clusters of narrow leaves, growing in an orderly arrangement, grouped together as if someone had planted them here like that. But who would plant them here like that? Then, I had an instant fear that I might've been riding into Uncle Theo's garden, and when he had specifically told me to stay out! I went for the brakes to stop the bike, whatever it took, even if I risked flipping over the handlebars, anything to avoid any more damage as I was moving at a rapid clip and taking out a whole host of these weeds or plants or whatever they were with me, some getting stuck in the spokes and in the cables. If these really were part of Uncle Theo's garden, I was going to be in some serious trouble with him.

But in that split-second before I could react, I heard a pop that exploded like a shotgun blast, and the front of the bike flew up. I went tumbling, end over end, entangled in the frame, unable to free myself. It was as if I was moving in slow motion, yet there was nothing I could do but wait and pray for this to finish. I rolled and spun and crashed, my head slamming against the solid earth, the sickening thud of the collision echoing inside my helmet. I had become this unrestrained mangle of metal and flesh hurling violently through space, completely out of control, which seemed to proceed forever, until mercifully, somewhat, I came crashing to an immediate halt against the trunk of a broad oak tree.

I lay there flat on my back—more scared than anything—to gather my wits and try to comprehend what the heck had happened. I saw twinkling stars dancing in front of my face before they gracefully faded. I stared up at the late-afternoon sky, a mass of ravenous clouds emerging to gobble up the sun, a large-winged bird, a hawk or a vulture, gliding by to casually inspect what was going on below. I took a deep breath, and I could still breathe, so that was good. I delicately sat up, bracing with my elbows, a dull pain throughout, dizzy, and lightheaded.

I managed to fold into a seated position where I took stock of myself to evaluate my injuries, to confirm I still had all my parts and that they were, more or less, in working condition.

I grabbed at my head, and I could feel a wide crack in the crown of the helmet before it broke apart in my hands. I checked the rest of my body and was generally comforted to discover only some minor scratches and scrapes and a lot of mud and dirt. There was, though, a serious gash on my left knee that was bleeding in a line of rich crimson. But I was pretty certain I would live. A couple more deep breaths and I wobbled to my feet, and I was pleased that I could do that too, and with, apparently, no broken bones or sprains. All and all, I had made out relatively unscathed, yet sadly, I couldn't say the same for my bike.

I examined the wreckage. The suspension fork was bent and the handlebars were twisted and the chain had snapped clean in two. And the front tire was absolutely shredded with the rim dented and the skewer broken off at the end. It was like I had hit a landmine or some bomb, because I couldn't imagine what would have done that kind of damage. I staggered back to the area of impact to see what it might have been, for any clues or indication, a stick or a stone or a bottle, though I doubted any of those would have destroyed the bike like this. I noticed a piece of wood, a two-by-four, with the tip sharpened into a point like a spear, poking out of the ground that I clearly had not seen before I rode over it, and I definitely would have seen that.

"What the heck…" I said to myself as I stooped for a closer look.

I was careful not to cut myself as I touched it. I found that it could be pushed back into the ground, which was probably how it had been concealed. It was on a spring of sorts that allowed it to be loaded like some type of booby trap. But why? And who would do that, and so close to Uncle Theo's garden? I immediately had a very bad feeling, and understood that this was maybe why Uncle Theo had told me not to come around here. And now, I needed to leave before anything else happened.

I picked up my bike and pushed it as best I could, leaning it onto the back tire since the front tire was done for. I was leery of any more of these hidden-spear booby traps. With what that thing had done to a sturdy mountain bike, I wasn't about to find out what it would do to me, an out-of-shape teenager, if I stepped on one. I just wanted to get out of this field, looking down as much as I was looking up. I caught glimpses of a few more of those spears poking through the soil, just waiting to be discharged. I steered well clear of them, my body trembling, as this was so weird and unsettling, but it momentarily made me forget about the pain I was in from the crash.

I practically held my breath until I was safely away. As I got out of that field and cut through Uncle Theo's garden, I noticed more of these odd plants creeping up in and around his crops. Perhaps that was why Uncle Theo was out here so often, because he hadn't yet managed to completely rid his garden of them. I remembered when Mama once had a garden in the backyard and she was always out there on her hands and knees weeding. I walked among full stalks of corn and climbing tomato vines and neat rows of lettuce and other leafy greens, carrots and beans, and altogether else I didn't quite know. Uncle Theo sure had an impressive setup. To me, it was more like a farm than a garden. But I couldn't dawdle to admire it. I had to keep moving. I wouldn't want Uncle Theo to catch me out here. I wasn't even going to tell him that I had taken the wrong split in the trail, which was why I ended up in his garden, and I didn't when he met me at the kitchen door, concern on his face, and he asked me what happened.

"I ran over something," I answered, lied, "maybe a stick or a stone or a bottle."

"This is more than from a stick or a stone or a bottle," he corrected me as he inspected my bike, pulling at the broken chain and feeling the shredded tire and touching the twisted handlebars. My heart was in my throat, and I dared not inhale, afraid of what Uncle Theo might find, or what else he would ask, if he wondered where I had the wreck. "And your helmet," he continued, and he seemed shocked by the sight of it, taking the pieces from me. "Gee-zus, what happened to your helmet?" Uncle Theo stared directly at me. "Where were you riding exactly?"

"Exactly?" I managed to say, and I heard my voice crack, and my mouth had become unbelievably dry, and it was difficult to get the words out. "Um…you know, where you told me to." I motioned over my shoulder while still holding eye contact with Uncle Theo. "On that trail, beyond the barn."

Uncle Theo stood back and studied me, then he turned in the direction of that trail, solemn and serious, while I just kept fixed on him. Time stood still as I waited, for something, anything, with Uncle Theo caught up contemplating. Then, he returned to me and said, "Well, all right, then. Sorry that happened. You okay?"

I told Uncle Theo that I was, except for my left knee that I held up for him to see, but the bleeding had mostly subsided, and it was just a pulsating pain.

"Come on inside," he said, putting his hefty arm around me and leading me into the house. "I'll clean that up for you. Can't have you getting hurt on my watch, that would be bad for the both of us."

I acted like I understood.

"Then after dinner, I've got some tools in the barn, I'll try to fix your bike. And there's an extra helmet around here somewhere." He stopped short, and my heart skipped a beat, wondering what else he might say or ask about my ride. "Did you have fun today at least? You know, aside from the wreck that nearly killed you and tore up your bike and shattered your helmet. Was it worth it?"

I nodded my head, and formed my face into a smile, and it was worth it.

"Mm-hmm," I said, "it was fun."

Uncle Theo paused, the way he did sometimes.

"I thought so." He seemed relieved with my response. "You're a kid, you know. You're supposed to have fun. Remember that."

"Uh-huh," I replied as I walked inside the house with Uncle Theo. "I'll remember that."

❧

Uncle Theo and I were seated at the table having dinner: the squirrels I had watched him unpack and stack into the freezer last night, their stiff and lifeless pink corpses, what his buddy had brought over in exchange for whatever Uncle Theo had given him in those two full garbage bags. The squirrels looked a little better when we were eating them, at least more appetizing. With the meat off the bone, I could pretend I was eating something other than Rocky the Squirrel. Uncle Theo had stewed them in the Crock-pot with onions, carrots, and potatoes, served with yeast rolls and milk for me and a beer for himself, and I hadn't yet seized upon the opportunity to ask Uncle Theo for a beer too.

I sort of hated to admit it, because I hated to admit that I was eating a squirrel, the same harmless creature I would feed my lunch to at the park when I was ditching class, sitting on the swings and smoking cigarettes, but it was tasty, and Uncle Theo was some kind of cook. He was the nearest I knew to a gourmet chef, with his collection of pots and pans hanging from the kitchen ceiling and a plethora of shiny knives and gadgets, columns of spices and herbs, how he chopped, how he sliced, how he knew just how much of whatever he needed to add in and for how long to cook it, no recipe books or any kind of instructions from what I could gather. Of course, hands down, I still preferred Mama's cooking to anyone's, but Uncle Theo undeniably knew what he was doing. If only he would ever cook normal food once in a while.

As usual, there wasn't much talking between us. That was, until I broke the silence.

"So what is it that you do, Uncle Theo?" I asked, summoning the nerve to ask him that, and maybe it was the elation I was still experiencing from having ridden that bike up through the coal trails today and narrowly escaping death on the way down, but I just had more confidence in me.

"Do about what?" he asked in return as he focused on eating, carefully cutting the squirrel meat with his knife and fork like he was performing surgery on it.

"I mean...you know..." I fumbled with how to put it. "I

dunno…you don't work, but, well, you don't appear to me to be a millionaire neither."

Uncle Theo seemed to think that was funny and kind of chuckled, and I took that as a positive response and that he wasn't angry at me for asking.

"How do you mean I'm not a millionaire?" he said with a subtle grin. "I live in a mansion. You said so yourself."

"It's just that…most people have to work for a living, go off to a job, nine-to-five or whatever. But from what I can surmise, you don't do that."

"I work," he answered, seemingly more concerned with his food than on this conversation. "I piddle about in my garden."

"Yeah, but that ain't your job, is it?" I kept on, and amended, "I mean, it's work, for sure. It's a big garden." And then I promptly backtracked so that Uncle Theo wouldn't suspect that I had been out there against his wishes, "from what I reckon, from how much time you spend out there. Not that I've seen it. Because I haven't." And just to be clear, I said, "I ain't seen your garden." Inside, I breathed a sigh of relief at that close call. "But that's not your job, is it? Like your *job* job? Is that what you do for a living, piddle about in your garden?"

Uncle Theo's smile slowly faded, and he grew still, and he rested his fork and knife on the edges of his plate. He wiped his mouth with his napkin, using both hands, then he did that thing where he sucked on his front teeth with his tongue as if he was trying to loosen a piece of food that had gotten caught there.

"I came into some money a while back," he offered, subdued. "I had a…um… I had an 'accident,' you could call it. And I got paid some money for it."

"What kinda accident?" I asked quickly, probably too quickly.

"Just, um, an accident of sorts, while I was at work."

"And now you don't ever have to work?" I said, and concluded, "That's not a bad accident to have."

"No, no," Uncle Theo grew serious, and he glared up at me, and I became fearful that maybe I had gone too far. "It was bad, Rhett.

It was, uh, pretty bad." He shifted in his chair. "And it's not so much that I don't have to work. It's more like…I can't work, least, not how I used to, what I did. I just don't have it in me anymore."

"What did you do?" I blurted, second-guessing myself as soon as I did because maybe I shouldn't have, but I wanted to know since there was too much about Uncle Theo that I didn't know, and I wanted to know something about him.

Uncle Theo sighed.

"I was a lawyer, Rhett."

"A lawyer?" I said with surprise, and I was surprised. I wasn't expecting Uncle Theo to tell me that. He sure didn't seem like the lawyer type to me, not that I knew many lawyers, or what their type was. Although, Mama had a lawyer come by the house and visit her every so often, and Uncle Theo was nothing like that guy, in his gray suit and shiny shoes and leather briefcase, hair slicked to the side and clean-shaven, smelling like musk and acting like I wasn't worth talking to, and Mama too, as I recollected. Being a lawyer just didn't seem to fit Uncle Theo, with how gruff and sort of messy he was, and hairy, all of his tattoos and his muddy hiking boots, and how he didn't seem to mind talking to me, to a certain extent, at least.

"Yep, a lawyer," Uncle Theo answered, and he fidgeted, and I sensed that he wanted to be done with this topic. "You'd make a fine lawyer yourself, what with your excellent cross-examination skills."

I took that as a compliment, even while I had nary a clue what cross-examination skills were. I still couldn't get a read on Uncle Theo, and I hoped I wasn't annoying him.

"But I wouldn't wish that on anyone," he mumbled under his breath as he returned to operating on his squirrel meat.

"But—"

"Now how's that squirrel?" Uncle Theo asked, pointing with his fork and knife at my plate, clearly desiring to change the subject, and I figured I had best oblige. "Enough jawing, let's eat. It's gonna get cold."

"Mm-hmm." I took a bite of squirrel, chewed, swallowed. "It's not bad. Tastes kinda like the rabbit we had." And I mumbled under my breath, "Which kinda tasted like the venison."

"Only sweeter," Uncle Theo added.

"Um…" I took another bite of squirrel, ran it around inside of my mouth to discern if it was indeed sweeter than the rabbit, before I chewed and swallowed, and also to show Uncle Theo that I was doing that. "Yeah, uh-huh," I replied, trying to sound convincing because that seemed to be what Uncle Theo wanted to hear, although in all honesty, I couldn't tell. It all kind of tasted the same, not bad, not with how Uncle Theo cooked it, but just kind of the same.

"Because of the nuts they eat," he chimed in, evidently taking pride in knowing that as he kept on eating the squirrel like it was the best thing ever.

I took another bite of squirrel, chewed, swallowed.

"These vegetables from your garden?" I asked, hovering my fork over the onions, carrots, and potatoes that were part of this squirrel stew.

"Mm-hmm, yep," he said, still eating.

"What else you grow out there, in your garden?" I asked.

"Lots of things. Green beans, tomatoes, lettuce, cucumbers." He took a gulp of his beer. "Peppers, garlic, rhubarb, beets. Corn. Got a lot of corn stalks. You like corn on the cob?"

"Uh-huh."

"It's not something I can eat, but I'll fix you corn on the cob one day. Butter, salt. Maybe a little chili powder, cilantro, lime juice. Spice it up for you. You'll like it."

"Anything else?" I asked him.

"Huh?" Uncle Theo seemed confused. "On the corn? I could melt some cheese on it…"

"No," I clarified, "in your garden. What else do you grow out there?"

"You name it. If it'll survive in this mountain dirt, I'll plant it in my garden. And if I can't eat it, I can always find someone who will."

I nodded like that had answered my question. But what I really wanted to find out was what those tall weed-like plants were out there, the bunch of which I had ripped out of the ground when I came racing through on the bike, partly because I wanted to make sure I wasn't in any trouble with Uncle Theo for doing that, and partly because I had never seen plants like those before. But I didn't know how to get around to asking about that since I wasn't supposed to be out there in the first place.

"I imagine it's difficult to keep the weeds out, huh?" I said, eyeing Uncle Theo to catch his reaction.

"It takes some work, sure."

"Do they get real tall?" I asked.

"What's that, bud?" Uncle Theo continued eating.

"The weeds," I said. "Because I could help you sometime, you know. Pull up the real tall weeds for you."

"The real tall weeds?" Uncle Theo peered from his plate, then used his adult voice to remind me that he was the one in charge. "Look, Rhett," he sat back in his chair, "I already told you, I don't need you wandering around in my garden. Not unless agriculture is one of your studies, and I went through your textbooks and your lesson plans, and it's not. You're here to focus on your schoolwork, getting that straightened out."

"But—"

"And I can't have you injuring yourself out there," he cut me off, "not on my watch." And before I could say anything further, "Now eat, before it gets cold. A boy as scrawny as you, you need to eat."

I thought about saying something else, but also thought better of it. I just lowered my head and did what Uncle Theo said and returned to my plate.

"Yes, sir."

Uncle Theo returned to his plate too, and we both continued eating, with no more words to be exchanged, until I finally spoke up once more, and it might've just been my turn today to initiate the conversation, to use my "excellent cross-examination skills," as Uncle

Theo called it.

"Uncle Theo," I said, cleaning my plate by running one last bite of yeast roll to sop up what remained of the squirrel stew and shoving it into my mouth.

"Hmm?" he said, cleaning his plate in a similar manner.

"Can we have something normal to eat sometime?"

He stared at me.

"Normal?"

"Yeah, like…" I stammered.

"You don't consider squirrel normal to eat?" Uncle Theo interjected. "Or deer? Or rabbit?"

"I, uh…"

"Because I think those are perfectly normal to eat. And I doubt I'm alone in thinking that. In fact, I'd venture plenty of folks would think that." He paused as if contemplating it further, rubbing his hand over his beard. "I guess it just falls on what your perspective is, wouldn't you say?"

"Um…" I didn't know what to say, what my perspective was, and I was afraid I might've hurt Uncle Theo's feelings, or worse, that I might've made him angry, before I saw a grin sneak across his face.

"I'm just joking, bud," he said, and kind of smiled. "Those meats can be acquired tastes. I get that, especially for a big-city boy like yourself." I blushed at that, and I certainly didn't consider myself a big-city boy. "I've got some chickens in the freezer. How's that? Is that normal enough for you? Although, I don't want you to go complaining that it reminds you of Foghorn Leghorn."

I hesitated as I thought about that, and then I said, "I was thinking more like pizza or tuna mac."

"Oh, *that* kinda normal," Uncle Theo replied, with a hearty laugh that put me at ease. "That's what you call normal."

"Yes, sir," I said, laughing along with Uncle Theo. "That's what I call normal."

"I'll tell you what," Uncle Theo said, leaning in toward me, and I got a closer look at the swirl and curlicue tattoos on his neck, "I'll see what I can do. How's that?" He took a last swallow of his beer, still smiling, and rose from the table. "I'll see what I can do."

જી

I got up in the middle of the night to fetch a glass of water, having been awoken by a powerful thirst, my mouth as parched as hot sand on a beach, gagging on nothing, unable to swallow. It could've been my allergies from having spent most of the day outside, something I wasn't particularly used to, the pollens and the grasses, the ragweed. Or maybe it was the spices Uncle Theo used to cook that squirrel. Whatever it was, I was dying of thirst.

I grabbed the glass I kept on the nightstand—and dumb me for forgetting to fill it before going to bed—and took it into the kitchen, shuffling along the hallway, as quiet as could be so as not to wake Uncle Theo. But I paused when I got to the front room when I saw Uncle Theo sitting there at the table, hunched over as if he was working on something.

I didn't want to disturb him, and I also didn't want him to know that I was up. I just didn't want to be a bother to him in his own house any more than I felt I already was. I poked my head out to see if I could tell what he was doing without him seeing me. Chekhov saw me though, as she lay at his feet. She noticed me right away, and what a good guard dog she was, raising her massive head, her pointy ears perked. I put a finger to my mouth to shush her and motioned for her to lay back down, that it was nothing, no one, only me. And she took the hint—she was a pretty smart dog too—and lay back down with a snort through her nose and a pat from Uncle Theo, who continued doing whatever it was he was doing at the table.

I couldn't tell what he was doing as I strained to see, to figure this out. I thought, at first, he might have been reviewing my lessons, going over my schoolwork. But I noticed that my texts and notebooks were still neatly stacked and out of the way on the edge of the table, Uncle Theo's whole "separation between school and home" thing. And so that made me even more curious, and then I really needed to know.

I kept watching as Uncle Theo wrote into a yellow pad of paper, and he was writing a bunch as if the words were flowing out of him. He would fill one page and then flip it over to write on the next page, and that continued: deep in thought, he looked to be, taking a moment to chew at the tip of his pen, and squint his eyes, and twist his head up as if whatever he was writing about was on the ceiling. Then, he would proceed to writing some more, and more at that pace. But what? What was he writing? What did Uncle Theo have to write about, and so much, and so fast, and in the middle of the night?

It was perplexing indeed, quite the mystery, but I didn't stand there and linger, not once I figured that it probably didn't concern me, and it made me think that maybe I was being nosy, and I probably was. Mama had always taught me how it wasn't polite to be nosy. Even so, I sure would've liked to get ahold of one of those pads of paper to find out what Uncle Theo was up to, writing away as he was, filling up the pages. I swore, my uncle: the more I was around him, the less I knew about him.

I quietly shuffled away to fill my glass in the bathroom sink, then to try and get back to sleep.

CHAPTER FOUR

I overslept again the next morning, although not technically this time either because it was Sunday, and I knew it, and I didn't have schoolwork today, so I didn't get up right away, didn't need to, even with the sun streaking through the curtainless window and Chekhov licking at my face. It was okay for me to sleep in, and besides, I was still sore from my bike wreck yesterday. Though, I suspected Uncle Theo would no doubt give me grief for sleeping late, until 10:15, earlier than yesterday, slightly, but still. Uncle Theo was probably already up and about, had done a dozen different things by now, and was certain to tell me all about it as soon as he saw me. I prepared myself for that—with a smile because I didn't mind it—as I finally pulled myself out of bed, this leg, then that leg, and ambled to the kitchen for breakfast. And sure enough, there was Uncle Theo, sitting at the table in the front room the way he did, in his sweaty workout gear, his glasses sliding down his nose, leaned back, legs crossed, hand on his head, drinking a cup of coffee and reading. As I approached, I saw that he was reading the Bible.

"Morning, sunshine," Uncle Theo greeted me as he kept reading before glancing over at that ticking clock on the wall. "You're up early."

"I know," I said with pride, until it occurred to me that Uncle Theo was making fun of me for sleeping late. "Didn't mean to disturb you and your Bible reading. Just gonna fix me something for breakfast."

"You're not a churchgoer?" he asked before I could completely slip away.

I stopped.

"Nah, not really."

"Because there's a nice little chapel down the road a ways if you ever wanna go some Sunday."

"I dunno," I answered, and then I asked him, "Is that where you go?"

"Normally." He took a pause and added, "When I'm not babysitting."

I couldn't rightly decide if Uncle Theo was joking or not—he wasn't much for revealing his emotions—but it nonetheless struck me that I felt bad for keeping him from church.

"You can go, Uncle Theo," I offered, "to that chapel. Don't mind me. I'm all right here by myself. Honest."

"I'm just messing with you." He brushed it off. "I'll probably go next Sunday. Just wanted to stick around this morning for Sleeping Beauty to wake up. Or should I call you Evel Knievel after how you tore up that bike yesterday?" He stared at me. "How are you feeling this morning after your daredevil ride?"

"I'm good," I said, smiled, then moved into the kitchen where Uncle Theo had already set out the boxes of cereal on the counter, along with a pitcher of milk, a banana, and a bowl and spoon.

"Doesn't your mother ever take you to church?" Uncle Theo queried from the other room. "Can't imagine she'd let you get away with skipping a Sunday."

"Oh yeah, she bugs me about going," I answered as I brought in my bowl of Cheerios and banana and joined Uncle Theo at the table. "All the time."

"I bet." He nodded like he could relate. "She was always like that." He turned to me. "How have you managed to resist it?"

"I've gone with her sometimes," I admitted, scooping a

heaping spoonful of cereal into my mouth, trying to talk but then waiting until I swallowed it first. "When she won't take no for an answer, and it's just easier for me to give in than to keep quarreling with her."

"Smart man. Remember that when you're married: pick your battles."

"Mm-hmm, um…okay." I didn't entirely know what Uncle Theo meant by that, but I pretended like I did. "For sure."

"Anyways…" He exhaled and stretched and went back to reading his Bible as I went back to eating my cereal, with Chekhov appearing at my side to sniff out if I was eating anything she wanted, and when she determined that I wasn't, she sauntered around to lie next to Uncle Theo.

"So, it's not for you?" Uncle Theo resumed after that short lull.

"What's that?" I asked him, as I had lost track of what we were discussing, holding the bowl to my mouth, and tipping it so I could slurp the milk that was left inside.

"Church, God, religion, all that," he went on. "It's not for you?" Then he held out his hands and said, "Not that I mean to pry."

"I don't mind it if you pry," I told him.

Uncle Theo snorted a laugh at that, brought his Bible down and rested it spread opened against his chest, and stared at me over his glasses.

"Oh, um…" I said when I realized that Uncle Theo was waiting for me to answer his question. "It's not bad, I guess, church and all that. I dunno. Reckon I'm not too into it, though."

"I see," he said, and he returned to his Bible.

"Why?" I asked him.

"Huh?" Uncle Theo looked back up at me.

"Why do you ask?"

"Just curious," he answered, nonchalant. "It's not for everyone, I suppose. No harm in that."

"Has it always been for you, Uncle Theo? Church, God, religion, all that?"

He again rested his Bible spread opened against his chest, moved a hand through his unruly hair, still wet from his exercising, and I noticed more tattoos under his arm that I hadn't seen previously, some kind of birds, maybe, or angels?

"No, not always," he replied with a sigh. "I came upon it later in life. I certainly wasn't like your mother. Growing up, she always had to go to church, every Sunday—sometimes twice on Sunday—and Wednesday evening too."

"Sounds like Mama." I smiled at that.

"I told her the preacher was gonna get tired of looking at her." He laughed to himself. "She didn't find that too amusing."

"That sounds like her too."

"When I was younger," Uncle Theo kept on, "I was probably a lot like you, didn't have much use for that sort of thing. Too preoccupied with all that I had going on in my world."

I nodded because I understood, and it was also neat to hear Uncle Theo say that he was a lot like me; there was something reassuring about that.

"But I got religion eventually, and that's what counts." He rubbed his face. "Circumstances change, you know. And stuff happens: good and bad." Uncle Theo paused as if he was picturing something in his head, and I couldn't tell if it was something pleasant Uncle Theo was picturing or unpleasant. "Some things'll make you find religion real fast." He had a faraway gaze in his eyes before he came back to me. "You ever hear that saying, 'There are no atheists in a foxhole'?"

I shook my head because I hadn't, and I wasn't even certain what an atheist was.

"Well, let's just say that sometimes your life becomes such that you reach a point where you've done all you could, and you find yourself in need of some extra help, some divine intervention as it were." He sighed. "There are some problems that are just out of your hands."

"And that's when you put those problems in God's hands," I

chimed in, remembering what Mama had always said about that.

"Yeah, that's right." Uncle Theo's face lit up, my comment connecting with him, and maybe I was connecting with him too. "Something like that, Rhett."

"I don't figure God has much time for me these days," I confessed to Uncle Theo as I gathered my empty cereal bowl and spoon and banana peel to carry into the kitchen.

"What are you talking about?" Uncle Theo's expression changed to serious.

"It's just…" I started, and I shifted in my chair, as I was beginning to get uncomfortable talking about this, didn't think I'd have to be talking about this—church, God, religion, all that—had only intended on coming in here for breakfast. "Why, just look at all the stuff that's gone on in my life."

"Like what?" Uncle Theo leaned in toward me.

"Well, like everything. Pops up and leaving out of the blue, for no reason. Mama having to take care of me and Ella Mae on her own, holding down a bunch of jobs." I hesitated and let out a long exhale because I didn't want to go any further, but I felt I had to because I was already in this far. "And look at me."

"Yeah, look at you," Uncle Theo said, stiffening to size me up. "Sure, you're scrawny, and you didn't know what venison was, but all in all, you're all right."

I laughed to be polite, and I knew that Uncle Theo was trying to help me, but I didn't answer anything back.

"Huh?" Uncle Theo clearly wanted me to answer back. "What do you say?"

I had another long exhale.

"God surely doesn't want to have anything to do with me," I responded, shaking my head. "With what a screw-up I am, and giving Mama so many headaches, and causing her to have to worry about me as she does, and her always getting angry at me, and me always letting her down. Heck, Uncle Theo, I got myself kicked out of school." I breathed out heavy again, and my chest was tight. "Can't properly say

I see God going out of his way to help me. And I've put all sorts of problems in his hands. I don't know what more I gotta do to get his attention."

"Get his attention?" Uncle Theo furrowed his brow.

"Aw, nothing," I said, and I waved my hand, and I truly didn't want to be having this conversation anymore. "Just forget I said anything."

"Now, look here," Uncle Theo asserted, using his adult voice and sounding like he was fixing to scold me. "You don't have to do anything to get God's attention. You already have God's attention. And thinking that God doesn't want to have anything to do with you, why, that's not how you're supposed to be thinking. That's negative, pessimistic. I'd go so far as to call that blasphemous."

"Blasphemous?"

"Yeah, sure. It's blasphemous, you acting like you know more about this than God, that you know what God might be up to, that you know better than him. That right there is pretty much the definition of blasphemous. Because you don't know what God's plan is for you, none of us do. He could be working his plan for you right this very instant, for all you know." He folded his arms. "In fact, I'd venture to say that he is."

"If this here is God's plan for me, he's more of a screw-up than I am. And I'm sorry if you think that's blasphemous, Uncle Theo, but that's just how I feel about it." I got up to leave, and my face was hot, and I was sure that if I saw myself in the mirror, my cheeks would be beet red. "I don't want to talk about this if you don't mind. I'll just leave you be to read your Bible. I'm sorry I interrupted you and kept you from going to church this morning."

"Rhett, you just wait a second." Uncle Theo held me back with his large hand wrapped around my forearm, not like he was upset with me, but just like he didn't want me to get away just yet. "One second, all right?" And he released his grip, and I sat back in my chair. "Now I'm not here to force religion on you. Every man has to find religion on his own. But I don't much care for your attitude about it either, and as your uncle, it's my vested duty, my responsibility, to set you straight."

"Straight about what?"

"Straight about you and who you are and your life. You're only twelve-years-old—"

"Fourteen," I interrupted.

"What now?" Uncle Theo stopped as if taken aback by that.

"I'm fourteen, not twelve," I corrected him.

"Oh, um…okay," and he appeared slightly perplexed, then had to pick up his train of thought. "So you're fourteen. All right, then. All the same. You've got your whole life ahead of you. Your *whole* life, Rhett," he emphasized. "You can't get discouraged now. You can't just dismiss things, just give up. It's too early in the game for that, bud. Way too early."

I didn't get it, and I told Uncle Theo that.

"Here…lemme find something." Uncle Theo flipped through his Bible, and as he did, I could see that that Bible was well-worn and broken-in and that Uncle Theo had obviously gotten a lot of use out of it over the years, with many of the pages dog-eared and folded, and there was writing, and yellow and pink and light-blue highlighting, and a bunch of curled sticky notes on the edges. "Okay, here it is," he said, apparently finding what he was searching for and pushing his glasses up off the tip of his nose and onto his face. "Isaiah, Chapter 49, Verse 11. This is one of my favorites." He cleared his throat and commenced to reading. "'And I will make all my mountains a way, and my highways shall be exalted.'" He looked at me, waiting for that to sink in. "You hear? I'll repeat it because it's a good one." And he read from his Bible once more, quoting that same verse. Then, Uncle Theo nodded with approval, staring at those words in his Bible like he was admiring them before he slid his glasses down on his nose and peered at me. "What do you think about that?"

I wasn't sure what to think about that, so I just shrugged and asked him, "Does that mean you want me to leave? To take the highway out of here, the four-lane? Because I wouldn't blame you none if you did, and you wouldn't be the first."

"Of course, that's not what I want," Uncle Theo was quick to respond, and he was abrupt about it, and that made me feel kind of dumb, but I didn't understand what he was getting at with his Bible verse. And he must have seen that in me because he softened as he set out to explain it. "This is telling you that God will provide a way, even if it doesn't seem like it at the time. Even if it seems impossible. If you can't find your way, God will find a way for you and get you to where you need to be. Even if there are mountains all around you."

"Like out here in the sticks?" I asked him.

Uncle Theo chuckled at that.

"Yeah, Rhett," he said, "like out here in the sticks." He took a sip of his coffee, and maybe also to collect his thoughts. "It means that God will perform miracles. Even if you can't believe it, if you think God might not wanna have anything to do with you. Because he does, God wants to have *everything* to do with you, and he is working for you. All the time, God is working for you. And you don't need to try and get his attention either, because you already have God's attention. The day you were born, you had God's attention. All you gotta do now is just trust God's plan for you." He pointed his finger at me, and I noticed a tattoo on the back of his hand of a star. "And trust me, God does have a plan for you. He's got a plan for all of us. I'm certain of it."

I took this in, and I could tell that this was something Uncle Theo seemed certain of, even if it only raised more questions for me.

"How are you so sure, Uncle Theo?" I asked him. "And what about you? Do you mean to tell me God has a plan for you, with your accident that made it so you can't work like you used to, and you have to live out here all by yourself?"

"Yes, Rhett," Uncle Theo became muted but remained just as confident. "That's why I'm telling you to trust me about this: because I've experienced it firsthand. I don't have anything to complain about. To the contrary, I've got everything to be grateful for. It worked out for me, and it'll work out for you too." He sat back in his chair and took another sip of coffee. "Why, it's already working out for you. I can tell. An uncle knows these things."

I sat there and stared at Uncle Theo, at the lines in his face and the glimmer in his eyes. He truly seemed to believe what he was saying, no doubt about that. I considered myself a decent judge of BS, since I dished out so much BS, and this was no BS coming from Uncle Theo. So, I guessed I had best believe him and what he was saying about God and God's plan for everyone. And maybe I already sort of did, somewhere inside of me, because deep down, I wasn't about to give up on myself either. It was just that in certain times, and particularly in the hard times—and there seemed to be an awful lot of hard times—I didn't fully know what to believe. But seeing Uncle Theo like this and how it was that he believed, it made me feel a whole lot better about my situation, and it made me want to believe.

"Anyways…" Uncle Theo closed his Bible and set it on the table and got up to take his plate and coffee cup into the kitchen. "I'm not here to preach to you," he said, and a slight laugh escaped under his breath. "Far be it for me to preach to anyone."

"I don't mind it," I said, and I didn't, as I followed after him.

He turned to me. "But if you ever need to talk about this or that or whatever, anything, well…you come find me. No matter what."

"Okay," I said, and I was rightly encouraged by that, because up until then, I didn't consider that I had anyone like Uncle Theo I could talk to. "For sure."

Uncle Theo lingered, and he kept looking at me, how he did, not really looking at me, more like his mind was somewhere else as he was looking at me, and I couldn't gauge if he was going to say anything further. But at that moment, Chekhov barked as if she was feeling left out of the conversation, not one of her vicious barks but just one to let us know she was still around, and that knocked Uncle Theo out of his trance.

"Yes, and you can talk to Chekhov whenever you want to also," Uncle Theo said with a grin as he gave Chekhov a sturdy pat and a rub along her back. "She's here for you too." He returned his attention to me. "Now, unless you want to study on a Sunday, I suggest you go outside and enjoy this nice spring day. Hit some more of those coal trails. I was able to fix your bike."

"For real?" I was shocked by that, figured that bike was done for.

"And I found you another helmet." He gestured out the kitchen window to where the bike was leaned up against that same tree as it was before, with a new helmet hanging from the handlebars. "But watch where you're riding this time. I don't have any more spare helmets or spare parts." He winked at me. "And you don't have any spare parts either."

"I'll be careful," I assured him, hurriedly washing my bowl and spoon in the sink so that I could leave. "I promise."

"I can't have you getting hurt when you're in my charge. That wouldn't be good for either of us if your mother found out."

"No doubt!" I agreed.

Uncle Theo moved to leave out the back door. "I gotta piddle about in my garden today," he told me. "This weather's got everything coming into bloom all at once." He shook his head, complaining to himself, yet I could still hear him, "I don't know where the time goes."

With that, Uncle Theo left the house and headed to his garden, Chekhov happily trotting along at his side. I watched through the kitchen window while he walked away, his limp. Then, I rushed into my bedroom to get ready for another day on the mountain bike.

As the days wore on and Uncle Theo and I grew accustomed to being around each other, we more or less fell into our schedule since Uncle Theo was so big on schedules and routines and regimens. During the week, I woke up in the nick of time to scramble out to the front table by eight o'clock sharp to work on my school lessons, while Uncle Theo did his exercises in the barn. He'd come in at lunchtime in his sweaty workout gear to review my studies from the morning, and after I ate a PB&J and some carrot sticks he had cut up for me and kept in a plastic container in the fridge—preaching to me how those were better for a boy my age than greasy potato chips, although I had to respectfully, and silently, disagree—he'd make me go outside and run around in the yard, often with Chekhov joining me, just to be active and doing something, for recess.

In the afternoon, I'd be back at it at that table studying while Uncle Theo "piddled about" in his garden, as he put it. Sometimes, he would also go off and run errands in that broken-down pickup truck of his that had to have been on its last legs, never letting on where he was going or why, and I never pried, though not to say I didn't think about it. He would leave Chekhov at the house to watch over me, but she usually just took a nap at my feet, sometimes farting and stinking up the whole front room so badly that I'd have to open a window to let in some fresh air. It had to have been because of all the table scraps that Uncle Theo fed her, but I never said anything because it wasn't my place to tell Uncle Theo how to raise his dog. It was something nasty, though.

On the weekends, I'd take that mountain bike out, ride it all around, explore this holler I was stuck living in, being careful not to wreck it again, and of course, watching where I rode and what I rode over. I definitely made sure to steer clear of that wide patch of tall weeds behind Uncle Theo's garden. Yet, I still remained rightly curious as to what those were and what all was back there, what it was exactly that Uncle Theo was growing, aside from the obvious vegetables and herbs or whatever. There was something else going on there, I just knew it. My gut told me so, and my gut was never wrong.

Whenever I allowed my curiosity to get the better of me, and I summoned the courage—or it could've just been plain stupidity—to return to that forbidden area, I would come to my senses and chicken out at the last second and turn away, mostly because I didn't want Uncle Theo to catch me out there, and I didn't want to disappoint him like I'd disappointed everyone else. But I was also just afraid of that unknown. I had a strange feeling about it. Once, Chekhov caught me a little too close to Uncle Theo's garden for her liking, and she sure let me know it, yipping and yapping and charging at me to nearly knock me off my bike. I got the hint, all right. Real quick. I acted like I was lost and told her as such, and she seemed to understand and to believe me, giving me a "no hard feelings" lick on the cheek, wet and sloppy.

In the evenings, Uncle Theo would fix us dinner: one of his weird mystery meats that someone had given him, with two sides, a vegetable and a starch, and yeast rolls, milk for me and a glass of beer for him, and one of these days I was going to ask him if I could have a beer too. We talked some when we ate, a bit more than we had been, though Uncle Theo was no Chatty Cathy. It was usually me driving the conversation, something I wasn't particularly used to doing, especially with adults. But I liked my uncle and found him genuinely interesting, and I wanted to get to know him better, despite him not being much for opening up. I had so many questions I wanted to ask him.

Uncle Theo reminded me of the squirrels I would feed at the park when I used to ditch class. If you came at them too fast, too hot and heavy, you'd scare them off, and they would go bounding away, never to return. But if you kind of eased into getting to know them, slow and steady like, then they would come around eventually, and they'd trust you, and they'd let you feed them and talk to them and such. And you could consider them your special friends. That was how I thought of Uncle Theo. He was like a squirrel: a big, gruff, hairy, tattooed squirrel who wasn't used to being around folks, but if I just went with the flow and at his pace and respected his space, he'd come around, sure enough.

After dinner, I'd do the dishes, and I was getting the hang of that as well. Uncle Theo hardly had to holler at me anymore to do it. I just knew that that was my job, and I didn't mind it, and really, too bad if I did. Uncle Theo would stay seated at the table to go over my schoolwork from the afternoon, deep in thought, hand on his head, his horn-rimmed glasses. If he didn't have anything he needed to discuss with me about that, no corrections or questions or revisions— and it was getting to be that I was handling my schoolwork well enough on my own—he would take Chekhov for a walk. I'd hear him out there talking to her, just idle ramblings about his day and hers, and it was actually kind of cute, but I'd never let on as such to Uncle Theo, didn't reckon he'd be receptive to me calling him cute.

I would go to my room and read for a spell before bed, Uncle Theo's wrestling magazines that he had so many of or a paperback book, and he had a lot of those also, a lot by some writer named Mickey Spillane about bad guys and good guys going after each other. I found those books loads more captivating than anything I was forced to read for English class, sort of like the black-and-white shoot-'em-up movies I would watch on TV with Pops. I'd drift off at some point, staring up at the galaxy of star stickers above me on the ceiling, just thinking about everything and nothing, how it wasn't so bad here, I supposed. Then, it would be the next morning, and I'd get up and start the day all over again, one day closer to getting to go back home to be with Mama and Ella Mae and my friends. Well, at least that was the plan I had in my head, and I was holding firm to that.

One evening, I had fallen asleep in such a manner when a knock at the front door, instantaneously accompanied by Chekhov's blood-curdling barks, frightened me from my slumber. I popped out of bed and hurried from my room to see what the commotion was. I got out there right as Uncle Theo was opening the door to let someone in, scolding Chekhov to be still. I stood hunkered against the wall and waited and watched as a police officer entered the house.

The very sight of him, in his official-looking uniform, his badge and holster and hat and everything, triggered something in me, some odd feeling, this mix of fear and foreboding, along with fragments of a memory, blurry snippets flickering through my mind of a night just like this when I was young, only a kid, and the police came to our house, the flashing red lights of the patrol cars outside pulsing through the windows into the living room, and me overwhelmed by this choking dread that life would never be the same. It was the strangest thing, and why I was remembering this now, I couldn't understand. Yet here it was, that faded memory, back with me, front and center, enough to nearly bowl me over. I held myself pressed against the wall.

"Is this your nephew?" the police officer, a burly man, solid and squat, removing his hat to reveal a closely cropped blond crewcut and a thick neck, asked Uncle Theo, nodding at me as he stepped inside.

"Oh, um…" Uncle Theo pivoted, surprised, and gave me that look that conveyed he wasn't pleased I was standing there, but he was stuck with me now, and he had to explain it. "Yeah, uh, that's Rhett." He reluctantly gestured me over. "Rhett, come here and say hello to Sheriff Hank."

I walked up to the sheriff nervously as if I was the one in trouble—but I wasn't, was I?—my legs clumsy, my belly aflutter. Chekhov apparently sensed my apprehension and took it upon herself to lean into me to lead me to him.

"Hello, sir," I said, and extended my hand to shake, not sure if that was the proper way to greet a sheriff but doing it all the same.

"Nice to meet you, Rhett." Sheriff Hank took my hand and shook it, firm enough to crack my knuckles. "I'm a friend of your uncle. He speaks very highly of you, son."

I glimpsed up at Uncle Theo, not expecting to hear that my uncle spoke "very highly" of me, and it had to have shown in my face, as Uncle Theo blinked, uncomfortable, and glanced away.

"Are you enjoying your time here in our little slice of heaven?" the sheriff asked me, with a broad grin that didn't so much put me at ease as it just made me more nervous.

"Yes, sir," I said, finding it peculiar that he knew about me staying with Uncle Theo. "It's very nice."

"Why, yes. It is very nice," the sheriff agreed with me, still smiling like I had said something humorous, and he turned to Uncle Theo and slapped him on the shoulder in a playful manner, yet it seemed like a rough slap to me, and that kind of slap would've sent me sailing clear across the room. "You hear that, Ted? It's very nice here."

"That it is, Hank," Uncle Theo responded with a smirk.

"Now, if you don't mind, Rhett," Sheriff Hank returned to me, bending down to look at me square, "I need to talk to your uncle for a minute."

I didn't mind it, and I just remained there like that. And I also didn't get the hint until Uncle Theo followed with, "Rhett, why don't you take Chekhov and go into your room? I'll come for you shortly and then we can, uh…watch some TV."

That shocked me almost as much as a sheriff showing up, because I hadn't seen Uncle Theo watch that old television since I'd been here, and I doubted that relic was even operational. But it also told me that he wanted me out of the room because he and Sheriff Hank had grown-up business to attend to, which only made me want to stick around, but of course, I knew better.

"Yes, sir," I said straight away, with a nod to Sheriff Hank. "Nice meeting you, Sheriff." And to Chekhov, "C'mon, girl." And with that, we retreated down the hall and into my room. I closed the door, but not too tight because I wanted to find out what I could about what was going on out there.

I shushed Chekhov to get her to settle down. Having company, and someone she seemed to recognize in Sheriff Hank, had her agitated something awful. With rubs behind her pointy ears and a pat on her back the way Uncle Theo did, I managed to get her to relax enough to where she lay down on the floor with an exhale out her nose, while I placed my ear to the door.

I could hear the two of them moving about in the front room. Uncle Theo shut the door, and the creaking of the floorboards stopped, and that indicated to me that they were standing. It was casual conversation to start. Sheriff Hank asked Uncle Theo how everything was going with me, and that still made me feel awkward, the sheriff knowing I was staying with Uncle Theo and asking about it, and why would he care? Uncle Theo answered, typical for him in as few words as possible, that it was "fine," with no explanation. There was chit-chat about the weather, and the Wildcats, and some other stuff that I didn't find particularly interesting, before Sheriff Hank said, in a lower voice, yet I could still make it out, what with how small this house was and how thin the walls were, "So, I heard tell those two fellas have come back around, asking 'bout you, this time in Birchmont Village."

"Yeah?" Uncle Theo responded, disinterested.

"Everything all right?" Sheriff Hank asked him. "You ain't seen nothing, I don't know...out of the ordinary?"

"Nuh-uh." Uncle Theo replied, and his footsteps made it sound like he was pacing.

It got silent, and if they were talking, I couldn't hear them, even when I cracked the door open, motioning for Chekhov to stay put, as that had caught her attention and caused her to stand, her massive body, thinking we were going out. Then, Sheriff Hank said, "Of course, I can't officially take anyone in just for asking questions about a person: nothing illegal about that, in and of itself."

Uncle Theo said, "I know."

"But we'll keep an eye out," Sheriff Hank continued. "And if anything happens, well, we'll be all over it. Don't you fret none."

"Appreciate that, Hank."

There was another momentary silence, and then Sheriff Hank added, in a voice exceptionally low, and I had to lean out in the hall and strain to listen. "Say, uh...you wouldn't happen to know of any reason why they'd be coming around now, do ya? You know, after all these years."

Uncle Theo didn't say anything, at least I didn't hear him say anything, and I imagined he just shrugged his shoulders and looked down, as he was accustomed to doing whenever he was done with whatever was taking up his time.

"All right, well..." Sheriff Hank sighed, and he asked, "How long's the boy staying here?"

"As long as it takes." Uncle Theo was fast to reply.

"As long as what takes?"

"As long as it takes for me to straighten him out," Uncle Theo answered, and then explained, "He's a good kid, just had some tough breaks."

"He ain't been out and about, has he?" Sheriff Hank questioned. "To attract any...attention?"

"Nah," Uncle Theo replied. "He's here inside doing his studies for the most part."

"He ain't leaving the house none?"

There was creaking of the floorboards, which I took as more pacing from Uncle Theo.

"He might take his mountain bike out," he said, "ride on some of these coal trails. But that's the extent of it. I'm keeping an eye on him, me and Chekhov both."

"You and that ol' mutt." Sheriff Hank chuckled. "Did you save her life, or is she saving yours?"

"Little bit of both, I'd say."

It got quiet again, and I couldn't tell what was happening because it didn't sound like either of them was moving or saying anything. And it could've been that they were both just thinking of what to say next. I couldn't lean out any farther because if I did, they were bound to see me, so I held tight, just around the corner from where they were.

"Well, okay then," Sheriff Hank finally broke the silence, with the floorboards creaking, which I took as him fixing to leave. "You promise you'll let me know if you need anything. And I'll send a car by every so often, whenever I can, to shine a light, have a look around. We're short-staffed, but I'll do my best."

One other pause, and I could picture Uncle Theo nodding, and then I heard the door open.

"You take care, Ted," Sheriff Hank said.

"Yep. You too, Hank."

"You're doing a good thing," the sheriff added, "taking care of that boy."

"Just doing what I can for family. I owe it to my sister. And I guess to the boy."

"Yeah, but...not everyone would be so gracious in your situation."

"It's fine, Hank," Uncle Theo said, short as if to cut Sheriff Hank off, and I was confused as to what the sheriff meant by Uncle Theo's "situation."

"All right, bud." Sheriff Hank's voice trailed off to tell me he was stepping outside, but before he left, he asked, "And how's the gardening going?"

Uncle Theo kind of laughed at that. "The gardening? It's fine."

"What's in season now?" the sheriff followed.

"Got some beans and tomatoes and potatoes, whatnot. My crop."

"Appears you got your hands full with that garden," Sheriff Hank kept on, "from what I can tell. Of course, I ain't never been back there to see for myself."

"I'd be happy to give you the grand tour sometime," Uncle Theo offered, and there was a tone to his voice that maybe he was amused, but then again, maybe not.

"What do you do with all that?" Sheriff Hank questioned. "All them beans and tomatoes and potatoes...whatnot? Your crop? Because it's gotta be more *produce* than for just one man. You offering it up to your neighbors?"

"Sometimes," Uncle Theo replied. "We got a bartering system: they might give me something they got on a hunt, and I might give them, you know, some of my...*produce*."

"Sounds like a nice little business you got there."

"Oh, I wouldn't call it a business, Hank," Uncle Theo corrected him, "just neighbors helping neighbors, looking out for each other. Being, you know, neighborly." There was another silence, and I couldn't figure if Sheriff Hank had left or what. But then Uncle Theo said, "Well, thanks again for stopping by."

"Mm-hmm," Sheriff Hank said, slow and drawn out like he was skeptical of something, which I distinctly recognized from how Mr. Smitherman would respond to me whenever I told him something—usually a lie—that he didn't entirely believe. "Just watch out for yourself, Ted, for you and the boy."

"Will do."

I heard the front door shut, and the movement of Uncle Theo walking in my direction. I scrambled back into my room and closed the door gently so that Uncle Theo wouldn't hear. I gave it a few minutes, in case Uncle Theo might call for me, but when it became apparent that that wasn't going to happen, I freed Chekhov from my bedroom, knowing that she would beeline it for Uncle Theo, and she did. I halfheartedly gave chase, faked calling her back into my room, to find Uncle Theo seated at the table, staring down at one of his pads of paper as if he was about to do some writing.

"Sorry, Uncle Theo, she got away from me." I glanced around the room as if I was searching for something. "Is Sheriff Hank gone?" I asked innocently enough.

"Hmm?" Uncle Theo appeared distracted. "Oh, um, yeah, he left. Hey, I apologize for sending you to your room. The sheriff and I just needed to discuss some things."

"What things?" I asked, just out of reflex.

"Nothing," he said, acting like it was nothing. "The sheriff just likes to drive around every so often and check on folks."

"Oh," I replied, acting like I thought it was nothing, because two could play that game. Then I said, "Neighbors watching out for each other."

"That's right, Rhett. That's what we do around here." Uncle Theo was defensive in his reply, but caught himself and breathed out, and sort of relaxed, and nodded to the TV. "Anyways, if you wanna watch something on that thing. I don't know what's on. I rarely use it. But you're welcomed to try."

I glared at that rinky-dink television set pushed into the corner, sitting there all pathetic and neglected, collecting cobwebs, and I knew it wasn't worth the aggravation to fiddle with those knobs and rabbit ears.

"That's okay," I told him. "I'll just go back to my room."

"All right. You can take Chekhov with you if you like, if you want her company."

"I'm good," I said, noticing how Chekhov was lying contented at Uncle Theo's feet. "She looks comfortable with you."

Uncle Theo looked down at the dog, and he agreed. "Yep,

guess so." Then back to me, "Well, good night then, bud."

"Good night, Uncle Theo," I said as I returned to my bedroom at a leisurely and deliberate pace, as I still had something on my mind, lots on my mind actually, as usual, but one thing specifically that arose during Uncle Theo's visit with Sheriff Hank. I was fiercely debating with myself during those fleeting seconds if I should chance asking him, before deciding to go through with it, figuring that I had better do so while I had the opportunity. "What business are you in?" I asked, stopping and turning around.

"What's that?" Uncle Theo peered up from his pad of paper, his glasses sliding to the tip of his nose.

I wavered, fearful, worried if I should be asking about this, and I probably shouldn't, but I did.

"Sheriff Hank said you got a nice little business. So what's your business?"

"Were you eavesdropping on us?" Uncle Theo raised his voice and shifted forward in his chair.

"No, sir," I said, lied. "I just might've overheard that part, when I was, uh…"

Uncle Theo let out a long sigh that caused me to shut up, and he went to talk like he wanted to say something to me, but he held himself back and ran a hand through his mop of hair. With a deep breath, and more measured, he just said, "I don't have a business, Rhett. I already told you: I just piddle about in my garden." He returned to his writing pad. "But by all means, feel free to ask Sheriff Hank what he meant by that the next time you see him."

That was my cue to shut up and not get into this anymore, so I just agreed with Uncle Theo, and said, "Yes, sir" and "Good night, again," and walked purposefully to my bedroom and shut the door tight behind me and got directly into bed. But try as I might, I couldn't get to sleep with my mind jumbled with thoughts after thoughts after thoughts, trying to piece this together, anything together, to figure out what was going on here, and getting nowhere. I tried to read, first some wrestling magazines and then another one of those Mickey Spillane paperback books, but all I kept thinking of was my uncle and all the things about him that I didn't know.

I had that dream again, that same weird dream, the one where I was playing ball outside with Pops as a storm rolled in, and no matter how hard I threw the baseball, it wasn't hard enough for Pops's liking. Pops was being exceptionally ornery about it, and irritated, and just plain mean. He was calling me all sorts of names and telling me that I wouldn't amount to anything in my life, not if I couldn't throw a measly baseball into his mitt with any gusto. That riled me up, Pops talking to me that way, like my feelings didn't matter, and him not understanding that I was throwing the ball as hard as I could, and I knew I was by how the ball kept landing square into Pops's mitt with a *smack* that had to have hurt his hand. But he didn't let on as such. He just casually plucked it out and lobbed it back and continued to belittle me and my efforts, saying some really hateful things, about how no son of his was going to be a weakling, and how I had to take responsibility for myself, and that I had best get my "shit together."

It was confusing for me because, in my head, I knew that Pops had already up and left, yet in my dream, Pops was here in the backyard, playing ball with me. And I didn't want to do anything to jeopardize that, to cause him to leave again. So, I kept throwing the ball with everything I had. My arm felt like it was going to pull out of the socket, and my shoulder pulsed and throbbed. And I was sweating and gasping and choking in air. My legs were weak and trembling. I feared I might pass out. But I kept at it all the same because I didn't want to do anything to make Pops up and leave, not again.

Once that storm had overtaken us, and the wind whipped, and the rain pummeled, and I could hardly see anything, I yelled out at Pops that maybe we should go inside until the weather passed. But Pops would have none of it. He just kept on, harassing me into throwing this baseball harder, despite all of my best attempts and the fact that I was already throwing it as hard as I could. Pops wouldn't take no for an answer. He would just lob that baseball back to me after it had landed with a *smack* in his mitt that had to have hurt his hand, and criticized me, saying how I could do better, that I wasn't trying, that I was giving in, that I was giving up.

I wanted to please Pops, I really did, and I surely didn't want to do anything to cause him to up and leave again. But there came a point, with the storm, and my exhaustion from throwing, and just everything, where I was fed up, and enough was enough. I told Pops that, and how we needed to go inside for a spell, all but begging him. Pops wouldn't allow it, though, and when I went to walk away, Pops came after me. He grabbed me about the shoulders and spun me around, and he shouted, mere inches from my face, that that wasn't how it would be, that we were going to stay out in the yard and play ball until I could get it right. I resisted, but I could tell that was only making Pops angry. I wanted to reason with him, but I couldn't. And I wanted to leave, but he wouldn't let me. So I had to do what I had to do.

"Stop!" I finally yelled at him. "Pops, cut it out! Just stop it! Leave me be!"

It was no use, as if he hadn't heard me or, if he had, he didn't care. He just kept his grip on me and said that we weren't finished playing ball yet. He plucked the baseball from his mitt and pushed it hard into my chest, and it hurt, and took the breath out of me. He had his one hand still clasped on my shoulder as he used his other hand to push the ball into my chest, like he could push it clear through me. I tugged back at him, to free myself, to loosen his grip, because this wasn't Pops. It couldn't be. It might've looked like him from the last I had seen of him, before he up and left when I was young, but it wasn't him. It was this shell of Pops, with something dark inside, darker than the sky from this raging storm and sinister in a way that scared me. I just knew I had to get away. I had to free myself!

I managed to wrench my right shoulder from how Pops had a grasp on it, and as soon as I did, I punched him in the face without thinking about it, because it was something that had to be done. That caused Pops to back off, and when he did, I punched him with my left hand too. And then with both hands, one after the other, alternating between right hand and left hand. I just kept punching Pops, everywhere, wherever my fists landed: on his face, on his chest, in his stomach. I was full of rage. I kicked him too, and I stomped him with my feet, and I drove my knees into his midsection. I just laid into Pops with this fury. I kept striking him as hard as I could, with an aggression, a ferocity, without tiring and, if anything, with an increasing intensity. I persisted, going after him, blow after blow after blow, not relenting, not backing off. I just kept hitting Pops with everything I had as the storm raged on around us.

Pops didn't fight back. He just stood there, and he took it as I beat the ever-living daylights out of him. His eyes were swollen, and his face was puffy, and his nose was busted. There was blood streaming from his mouth. He doubled over with my body blows, and he flinched, and he recoiled. He dropped the baseball at his feet, and his mitt too. But I refused to let up. I wouldn't. I couldn't. I was flailing my arms and kicking my legs and screaming at the top of my lungs, my throat scratchy, spit flying out.

"I want to go!" I yelled as I unleashed on him. "I want to leave!"

I was unstoppable, fighting Pops the way I was. It was almost as if I was gaining strength, that I had even more vitality. I wasn't even close to letting up. This went on for so long that I lost track of the time, and I forgot where I was. And I didn't mind the storm any either. I just kept on like that, and on like that, with this violent assault, shouting and screaming at Pops.

"Why did you leave me?" I cried out, my body shaking, lashing out at Pops with all my might. "Why did you leave? Why did you leave? Why did you leave me, Pops?"

I continued yelling like that and beating up on Pops, over and over and over. It seemed as if it would never end because I wasn't anywhere near to stopping, until I awoke with a shutter and a tremor, like I was tumbling out of that weird dream and landing a hundred feet below it, the pillow soaked, the sheets wrapped tight around me. I sat up quickly, panting and gagging, staring wildly about before realizing, with a solace that allowed me to breathe, that I was in my bed in my bedroom at Uncle Theo's house. Chekhov was standing beside the bed, watching and whimpering, no doubt confused—and maybe a little scared—as to who this crazy person was. I felt the same.

I reached over to pet her, and she licked my hand, and I moved in closer to let her lick my face, wet and sloppy, her way of reassuring me that everything was all right, and I needed that, and I wanted to believe that.

CHAPTER FIVE

I couldn't fall back asleep. I was too shaken. I was too wired. My thoughts were racing. The adrenaline was still pumping. And even if I could fall back to sleep, I was afraid to for fear I might end up right back in that weird dream. What was that dream about anyway? And why did I keep having it? Why now? Everything was so strange these days, nothing I was used to. What was happening to me?

Instead of just lying there, staring up at the galaxy of star stickers on the ceiling and making myself crazy, or crazier, my imagination getting the better of me, I decided to fetch a glass of water from the kitchen, maybe that would help. As I walked out into the front room, without really thinking about it, without considering that anyone else might be awake, I stumbled upon Uncle Theo sitting there at that table, writing. Chekhov, clearly having had enough of me and my shenanigans, had already bolted from my room and was lying at Uncle Theo's feet. She perked her head up when she saw me, as did Uncle Theo, and I cringed at the notion that I had disturbed him yet again. If I kept on like this, I was sure to get on his very last nerve.

"What's up, bud," he said when he saw me, and he didn't seem angry about me barging in on him so that was a relief. "Can't sleep?"

"Nuh-uh," I answered, rubbing my eyes, groggy. "Weird dreams."

"Yeah, I get those," said Uncle Theo, and he reached down to pet Chekhov. "So does Chekhov, from what I can tell, whenever she starts turning and twisting in her sleep."

Chekhov grunted to let us know she was listening and that she had heard that, and maybe to also agree with Uncle Theo's observation, because she was a pretty smart dog, after all.

Uncle Theo kicked out a chair. "Have a seat."

"Nah," I said, reluctant to do that, glancing down at how Uncle Theo had his writings scattered about, "you look busy, and I don't want to bother you none. I feel like I'm always bothering you."

"You're no bother," he tried to assure me. "I'm just sitting here noodling."

"Noodling?" I asked as I shyly took a seat. "What's 'noodling'?"

"Just…"—he shrugged, staring at his papers—"I don't know. I sit here and write at night. When I can't sleep." He sighed. "Which is most nights."

"Why can't you sleep?" I wondered if Uncle Theo was having the same weird dream as I was.

He shook his head. "Who knows? This and that. Aches and pains accumulated over the years, and an overactive mind."

"I've got that too," I said, and I could definitely relate. "An overactive mind."

"Maybe it runs in the family," he replied. "It's not easy having the weight of the world on your shoulders, huh?" Uncle Theo gave me a knowing smile, then he grew quiet.

"What is all this?" I questioned, with a nod to his pads of paper. "What are you writing?"

"Oh, um…" Uncle Theo reached out and gathered his writing pads, pulled them in together and stacked them into a pile, like maybe so I wouldn't snoop around and read any of it, which was what I was trying to do, subtly, though obviously not subtly enough if Uncle Theo caught on to that. "Whatever happens on in my head." He swallowed hard and looked back up at me. "Lately, you could say I've been putting my memoirs together." He shrugged once more. "I don't know why.

Just started thinking about my life in that way recently." Then, as if he was embarrassed, he said, "It's silly, I know."

"It ain't silly," I told him, and I meant it. "I think that's neat, that you've done enough in your life that you can write it all down. Like a bona fide writer. Like that fella, Chekhov, the great writer, and not Chekhov, the giant dog." Chekhov grunted at that, and it could've been she only grunted when she heard her name.

"I wouldn't go that far," Uncle Theo leaned forward and casually covered his stack of writing pads with both arms, and when he did, I noticed a tattoo on his left forearm of the name "Sadie" in cursive. "I'm just writing to get it out of my head. Guess it's like therapy for me that way. Better on paper than in my head." He paused as if contemplating. "But then again…who knows, someone might find it interesting someday."

"For sure. Heck, I'm interested in it now." As I said that, I went to reach out to where Uncle Theo still had his arms on his writing pads, to see if he'd let me take one to look at, but he kept tight over it, so I backed off. "Anyway," I said, just to be saying something because I suddenly felt awkward.

"You know, you're a good writer," Uncle Theo broke the stiffness in the air, and probably also to change the subject, which I found he had a knack for doing, and it worked, as that comment had come out of nowhere and taken me by surprise. Uncle Theo went on, "From those assignments of yours I've read, for your English Composition class."

"Oh, yeah, those. Well, that's just because I've got to, on account of that's what's in the assignment."

"Even so, they're good."

"Yeah?" I was having trouble believing that, had never received a compliment on my writing before, or on any of my schoolwork for that matter. "For real?"

"Sure," Uncle Theo said like he meant it, "you got a real gift there, Rhett. You oughta stick with it."

"Maybe I'll write my own memoirs someday," I joked, "when

I've done enough with my life. Or at least done something with my life."

"Why not?" Uncle Theo said, and he didn't seem to be joking. "'An unexamined life is not worth living.'" He waited a second, then added, "Socrates."

"I, uh…" I wasn't sure what Uncle Theo was getting at with that, if maybe Socrates was like "capeesh" and Uncle Theo was giving me another directive, so I repeated it back to him, "Socrates."

Uncle Theo sort of grinned and asked me, "What have you thought about doing?" and then he held his hands out and sort of retreated, "Not that it's any of my business. I don't mean to pry."

"I already told you, I don't mind it if you pry," I said.

Uncle Theo snorted a laugh and folded his arms across his chest, and just stayed like that.

"Oh, um…" I said when I realized that Uncle Theo was waiting for me to answer his question. "What do you mean exactly?"

"With your life and whatnot," Uncle Theo explained. "I know it's too early to have your life planned out. Hell, I don't have my life planned out, and I'm an old man." I laughed at that, could've been louder than I needed to, but I thought it was funny, Uncle Theo calling himself an old man. "But…what interests you?"

"What interests me?" I sat back and considered that, but it was nothing I had really ever considered, and I didn't rightly have a response. "Beats me."

"Well, what do you like to do?"

I scratched my head, to continue to ponder, before I answered with the only answer that came to mind, "I like to ride that mountain bike you got me."

That seemed to amuse Uncle Theo, the way I seemed to amuse him without trying. "That's something."

"Are you meaning like school-wise?" I questioned, confused.

"Sure, or… I don't know, what you might be thinking of doing after school."

"Gosh, I just want to get out of school first, as soon as the

State'll let me. I'm counting down the days."

"Be careful thinking like that," Uncle Theo cautioned, "that's a sin, you know—counting down the days, squandering time—because time's the best thing you got right now, and you don't know how much of it you have, no matter your age. You can't presume to know more than God does, about how much time God has granted you." He took a breath, then resumed, somewhat subdued. "Then, when you do get to be an old man like me—if God has blessed you with that luxury, if no one has tried to steal your time—you find that time's running out, and it's too late to do much of anything."

"Yes, sir," I said, as I felt I needed to take this conversation serious, as it had taken a sharp turn toward the serious.

"Anyways," Uncle Theo said with a grin and a wave of his hand that he then ran through his tangled hair, to lighten the mood like maybe Uncle Theo also caught that he was getting serious. "I was just curious. You'll figure it out in due course. We all do."

"How'd you figure it out?" I asked since this had piqued my interest in Uncle Theo, although I already was well interested in him, but this was as good a chance as any to get to learn more about him, whatever I could. "Like, how'd you know this was for you: living out here in the sticks, piddling about in your garden and such?"

Uncle Theo reacted with a chuckle, not that that was my intent, but at least he wasn't annoyed with me for my prying. He took off his glasses, held them in front of his face, dangling, as he appeared deep in thought.

"This is just how it played out for me, Rhett," he answered, and added, "but I don't mind it."

I nodded like I understood, and waited to see if there would be more, and when there didn't seem to be more, I asked Uncle Theo, "What about when you was my age?"

"Hmm, what's that?" Uncle Theo said as if he had been deep in thought.

"Did you know what you wanted to do when you was my age," I followed, "with your life and whatnot? Like, did you always want to

97

be a lawyer?"

"Oh God, no," Uncle Theo responded quickly and convincingly. "No, no. Nuh-uh. I just fell into that." And more to himself, though I was sitting right there so I heard him, "God, no." Then he went on, as if he figured he owed me a better explanation. "I only went to law school because I thought I had to, because I thought that was what was expected of me. And I applied myself. An overachiever, I was. I worked hard, putting that job before anything else." Then lower again, and with a drawn-out sigh, "And what did that ever get me." Uncle Theo became silent, and it made me feel awkward, and I didn't know how to respond, or if I even should, so I remained silent as well, and still, and I just waited for him. "Anyways," Uncle Theo resumed, breaking loose of whatever had a hold on him, "you'll figure it out, at some point. Just don't overthink it. Do what interests you."

I nodded like I got it, and maybe I did, but I still had more questions, as I always did.

"What interested you," I asked him, "when you was my age?"

"What interested me when I was your age?" Uncle Theo repeated, and he waited, and repeated again, softer. "What interested me when I was your age?" He took a moment to ruminate before he answered, being sure to make eye contact with me, "I liked riding my bike too, Rhett. And hanging out with my buddies. And ditching class to go smoke cigarettes." That last part particularly connected with me, but I didn't let on as such to Uncle Theo because I didn't want him knowing that I ditched class or smoked cigarettes, even though I had a sneaking suspicion that he somehow already knew. "And I liked writing, making up stories, telling tales, going on these elaborate adventures in my head." He winked at me. "I wasn't half bad in English Composition, either."

I watched Uncle Theo, and a smile drifted across his face as if he was picturing something pleasant.

"And now look at ya," I told him, "writing your memoirs."

"Yeah," he said, "suppose that's right." Uncle Theo focused

back on me. "See how things play out: a person always seems to end up where he needs to be."

"Yes, sir."

"Which is why," Uncle Theo continued, pointing his finger at me, "you don't give up on what it is you want to do. If you want to ride that mountain bike for the rest of your life, then by all means, you ride that mountain bike." Uncle Theo lingered, how he did, like he had something else going on inside him. "But I suspect you'll aspire to more than just riding your mountain bike."

"Yes, sir," I replied, as I sat there and continued to watch Uncle Theo. This was the most I'd gotten him to open up to me, and I wanted to take it all in and to appreciate the moment and not do anything to spoil it, like those squirrels at the park.

It might've been that Uncle Theo realized he was opening up to me too, and maybe he didn't want to, because he seemed to catch himself, and then he went back to his usual self, guarded and reserved, and he returned to his writing pads, and he picked up his chewed-up pen, all of which I took as signs that this episode was over. And I didn't want to keep him from his writing any more than I had, and I didn't want to impose on him any further. I needed to fetch my glass of water anyhow, and go back to bed, to see if I could fall asleep since I wasn't near as tense and agitated now. So, I told Uncle Theo as I stood, "Well, I'll leave you be then, to your writing."

"All right," he said without stopping me. "Good talk, bud." And more to himself, "Good talk." He put his glasses on and focused on his pads of paper.

"Yeah," I said as I went into the kitchen, and more to myself too, "good talk."

I filled up a glass of water in the sink, doing my best not to be noisy about it, and quietly went to my bedroom.

Uncle Theo was right about a lot of things, but especially about me getting out and moving about and being active for a kid my age, which was what I was doing this day during recess. I was running around in the yard with Chekhov, a made-up game of tag between us. She would chase me for a spell, and then we'd switch off, and I would take my turn chasing after her. For a dog her size, she was deceptively fast. We'd go back and forth like that, neither one of us actually catching the other, but that didn't matter. It was fun, and it felt all right. I felt all right. I was energized and alive. I could breathe, full and deep and satisfying breaths. There was just something about this mountain air.

I hadn't minded these past few weeks with Uncle Theo. Of course, I was still eager for Mama to let me come home, but I wasn't hating it here like I feared at first. Uncle Theo was okay, in his own way. He wasn't the most talkative or outgoing or friendliest person, and I reckoned that if he had his druthers, he'd prefer to be by himself, just him and Chekhov, but he didn't intend anything by that: it was just how he was. And when he did talk, he said a lot with few words, which was more than I could say for most of the adults who talked to me.

I was careful not to bother him too much, and I had been doing a better job of that, though Uncle Theo might have disagreed. It must have been awfully strange for Uncle Theo to have his living arrangements upended too since it wasn't just me affected by this change. I had to cut Uncle Theo some slack, and I couldn't fault him for wanting his alone time. We were both doing the best we could to live together, neither one of us having really known the other prior. I appreciated all that my uncle was doing for me, which, as I considered it, made me want to do something for Uncle Theo in return.

I racked my brain to think of something special, because it had to be something special. Uncle Theo was unique to say the least, and it couldn't just be any old thing. What I really wanted to do was help him in his garden, but that remained out of the question, and he told me as such using his adult voice. I thought about washing his truck, but that old beater was so worn that the dirt was probably what was holding it together. And I was already picking up after myself and doing the dishes without Uncle Theo having to holler at me, so that wouldn't have been much of a favor either.

I pondered it, and I pondered it, as I ran around the yard with Chekhov, for something special I could do for Uncle Theo, something to show my appreciation for everything he was doing for me without getting sentimental, and definitely not corny because Uncle Theo did not strike me as the type to go for something corny, and really, neither was I. Once, for Valentine's Day, I gave Mama a card and some flowers and a heart-shaped box of chocolates, and that felt corny to me, and when the guys at school got wind of it—and I suspected that Mama had told one of their mothers and then that one mother told her son and he blabbed to everyone, which was how the rest of my buddies found out—they didn't let me hear the end of it for the whole rest of the semester. So, I wouldn't be getting Uncle Theo any kind of a card or flowers or chocolates.

While I was managing to eliminate all of the things not to do for Uncle Theo, I had nary a clue as to what I could do for him. And I pondered it, and I pondered it, and I pondered it, until it hit me, as I was thinking about Mama, that I could make Uncle Theo my favorite meal that Mama made: tuna mac! With Uncle Theo cooking for me every night, I could give him a break, and one night, cook for him. It wouldn't be the same because I obviously couldn't cook like him—his gourmet dinners with his mystery meats and complementary sides and yeast rolls—but he'd eat it up just fine because who didn't like tuna mac?

I set about to track Uncle Theo down and give him the good news before recess ended. My uncle and his schedules. I started in the barn, figured he might still be doing his exercises. Yet when I got out there, Chekhov at my heels, assuming this was part of our made-up game of tag, he wasn't to be found among the weights and other equipment, a stationary bike and treadmill, some elliptical machine, with one wall nothing but mirrors, and the other walls covered by posters of wrestlers. I was going to have to ask Uncle Theo what it was with him and professional wrestling—an ever-expanding list of questions I had for him—along with asking if he'd ever let me exercise in here, particularly with how he was always saying how scrawny I was.

For now though, I just needed to find him.

I left the barn and peered over toward Uncle Theo's garden to see if that was where he was, piddling about as it were. But I wasn't about to go over there, still leery of that particular section of the property, and Chekhov wasn't about to let me anyway. She seemed to guard that area like it was hers, no doubt on strict orders from Uncle Theo, and he had trained her well. I only stopped to glimpse in that direction, and Chekhov became antsy, fidgeting and twitching and speeding up her breathing, on the verge of setting me right with her barking and growling and the baring of her razor-sharp teeth. I swiftly moved to calm her. "Don't worry, girl," I said with a rub behind her pointy ears, "I ain't going to the garden."

When I concluded that Uncle Theo wasn't in his garden, and to double-check, I shouted for him and no response, I took off for the house, thinking he must've slipped in without me noticing as he sometimes did. I entered through the kitchen door, in a huff and a hurry, beads of sweat dripping down my face, and I had best keep with the moving around and being active to get in better shape. Uncle Theo wasn't seated at the table in the front, so I continued on down the hallway and peeked into his bedroom, but that was empty too, with his bed neatly made. Uncle Theo was all about making the bed, and he insisted that I make my bed every morning, preaching over and over how making your bed was the first and simplest thing you could achieve for the day.

I felt strange being in Uncle Theo's room without him. And I certainly wouldn't want him to find me here and accuse me of snooping. Even Chekhov seemed uncomfortable, as if she knew this room was off-limits. She loitered in the doorway without so much as an oversized paw passing into the other side, and she gave me that look, the tilt of her head, to question what I was doing. I was about to leave when I spied Uncle Theo's writing pads on the bookshelves. I wavered, and I hesitated, and I deliberated, knowing full well that I shouldn't, but I did anyway, my curiosity getting the better of me, and I took one out. Chekhov released a low, rumbling growl to express her displeasure, but I just had to read it, just a little.

Uncle Theo's writing, and longhand at that, was surprisingly neat considering how rough around the edges he tended to be, much better penmanship than mine, though that wasn't saying a whole lot. I read through this particular story he had written, and it reminded me of the Mickey Spillane paperback books I had been reading at night before bed, about a couple of bad guys who gunned down a good guy on the steps of the courthouse in broad daylight with all sorts of people around. For someone who wasn't much for reading, I was riveted, flipping through the pages, front and back, fascinated with how detailed Uncle Theo described everything, hanging on every word about the good guy being in the hospital, struggling to recover from his wounds. It was like I was experiencing it myself, could practically see the flashing and beeping monitors and the gaping wound on the good guy's belly. I couldn't put it down.

Uncle Theo was some kind of writer, no doubt about it, not that I was any sort of an expert or critic, anything but. Still, he could sure make up a story, that much I did know, and I wanted to read more. I could have sat on the edge of Uncle Theo's bed for the rest of the afternoon, reading his writings, if not for the fact that recess was over and I had to begin my studies in earnest, and that was certainly disappointing in many ways, but primarily because it meant I would have to catch up with Uncle Theo when I finished my lessons for the day to let him know that I'd be cooking dinner for him.

But right as I was thinking that, I heard movement in the hall. That had to be Uncle Theo, and I also had to get out of his room before he caught me. I rushed to put the writing pad back with the others, and when I did, I noticed a framed picture, facedown, on the shelf. I wasn't sure if I had knocked that over, so I picked it up. It was a picture of some young guy, clean-cut, clean-shaven, dressed in a dark suit and tie, broad smile from ear to ear, like in a school picture, only he was older, out of school, maybe a work picture. I inspected it closer, and that person in the picture was…Uncle Theo!

It must have been taken thirty years ago, but that was him all right. I could tell by his eyes, and I recognized his features that were now hidden by his long hair and unkempt beard and ratty t-shirts and tattoos. He was slender back then, and dare I say, scrawny! I guessed it was taken when he was a lawyer because the person in that picture looked exactly like the type of person I thought of when I thought of lawyers. But it wasn't the Uncle Theo I knew, or was getting to know, nor was it the person he was anymore. I couldn't fathom Uncle Theo ever looking like that and wouldn't have believed it if I wasn't staring straight at it. And I just kept staring at the picture, I couldn't help myself, until a yelp from Chekhov told me I needed to go. I returned it face down on the shelf and darted out of there.

The bathroom light was on, and the door was partially opened. I scuttled down and stuck my head in, expecting to find Uncle Theo brushing his teeth or combing his hair—though I doubted he combed his hair—but just something that wasn't enough for him to need to close the door completely. Yet, what I saw inside was nothing I would have ever expected, and I couldn't properly explain what I was seeing. I just had a sickening feeling it was something I shouldn't be seeing, with a queasiness that made me want to retch.

There was Uncle Theo, seated in a metal folding chair with his t-shirt pulled up to expose his stomach, and near his waistline was this thing: this fleshy, thick earthworm-like thing poking out of his body that Uncle Theo was trying to put a plastic baggie over. It didn't seem real, more like something from a horror movie, or a zombie film. Was that thing kind of slithering? And as gross and unnerving as it was, I couldn't force myself to turn away. I couldn't move. And I couldn't understand, but it looked to be this piece of Uncle Theo's insides protruding through his belly to the outside.

I made a gagging noise, an automatic reaction that I wasn't aware I had made until Uncle Theo glanced up when he heard it to find me standing there in the doorway. His expression dropped, a mix of shame and disbelief, as if I had just stumbled upon one of his most secret of secrets.

"Um, just a minute," he said, rattled, fumbling to cover

himself.

"Oops, sorry, I didn't, uh…" was all I could offer as I turned tail and dashed out of there, the sound of the bathroom door slamming shut behind me.

I got out to the front room and to the table, and I took a seat, any seat, as stiff as a board, except that I was trembling. I was trying to process what I had just seen, and I tried to shake that image out of my head, but I couldn't do either. I went to study, with civics the first class of the afternoon. I opened the textbook, and I stared blankly at the lesson plan, but that was the extent of it because studying was out of the question too. And to boot, I just knew that I was in a world of trouble for walking in on Uncle Theo in the bathroom doing that, whatever it was he was doing, and he was most assuredly going to kick me out of his house, and I wouldn't blame him one bit. I probably needed to leave before he kicked me out. I decided right then and there that I had no choice but to put my schoolwork aside and proceed to packing up my stuff to leave, with no idea where I would go, only that I had best leave. I got up to do just that when a hand on my shoulder gently nudged me back down in my seat.

"Sorry you had to see that, bud," Uncle Theo said, joining me at the table. "I should've closed the bathroom door. Thought you were still outside with Chekhov and, well…guess I'm still not altogether used to having company."

I couldn't look up. I couldn't dare look up at Uncle Theo. I couldn't look at anything other than my opened civics book and the lesson plan for the day and whatever else was on the table before me, but I couldn't look up. There was no way I was looking up. I sat there, not moving a muscle, preparing for the punishment that was certain to follow. And I deserved it. I sat there, and I waited for it, and I waited, and I waited, only there didn't seem to be any punishment coming. I still wasn't about to move though. I just sat there, until Uncle Theo did something.

"Do you want to talk about it?" he asked, to end this stalemate, and I was still too scared to look up at him, yet I could tell that he was looking at me, could feel the heat of his gaze.

"I shouldn't have been in there," I started, staring at the table, my eyes focused downwards. "I shouldn't have just barged in on you like that, when you were, um…well…when you were…" I stuttered because I didn't know how to put it, and I struggled to hold back the stubborn tears that were intent on forcing themselves out, feeling sad and scared and sorry all at once. I knew that I was in trouble and that I would have to pack my bag and leave. I didn't want to, but I knew I had to. "I'll leave," I told Uncle Theo, and I went to get up again, and again, Uncle Theo put his hand on my shoulder to nudge me back in place.

"Leave?" Uncle Theo asked like it was a ridiculous thing for me to say. "Why leave? Where are you going?"

I shrugged. "I dunno. I just gotta leave after that, after what I just did to you. Disrespecting you in your own house like that, in your bathroom. What was I thinking?" And frustrated, at myself, at the situation, at pretty much everything, I put my head in my hands, and I exclaimed, "I'm such a screw-up!"

"You're not a screw-up, Rhett," Uncle Theo tried to console me. "C'mon, now," and as he did, he kept his hand on my shoulder and sort of squeezed, and it made me feel warm in my heart. "I don't want you to leave. You didn't do anything wrong."

I swallowed hard, a lump the size of a softball, and I kept looking down, and I continued to fight back those stupid, stubborn tears that were intent on coming out, only I was determined not to let them. I didn't understand this. I didn't understand any of this. If I didn't do anything wrong, then why was I feeling this way, like I had done something outright terrible? And I was even more confused because Uncle Theo wasn't giving it to me, yelling and cussing for disrespecting him, and when he had every reason to be angry. Heck, I was angry at myself for being so inconsiderate as to burst in on Uncle Theo the way I had. Why wasn't he angry too?

Uncle Theo was still staring at me, I could tell. And I knew I wouldn't be able to not look at him for much longer. We were both hardheaded, but him more so, and plus, he was the adult. I was going to have to address him face-to-face, that much I did know. So, ever so slowly, I raised my head, and I looked my uncle square in the eye. And to my disbelief, there wasn't a scowl or a frown or a pissed-off glare or anything like that from Uncle Theo. He didn't appear upset with me in the least. Just the opposite in fact: he seemed concerned and worried as he leaned in toward me while he kept his hand on my shoulder.

"I sure feel like I did something wrong," I confessed, my voice quivering. "I just feel plumb awful."

"Nah, bud." He rubbed my shoulder, then took both his hands and folded them in front of him on the table, and I saw a tattoo on the inside of his wrist that said "writer" how it might be written in a dictionary. "It was my fault for not closing the door all the way. That's on me. I wasn't thinking. And I apologize."

I wasn't expecting Uncle Theo to apologize to me, and I certainly didn't need him to. And why would he? That caused me to scrutinize him more closely, to see what he might have been up to, but he didn't seem to be up to anything. He grew still, and he lowered his head. I just sat there, and I wasn't about to move until Uncle Theo was ready, until he lifted his head and focused on me.

"Suppose I owe you an explanation," he began, "for what you saw in there."

"You don't—" I went to tell Uncle Theo that he didn't owe me nothing, but he kept on talking, and I knew enough about him by now to let him talk when he felt like talking, because that was a rare occurrence.

"You know how I told you about that accident I had, which was why I stopped working?"

"Mm-hmm." I nodded.

"Well, it's because of that, um…that accident, why I'm like, uh…what you saw." He ran a hand through his hair, and he shifted in his chair, and he looked uncomfortable and nervous, neither of which I had seen from my uncle, nor did I care to. I wanted to tell him to stop, to not go any further, that there was no reason for him to go on and that he should just stop, that we were all right as far as I was concerned. But I didn't, and he wouldn't have paid me any mind anyhow. I just sat there, and I listened to Uncle Theo.

"It happened while I was at work," he went on, "the accident, actually, while I was on my way to work." He cleared his throat. "I was a federal prosecutor, and my job was to help put away the bad guys."

"What kind of bad guys?" I was eager to ask since this was the first I was hearing of this. I just figured Uncle Theo was one of those boring lawyers, the type that advertised on TV late at night when I couldn't sleep, not that I had any reason to think that, but that was just how I thought of lawyers.

"Just…just…" he sort of stammered, "bad guys: drug dealers, money launderers, racketeers—"

"Murderers?" I interrupted.

Uncle Theo hesitated and sat back in his chair and let out a heavy exhale. "Let's just say they were people involved in some bad stuff." He paused to regain his train of thought. "Anyways, once the bad guys got arrested, they went to court, and they were put on trial. And I had to argue as to why they needed to be sent to prison. And if the jury and the judge agreed with me, well then, the bad guys would go away, usually for a long time."

"Uh-huh, okay," I said, and I got it then because that reminded me of the shoot-'em-up movies I used to watch with Pops.

"Which didn't make me very popular with the criminals," he added.

"Uh-huh, for sure."

"And some of them had friends, and colleagues, associates, and these were some pretty bad individuals too. And they would get angry at me for sending their buddies to prison."

Uncle Theo paused once more, and I watched as he rubbed his hands together and then folded them and unfolded them and rubbed them some more. Seeing how difficult this was for Uncle Theo only made me feel worse for what I had done, which made it so that now Uncle Theo had to explain everything to me—even though I didn't feel like he needed to explain anything, but he apparently thought he did—as he shifted and squirmed, searching for the right words.

"One particular bad guy that I put away," he resumed, "had friends on the outside, and these were *really* bad fellas," he stressed, "who I was going to put away too." Uncle Theo held up a finger, how he did when he was making a point. "And I would've, mind you, except…well…except one day, when I was going in to work, walking up the steps into the courthouse in broad daylight with all sorts of folks going in to work, just a regular day like any other day, they jumped me, these two bad guys, came out from nowhere." He sighed, and his voice got soft, and it seemed like he was remembering something that was difficult for him to remember. "I didn't see them coming, and…and…they shot me."

A lightbulb went off in my head like one-thousand watts because I had just read about that in Uncle Theo's writings. Yet, I couldn't let on to Uncle Theo because I couldn't let on that I had been in his bedroom reading his writings. I was already in enough trouble with him, even though he told me I wasn't. I just covered up any reaction and acted as if I had never heard this before, which was technically true, only I had a hunch I knew how this story went.

"They shot me right in the gut." He lightly patted his stomach. "And I thought that was it for me, that I was done for, a real goner." Uncle Theo shook his head. "But after a long hospital stay, and lots of soul searching, and," he said, being certain to make eye contact, "praying, because, you know, you don't find any atheists in the foxhole—and I was most definitely in the foxhole, and, well, up until that point, hadn't been very religious—I managed to pull through, which is why…" Uncle Theo pointed at me and squinted and used his adult voice, "you don't squander your time, and you don't take *anything* for granted, because you never know how much time you have left, no matter how old or young you are." I couldn't help but think that Uncle Theo was scolding me then, but I paid attention all the same. "Anyways," he continued, "I did recover, by the grace of God." He snickered. "Or maybe God just didn't feel like dealing with me yet, so he kept me on this earth a little while longer. And once I was well enough, I left Louisville."

"You up and left," I said, and I remembered.

"Yep," he replied assuredly. "I was done. I was done with that career. I was done with that life. I was done with people. I was done with all of it. And I just left, with a little chunk of change—from disability, and there was a settlement—enough for me to live comfortably, and that was the only thing I wanted, was to live comfortably. And I moved out here," he said with a wink, "to the sticks." Uncle Theo peered about the room, at nothing in particular. "This was my uncle's house. Gramps's brother. He was in failing health, and needed someone to help him take care of the place, particularly his garden. Folks around here relied on him for what he grew."

"All those vegetables?"

"Yeah, uh…" Uncle Theo wavered for some reason, "that's right, something like that. And this house was run down, and the barn was about to topple over. I helped him to fix things up, straighten things out, and when he passed, he left it all to me." He sat back in his chair, exhaled, and spread his arms out with a wide grin. "My mansion. And this has been my life ever since." He sighed once more, but a satisfied sigh, "This is home, and I don't mind it."

With that, Uncle Theo stopped talking, and it seemed like he was done, but, as usual, I had questions.

"Did they catch the bad guys?" I asked him. "The ones who shot you?"

"Yeah, they got 'em," he kind of dismissed, like this wasn't something he was as interested in discussing.

"Who were they?" I followed, undeterred, and I really wanted to know. "And who was the bad guy they were angry at you for putting away, sending off to prison like you did?"

"Oh, um," Uncle Theo replied as he fidgeted in his chair, "that doesn't matter. It's all in the past. Bygones."

I could tell that Uncle Theo didn't want to talk anymore, but I was nowhere near to being done with my questions because I wanted to know more about this, all about this, this real-life Mickey Spillane paperback book that my uncle had lived through. But as I sat there, with so many questions, I gauged him, and Uncle Theo seemed like he wanted to be done with this, and I surmised I had best let him. I nodded like I understood, and I sort of did. Yet, that still didn't exactly explain what I had seen him doing in the bathroom with that thing on his belly. I wasn't going to ask him directly. I just glanced down in that direction on him, and Uncle Theo caught me doing that, and he got the hint.

"Oh yeah, and this," he said, staring down at his stomach, at that thing that was covered back over by his sweaty gray t-shirt. "When they shot me, it tore through my guts, damaged them beyond repair." He shrugged. "This is how I get by now."

I crinkled my face because that part didn't make sense to me, especially given that I rarely paid attention in biology class.

Uncle Theo waited to see if I was going to get it, and when it was obvious that I wasn't—and I wasn't—he explained, "It's how I gotta, uh, take care of things now, Rhett: bodily functions, so to speak. Basically, just a piece of my intestine that's sticking out, where, you know…and I gotta keep this little plastic bag over it that has to be emptied and cleaned and changed every so often. And that's what you caught me doing."

Uncle Theo focused on me to make sure he wasn't losing me as I was just trying to wrap my head around this.

"That's how you shit?" I questioned, and it just came out like that, as I pointed to his stomach.

He chuckled the way he sometimes did that made me wonder how I could amuse him without meaning to. "Yeah, uh-huh…sorta." And he must've recognized the look of disgust on my face, though I was straining my hardest to hide it. "It's my life now, Rhett. It's just how it is. Everybody's got something thrown at 'em, and this is what I've got."

I nodded, and I could definitely relate to that last part, as I already felt like I had had a lot thrown my way, although not as much as Uncle Theo, but I understood all the same.

"And that's why you limp too?"

"That's right, Rhett"—and slightly to himself, though I could hear him—"you sure are an inquisitive one." But he didn't seem bothered with me when he said that, just more of him being amused by me. "That gunshot weakened my core muscles," he went on. "That's how come I'm always exercising, to keep them strong. Also, when I was lying in that hospital bed, I vowed that I would never feel weak and helpless the way I did then, ever again." And once more, he pointed at me, and this was turning out to be a lecture to me, although I didn't mind it. "I don't want you ever feeling weak or helpless either, no matter what." Then he kind of smiled, how he did. "Even with how scrawny you are."

"So can I lift weights in the barn with you?" I spoke up.

Uncle Theo seemed to be caught off-guard by that, but he didn't immediately dismiss it as I feared he might. "We'll see," he said. Before I could ask another question, and I had so many questions, Uncle Theo cut me off. "That's all for now, all right, what do you say?" He looked over at that clock on the wall, steadily ticking, and with a jolt, told me, "You're late for class."

"Oh yeah, you're right," I said, mimicking the same sort of urgency that Uncle Theo had, although going back to my studies was the last thing I wanted to do today. Even so, I promised him, "I'll make up the time, Uncle Theo—I'll work late."

"That's okay, bud," he told me, putting his hand on my shoulder as he got up. "We can let it slide this once. Consider it part of your history lesson. And maybe a bit of biology too."

"That's fine by me," I said, and it certainly was.

"Just do what you can with the time that's left. I'll be out back in the garden," Uncle Theo said, walking off, with Chekhov following him closely, as she probably sensed he could use the company. "I'll be in a little later to fix dinner."

"Yeah, that," I uttered before Uncle Theo could go any further.

"That's why I was looking for you. I want to cook us dinner."

That froze Uncle Theo, and he gave me a curious look.

"*You* want to cook *us* dinner?" he asked as if he hadn't heard me correctly.

"Mama's tuna mac," I offered, excited but also apprehensive. "If that's okay. If that's something you can eat with, well, you know." And I nodded at his stomach.

"Yeah, I can eat tuna mac," he answered with a grin. "Who doesn't like tuna mac?"

"Exactly!" I wholeheartedly agreed. "Least I can do for all you've been doing for me and how I've disrupted everything for you here, bothering you and such."

"Rhett, I've told you before, and I'm not going to say it again, you're no bother. I'm serious." Uncle Theo was stern when he said that, then he relaxed enough to say, "But yeah, tuna mac. That sounds good."

"All right!" I said.

"All right," Uncle Theo agreed, and he turned to leave. "Well, we got our afternoon set for us. I'll be seeing you in a bit." He gestured toward my schoolwork. "Hit the books now. The school day's not over."

And with that, Uncle Theo went through the kitchen and exited out the back door. I watched from the window as he walked across the yard, his limp, which seemed a little more pronounced— and maybe Uncle Theo didn't feel the need to hide it from me anymore—to his garden, Chekhov in step. I kept watching him for no real reason, just to watch him, before returning to my studies, but it was going to be difficult to study civics after that.

My uncle, I swore, just when I thought I was getting to know him, something else turned up that I had no idea about. It caused me to wonder if I would ever really get to know the man. But I was most determined to try.

CHAPTER SIX

It was Friday afternoon. I had almost made it through another week, and the weeks seemed to be piling up, one after the next, and I could get what Uncle Theo meant about losing track of the time and how time flew by. I didn't know if it was something about being out here in the sticks, in these mountains, secluded and set away in this holler, but I was beginning to notice time slipping away from me.

While I didn't mind being with Uncle Theo, I feared that the longer I stayed with him in his home, the further away my home in Louisville became, like driving in a car when the street signs and scenery grew smaller and smaller in the rearview mirror, until they eventually disappeared, and you found yourself somewhere else. I didn't want that to happen to me with my home, my *real* home, but there was something inside me cautioning that it might, and that it already was. I had my fingers crossed tight though, and I said my prayers every night, that Mama would send for me soon.

I was finishing my last lesson for the day, and for the week, for that matter: the loathed math class, and how boring. I was having to learn fractions, which I found a lot more complicated to figure out with the calculator on my phone than addition or subtraction. And I was fading fast. It was a battle just to keep my eyes open. All I wanted was for this day and this week to be done with so that I could spend the weekend on my mountain bike exploring the old coal trails, which was my new passion, and who would've thought? But that clock on the wall, even with its constant ticking that liked to drive me crazy, didn't seem to be moving forward in the slightest, as I still had another thirty-five minutes to go.

It was right about then, with me thinking that nothing was going to save me from studying math, when Chekhov, who had been asleep at my feet and farting up a storm in her dreams—and Uncle Theo seriously needed to stop feeding her table scraps and give her regular dog food, and I had a mind to tell him that—jerked to attention, her gargantuan head rising like a bulky periscope, her pointy ears perked, her eyes focused on nothing I could discern. Then, she up and hightailed it out of there, through the kitchen—her oversized paws sliding on the slick linoleum floor—and out the back door.

I had no idea what that was about, and so of course, I had to investigate in the middle of my math class; all the more reason. I rushed into the kitchen under the guise of refilling my glass of water, as if I needed an excuse since it was only me in the house. But it was just out of habit, I supposed: always covering my tracks. I looked out the window above the sink, and I spied that same pickup truck that I had seen come around before, now with two men, the one who had been here prior and someone else, both equally scraggly, carbon copies of each other: denim shirts buttoned partway to reveal dirty t-shirts underneath, dusty jeans, muddy boots, sweat-stained ball caps, with their hair curling up and around in tangled wisps out the back. They were stepping out of their truck to meet with Uncle Theo, who was walking toward them from the barn, Chekhov leading the way like she was his bodyguard.

I stared attentively at this encounter, as this was, without question, more interesting than anything I had going on at that table in the other room with my school lessons, but I couldn't make out what anyone was saying. Their conversation appeared cordial enough, however. The scraggly men exchanged handshakes and pats on the back with Uncle Theo, and they joked around about something that must have been humorous to them, because they were all smiles, before they slowly headed in the direction of the barn. My curiosity got the better of me, as it was so apt to do, coupled with the fact that I was done with studying fractions, the type of knowledge I was convinced would never serve me in real life, and why fight it this late in the day, and the week? Once the three of them—plus Chekhov—went inside the barn, I sneaked out of the house and across the yard to try and get a better view as to what was happening.

While Uncle Theo might have claimed to have saved that rickety barn from toppling over, there were still gaps and splits aplenty in the walls. I crouched low and peered through one such opening like I was a detective in a Mickey Spillane paperback book, pretending to case the joint, creeping quiet as a church mouse so as to not be found out. But of course, Chekhov immediately noticed me because nothing seemed to get past her. I put a finger to my lips to shush her, and luckily, she seemed too preoccupied with whatever was going on in the barn and her role as Uncle Theo's protector to pay me much mind.

As I continued to look on, I watched as Uncle Theo moseyed to the back of the barn, past his exercise equipment, and disappeared behind a fabric partition—some sort of heavy-duty curtain—to a section of the barn I hadn't known existed. The two scraggly fellas waited at the front for Uncle Theo to return, admiring his wrestling posters and array of weights, until, after a few minutes, he emerged from that secret room lugging two plastic garbage bags of the same type I had seen him give to that one man when I had witnessed their last exchange. When Uncle Theo brought the bags out, he opened them both to reveal the contents. I pushed my face flush against the outside of the barn, hands flat against the wood slats, and squinted to see if I could make out what was inside the bags.

It appeared to be, from my vantage point, which wasn't the best, that the bags were just full of plants, but not freshly picked plants. These looked to be dried out and wrinkled and weathered. I focused harder, and I could have sworn those plants were a sampling of the tall weeds that grew beyond Uncle Theo's garden, only in rather poor condition. Why these two men drove all the way out here for two bags of dead weeds I had nary a clue, but they seemed happy enough about receiving that: quite pleased indeed, with one of the men punching his fist into the air in jubilation. Uncle Theo closed the bags, knotted them at the top, and handed them over to the men who turned to leave, Uncle Theo and Chekhov with them. That was my clue to get the heck out of there before I got discovered.

I pivoted on my heels and dashed back to the house, making it inside right as the men were exiting the barn. I poured myself another glass of water—which I truly needed after that run, and I had best stick with my conditioning—and stood at the sink, staring out the kitchen window. I saw the men toss the garbage bags into their truck, and then one of them pulled out a Styrofoam cooler that he presented to my uncle. The other man slapped Uncle Theo on the back once more as Uncle Theo just nodded. They talked a bit longer, something else funny as they smiled and laughed, before the scraggly fellas got into their truck and drove off, the engine backfiring like a shotgun blast, and the belts screeching and squealing something awful on my ears. Chekhov gave them a singular bark to let them know that she was still there and she was watching as she trotted off to catch up with Uncle Theo, who was already making his way to the house.

I took my glass of water and scurried back to the table, got seated to learn about fractions, or to give off the impression that I was learning about fractions, when Uncle Theo and Chekhov came in through the back door.

"Hope you like steak!" Uncle Theo shouted to me, excited, with a bark from Chekhov, as she probably knew she would be getting those table scraps.

"Yeah, I like steak, all right," I replied, and I got up to meet them in the kitchen, not as enthused about it as Uncle Theo was, mainly because I was suspicious as to what type of mystery meat these steaks were made from and not entirely wanting to know.

"We're gonna eat like kings tonight, bud," Uncle Theo said, setting the Styrofoam cooler on the counter, then he briskly brushed past me. "I'll put these away in a sec," he uttered with an urgency.

"First, I gotta piss like a Derby contender."

Uncle Theo hurried down the hall and into the bathroom, shutting the door behind him.

"What kind of mystery meat is this?" I muttered as I lifted the lid off the box to have a peek inside. Chekhov barked at me, either because she didn't want me messing with this without Uncle Theo or hinting that she wanted to eat the steak right now. Sometimes, she was difficult to read. "Just you wait," I scolded her, "you'll get your table scraps in due course." She barked once more so I wouldn't get the last word in; that much I did know about her.

I looked into the box, and there had to have been a dozen steaks, wrapped tightly in plastic and frozen hard as bricks. I didn't notice any arms and legs or heads on them, so that was a relief. Yet, I still couldn't rightly determine what kind of meat it was, even with picking one up for a closer examination. I grabbed a couple more of these meat bricks, and they all just seemed like regular steaks to me, not that Mama ever cooked us steak, but I had seen these in the butcher's section of the grocery whenever I went shopping with her, which we would bypass to grab a package of hamburger. My stomach growled at the mere sight of these steaks, along with the thought of how Uncle Theo might fix them for dinner and what kind of sides he would serve. Perhaps we *would* be eating like kings tonight.

I went to put the steaks back inside the box when I noticed something tucked in at the bottom, crammed underneath the meat, something green and papery. I reached in farther and pulled it out, and to my shock, it was money—and a lot of money!—cash rolled up with a one-hundred dollar bill on the outside, fastened by a rubber band.

"What the heck…" I said to myself, and just as I did, I sensed a massive presence looming over me.

"You sure are an inquisitive one, aren't you?"

I whipped around, and it was Uncle Theo, catching me red-handed.

"I, uh… I, uh…" I sputtered, my mind having gone completely empty.

"It's nothing, Rhett," my uncle remarked casually, taking the money from my hand and stuffing it into his front pants pocket. Then, he stepped around me to unload the steaks and store them in the freezer, leaving two on the counter to defrost to eat later and tossing the empty Styrofoam cooler into the pantry. "How do you like your steak?"

I just stared at Uncle Theo, observing him go about his business, dawdling about in the kitchen as if it was nothing, as if he didn't have a million dollars burning a hole in his pocket, though, probably not a million dollars—I was bad at math but not that bad—yet it might as well have been a million dollars to me because I had never encountered that much money in the flesh before. The only thing that came anywhere close was one time at school when Timbo held up a crisp fifty-dollar bill that he had swiped from his old man. But that was nothing like that roll of cash that just happened to be in the bottom of a Styrofoam cooler filled with steaks.

"What was that about?" I asked Uncle Theo, his back to me as he washed the dishes that were in the sink, which was my responsibility, so that really made me question that something wasn't quite right because he wasn't hollering for me to do it.

"Hmm?" he said, continuing to perform my chore without complaint, using the soapy sponge, rinsing, then setting the dishes and the glasses and the silverware on the plastic mat next to the sink to dry. When he was done, he turned to me, towel in hand, a blank expression on his face as if he had no earthly idea what I was talking about.

"That money," I said abruptly, motioning to the lump in Uncle Theo's front pants pocket where the cash was. "Why was it in the box of steaks like that?"

"Oh, um…" Uncle Theo began as if only then understanding what I was asking. "Those fellas owed me money." He tried to play it off like it was no big deal. "That's all." He glanced over into the other room at the table where my math book was folded open and at that ticking clock on the wall. "Are you finished with your schoolwork?"

"Yep," I said, lied, because I had more pressing concerns at the moment. "Got done early."

"Okay, well…why don't you go out and run around in the yard some, take advantage of this nice weather we're having before the humidity sets in, while I have a look at your lessons." He went over to the table. "Take Chekhov with you," Uncle Theo directed as he sat down and got himself situated. "I'll fire up the grill here in a bit."

I didn't move a muscle. I just remained there as Uncle Theo put on his horn-rimmed glasses and went about to review my math assignment, pulling out this bulky metal calculator that had to have been older than I was, with a spool of paper on it like he was going to print out receipts. Had I not been so perturbed, I would've told him that calculators didn't work so well on fractions, at least as far as I could surmise. But I had presently had enough with my uncle and his secrets, him never telling me the whole story on anything and assuming that I would just let this go like I let everything else go: two strangers showing up out of the blue and giving my uncle a wad of cash in exchange for a couple bags of dried-up old weeds. No way was this something I was content to just let go, even at the risk of whatever was to follow. I had to get to the bottom of this.

"Was it for the bags of weeds you gave them?" I inquired, and as I did, as those words floated out of my mouth, almost as if I could see them, fat and lazy and tumbling into the air, everything seemed to downshift. Uncle Theo shot me a glare that could've knocked me flat on my back, but I stood my ground. "Huh? Was it?" I kept on, taking a step forward and trying not to tremble, because I was already in, and there was no retreating.

"What bags of weeds, Rhett?" he asked deliberately, pulling his glasses off and squaring up with me.

"I saw it," I admitted, and I was nervous to admit it, but I admitted it all the same. "I went out to the barn—"

"You were spying on us?" Uncle Theo interrupted, and he was getting heated, that much was certain.

"I just, uh…" I briefly considered making up an excuse but thought better of it, because I had to come clean, there was no other way. "Yes, sir. I was," I said, swallowing hard, self-assured on the outside, not so much on the inside. "I wanted to find out for myself what was going on, on account of I'd seen that one man come around before, and you gave him garbage bags just like you did today. I wanted to know what was in 'em. It's my right."

"It's not your right," Uncle Theo snapped, and that startled me, for he hadn't spoken like that to me before, that tone, that tenor, no matter all my screw-ups, and with how his face was red and his jaw clenched and his eyes got small. It froze me, deer in the headlights. Uncle Theo must have recognized that, because he pulled back slightly, bent his head backward, and massaged the bridge of his nose with his thumb and forefinger like he was in pain, like I was causing him pain, and he sighed, long and drawn out. "Have a seat," he told me, a reluctance in his voice, with a flick of his wrist at the empty chair catty-corner to his.

I hesitated, not altogether confident about sitting at the table with Uncle Theo right then and there, with how he was, and that close, within arm's reach, wondering what he was up to, what he had in mind, if he was really angry and annoyed and aggravated at me, because he sure seemed that way, and then some. But he took another deep breath, to compose himself from what I could gather, which I recognized from how my teachers would do the same whenever I was getting on their last nerves and they needed to compose themselves to talk to me.

"It's all right," he said, making eye contact to convince me, as he could no doubt perceive my apprehension. "Take a seat, bud. I'm not angry with you…not really. Suppose you do kinda have a right to know what goes on here, considering you're sleeping under this roof as well, *my* roof, but even so." He sort of chuckled to himself, "I'm telling you, with your excellent cross-examination skills, you'd make a good lawyer someday." And he included his usual caveat, "Not that I would wish that on anyone."

I was tentative as I took a seat at the table, not scooting the chair in just in case I might have to get up fast and run off. I didn't suspect Uncle Theo would blow up on me, had never seen that side of him, nor did I expect to, but I also still didn't know him all that well either.

"So those *weeds*," he began with an emphasis on the word, "are some of what I grow in my garden."

"Beyond your garden," I noted.

Uncle Theo stopped and sat back in his chair as if that caught him off guard, me indicating how I had already been out there. And that wasn't very bright of me for doing that, and I knew it wasn't as soon as I said it, but I did so all the same, and I was all in now. He just shook it off as if nothing about me surprised him anymore.

"Yes, that's correct, Rhett," he went on, visibly forcing himself to be restrained. "Those weeds grow beyond my garden. And in and among my garden. And they've grown there for as long as that garden has been there. Actually, longer. Those weeds were there first, and then my uncle planted the garden in front and around them to conceal them."

"Why would your uncle want to conceal weeds?" I asked. "Why not just pull 'em up? They're weeds. Heck, that's one of my jobs at home: to pull up the weeds in the flowerbeds and between the cracks in the walkway."

"Because those aren't typical weeds," Uncle Theo clarified. "Those are marijuana plants. It's marijuana that I'm growing out there. You know what marijuana is, right?"

Of course, I knew what marijuana was—at least, I sort of did. One time at school, Timbo showed us a skinny, wrinkled cigarette that didn't look like a regular cigarette but rather as if he rolled it himself, twisted on both ends, that he said some older kid from his shop class gave him in exchange for a stack of his dad's nudie mags. Timbo told us it was a marijuana cigarette, and if we smoked it, it would make us feel good, calm and airy and relaxed and chill, and he kept saying "chill" like that was something, like that was the main point. He talked it up such that we were game to give it a try, and particularly because if one guy smoked it, then all of us had to smoke it or risk getting teased to death by the other guys. We were fixing to do just that when Mr.

Smitherman showed up, as he always seemed to do, always eyeing us the way he was. Rather than get caught holding a marijuana cigarette and face whatever punishment came with that, Timbo ate it, the whole thing, in one gulp, nearly choking. So I knew what marijuana was. Sort of. But that still didn't explain why Uncle Theo was growing it.

"Are you a drug dealer, Uncle Theo?"

Uncle Theo smiled, not one of his actual smiles but more like a made-up one, to maybe make light of this, but beneath that smile, he appeared a little perturbed.

"No," he said, and he was resolute, "I am not a drug dealer, Rhett."

"But you're growing marijuana," I continued, "and giving it to fellas in exchange for wads of cash. If that ain't a drug dealer, I don't know what is." And perhaps I was an inquisitive one, after all.

Uncle Theo laughed weakly, though I couldn't decide if it was a funny laugh or a frustrated laugh.

"You are definitely destined for law school, boy," he said with a snicker. Then, he sighed and turned serious as if there was a lesson coming for me. "It's not quite that simple." He stopped. "Like I said, that marijuana has been out there for"—he shrugged—"who knows, probably longer than this property has been in our family. My uncle just took it upon himself to...to tend to it. And when I moved in, he taught me." He lightly pounded his fist on the table to punctuate. "That marijuana's part of this land. It belongs to this land. It's gonna grow regardless. It's nature."

"So you're just allowing the marijuana to grow on your property?"

"Uh-huh, that's right."

"And then you sell it to folks?" I asked, as I was trying to piece this together. "And yet then, how don't that make you a drug dealer, even if the marijuana is growing in nature?"

"It's um...well...the thing is..." Uncle Theo stammered, like I had gotten him on that one, which wasn't exactly my intent. I was just trying to understand this. "Yes, that marijuana is growing out there, and folks are getting it from me, and if that makes me a drug dealer, well…that's open to interpretation."

I had no reaction to that because I didn't know how to react to that, didn't rightly know what Uncle Theo had in mind by that.

"Listen, Rhett," Uncle Theo picked up, scratching his head through his matted hair, then holding his hands out to explain, "people are gonna want this marijuana anyway. And they'll get it however they can. They'll come out here, trespassing and trampling and fighting and causing all sorts of ruckus to get at it. But there's an understanding, what my uncle established, and what I'm carrying on, what we consider to be a neighbors' agreement, where I'm the only one who tends to the marijuana, for the benefit of everyone in this holler."

I sat there, and I allowed this to sink in, but it was still about as clear as dirt for me.

"So, you're like…the marijuana farmer for this holler?" I questioned.

Uncle Theo acted like that tickled him, and he nodded, and he replied, "In a way, yeah, sure. You could say that."

"But you ain't selling it to folks? You ain't a drug dealer?" I asked. And before he could respond, I followed with, "Then what was that money for?"

Uncle Theo sighed once more, and this must've been a difficult conversation for him to have if he was sighing as much as he was, and I felt slightly bad about putting my uncle through this, but all the same, I had to find out. "People give me what they can for it," Uncle Theo answered, "as a courtesy, in appreciation for what I'm doing, as part of this neighbors' agreement. It's usually these *mystery meats*, as you say, whatever extra they got left after a hunt. Although"—he became momentarily excited—"those are prime Angus steaks we got tonight, mind you. The real deal." Then he returned to more settled. "But sometimes, I get other things, aside from mystery meats. Could be new tires for my truck, or gym equipment, tattoos." He held his arms spread to show me—as if I hadn't already seen his tattoos—and I wished he would sit still long enough for me to admire them all. "And yes, Rhett, folks do give me cash on occasion, which I just put back into what it costs me to tend to my *crop*. Like an investment."

I was starting to get it, but not totally, and I suspected that Uncle Theo could tell.

"You see, bud," he leaned in once more, got right up to me, "folks in these parts have had it tough, with the mines shutting down and businesses closing and companies moving out. Some people can't afford to leave, or they don't want to because this has been their home forever and they don't have anywhere else to go, maybe they don't want to go anywhere else. And why should they? But they still gotta get by. My uncle helped them out that way, and I'm doing the same."

"So these folks are selling the marijuana you're growing. They're the real drug dealers?"

"What these folks do with it is their own business," Uncle Theo was adamant in his response. "I don't ask any questions because it's none of my concern. They use it however they see fit. Could be for medicinal purposes: to take away the aches and pains accumulated over the years. Maybe they give it away, same as I'm doing." He withdrew and conceded, "And maybe some do sell it. Of course, that's a possibility. I'm not naïve. But do I know that exactly? Nope. Whatever it is, it is."

I scratched my head, and sorted through all the questions that were racing through my mind.

"Okay, but so the ones who are selling it—*if* they are selling it—" I stated it that way just to align with what Uncle Theo was telling me, though I was aware of enough to figure that some of these folks had to be selling it, "they're...well..." I was getting thoroughly confused, and I didn't know if that was what my uncle was trying to accomplish, but that was the result. "I don't get it, Uncle Theo, because you used to put away bad guys, like drug dealers; you told me so yourself." I threw my arms out. "How is this any different?"

Uncle Theo took his time to answer, and maybe I had stumped him, and I was definitely stumped myself.

"Could be," he started, sort of uncertain, "that it's not so different at all, in the grand scheme. Could be you're right. Under the letter of the law, these folks who might be selling it, sure, they could be considered the bad guys, and me too, for that matter." He ran his hands once more through his hair. "But once you get out into the world, you'll find that it's not always so easy to tell the bad guys from the good guys. The line can get pretty blurry at times. That's just how life is, bud."

That was the only thing that I was sure of from this conversation, and I had to agree with my uncle: life was certainly blurry at times. The issue was what to do to make it not so blurry, and I didn't rightly have the answer, and it seemed that neither did Uncle Theo. And so, I just reckoned I was done for now, and I put all those other questions I still had aside because this clearly wasn't something we were going to resolve today.

"Okay," I capitulated.

Uncle Theo reached his hand out, grabbed me on the shoulder, and said, "I know it's a lot to take in, and this isn't something you should have to deal with. I tried to keep this from you, Rhett. For your own good."

"Mm-hmm," I said, and I braced myself, in case I was in trouble with Uncle Theo and he was about to lay into me.

"Remember that stick that tore through your mountain bike tire?" he asked.

"Yeah?"

"That was a booby trap you rode over. They're set up all over back there, to keep people from sneaking in and stealing those plants. Because even though we have a neighbors' agreement, there are still some folks who aren't inclined to abide by any such understanding."

I knew I was right about those things, but that didn't make me feel any better about it, and in fact, I suddenly felt very frightened at the thought of how close I might've come to having one of those sharp sticks tear through me. I could feel my cheeks get flushed, and my mouth was dry, and I wanted another glass of water, and this was more than I had bargained for. I was learning perhaps too much about my uncle, even if I probably needed to.

"That's why," he said, pointing a finger at me, "when I tell you something, like not to go roaming around this property, you need to listen, okay? Because it's for your own good. Everything I do for you is for your own good."

I nodded like I understood, and I did, and I also appreciated hearing that.

There was a stillness that fell over us, neither one knowing what else to say, what else was needed to say, if there was anything else to say, before Uncle Theo said, "Needless to say, you can't let on about this to anyone. Not that you would." He wavered, and I had a notion as to what he was getting at. "Like your mother."

"I won't," I spoke up quickly to promise him. "You got my word, Uncle Theo. I won't tell anyone."

"I didn't think you would"—he sat back—"but, like we've said, the line between bad guy and good guy, well, it's not always clear…and we wouldn't want anyone getting the wrong idea."

"Mm-hmm."

Uncle Theo lingered on me, like he did, and then let out a long exhale as if that had been a burden for him to get out and it was a burden for me to take in, and we both breathed a sigh of relief that this was over. I needed more air, though.

"I'm gonna go outside," I said, standing up, "run around some, take advantage of this weather, ya know?"

"Excellent idea." Uncle Theo seemed glad at that, and maybe just glad that I was going to leave him be. "And I'll look over your math homework. Although, truth be told, fractions aren't my strong suit."

"Yeah, they ain't easy," I agreed, "and the calculator's not much help neither."

I said that last part before realizing I had said it, but Uncle Theo didn't seem to mind. There was a lot heavier stuff that we had been discussing than me trying to cheat on my math lesson. Uncle Theo put his glasses back on and went about to review my schoolwork as I left the house, patting my leg for Chekhov to follow, which she did without hesitation, as she was always up for a good run around in the yard, and it could've also been that she sensed the tension.

"I'll fire up the grill here in a bit," Uncle Theo called out to me. "Then we'll eat like kings tonight."

"Yes, sir," I said, leaving through the back door. "We'll eat like kings."

❧

I was out in the yard with Chekhov, waiting for Uncle Theo to call us in for dinner, but I wasn't being very active, and I wasn't running around. I was really hardly moving, in spite of Chekhov's usual enthusiasm and insistence, nudging up against me with her massive frame, her cold wet nose, begging to play our made-up game of tag, for me to chase her, and then she would chase me. I didn't want to. I wasn't in the mood for that. I wasn't in the mood for much of anything. I had only come outside so that I could get some fresh air and think, or maybe not think for once, at least not think about what my uncle was up to with that garden of his and the neighbors' agreement and his "crop." Yet, it was impossible to erase it entirely from my mind.

Perhaps Uncle Theo truly believed that the line between bad guys and good guys was blurry, and I wanted to give him the benefit of the doubt on that. But the line seemed pretty well-defined to me. And I had to admit, my BS detector was going off a touch when he was saying all that. Then again, I didn't want to believe that my uncle was a bad guy either, because he had been nothing but good to me. He was taking care of me, and he cooked me dinner and made me do my schoolwork. He was trying to straighten me out. And apparently, he was being good to his neighbors too, tending to those raggedy old weeds for them to use however they saw fit, to help them get by, whatever they needed of him. Even so, something about this just didn't sit well with me.

I wondered what someone like Mr. Smitherman would think about it, considering he always seemed to know the difference between wrong and right, particularly when it came to me and my buddies, when all we wanted to do was shoot the shit out back behind the dumpster that smelled of sour milk, and he would inevitably bust us for one thing or the other. And Mama most certainly would not have approved. Uncle Theo didn't have to warn me not to tell her about it because I already knew better than to do that. She freaked out once when she caught me drinking one of her beers that I had sneaked from the fridge. Finding out that Uncle Theo was the holler's marijuana farmer would for sure put her over the edge, and who knew where she would send me after that?

I didn't know what to make of any of this, and Uncle Theo was right: this wasn't something I should've had to deal with. Yet here I was, dealing with it anyway. If only I would've just minded my own dang business. It could've been that I really was too inquisitive for my own good. But I only wanted to get to know my uncle better. Was that so wrong? I reckoned that old saying held true: "you best be careful what you asked for."

"Hush now, girl, I'm serious. I'm trying to think!" I yelled at Chekhov as she was still impatiently trying to get me to play with her, resorting to that low grumbling growl that had scared the daylights out of me when I first met her, until she finally took the hint from my rebuking with a snort and a whine, and wandered off, tail between her legs.

I stayed outside for a while, somewhat disinclined to go inside and be around Uncle Theo, kind of letting things settle between us as I contemplated life and whatnot, bad guys versus good guys, with those ugly marijuana plants waving in the breeze off in the distance like they were mocking me, hidden how they were behind the full stalks of corn, and the climbing tomato plants, and whatever else was growing in that garden, but I knew where to look for them, and I knew they were there, those stupid, disgusting weeds. What was it about those weeds?

I was eventually drawn back to the house by the tempting aroma of steak being grilled over an open fire with hickory chips. I couldn't stay upset with my uncle for too long because, say what you would about him, the man knew how to cook. And we were family. I was heading that way, letting that sumptuous smell lead me, when I noticed a car way down at the end of the driveway. I assumed it was just more of Uncle Theo's neighbors coming to get their share of the marijuana, though it wasn't a beat-up truck like before but some slick, black sedan with tinted windows. I strained to see but, with the distance and those windows, couldn't make out who was inside, not that I probably would've known who they were anyhow.

I stood there and waited for the car to drive up to the house, but secretly hoping that it wouldn't because I was hungry, and I needed to eat and didn't feel like having to wait around for another one of those transactions to be consummated. This day was already turning out to be endless, when all I wanted was to go in for dinner, and it seemed that Chekhov did as well because once she saw that car, she came running out from wherever she had been and unleashed some furious barks, deep and guttural, and she tore off toward it, her legs thundering on the ground, kicking up dirt like a Derby contender. I ran after her, as fast as I was able, but I had no chance of catching up. I called for her to stop, for what that was worth, and it was worth nothing because she just kept on in hot pursuit.

I wasn't sure what her intention was once she got to that car, but it most assuredly wasn't to welcome whoever was inside to Uncle Theo's house. And whoever was in that car didn't stick around to find out. They slammed it in reverse, spun around, and peeled the heck out of there, the tires spinning out in the gravel, flicking out cascades of crushed limestone. When Chekhov got to the edge of the property, she stopped on a dime as if she knew precisely where the boundary line was, yet she kept on barking until the car was out of sight. By the time I got down there, there was nothing but the burnt smell of exhaust and a scattering cloud of dust.

Once that car was gone, Chekhov went back to being her normal, likeable self, her long red tongue hanging out of her wide mouth, panting, her hot and stinky breath, tail wagging, wanting to play. I bent down to rub her behind her pointy ears, and she licked me on the cheek to let me know she was all right.

"You're an odd dog sometimes, you know that, Chekhov?" I told her, not understanding what that outburst had been about but doubting that Uncle Theo would be happy with her chasing away one of his marijuana customers, or neighbors, or however he considered them. And I wasn't about to say anything. "We'll just keep this our little secret, girl," I promised Chekhov as I patted her down the back, and we returned to the house to eat.

That night, I lay in bed, still trying to come to terms with everything Uncle Theo had said earlier, staring up at the galaxy of star stickers on the ceiling. He and I didn't speak any more about his garden and all the rest of that at dinner. We just sat there at the table, with few words exchanged, and we ate like kings, as Uncle Theo had promised. Along with the steaks, which he had seared crusty brown on the outside and pinkish and tender on the inside, he served baked potatoes with sour cream, roasted asparagus, and cheesy garlic-butter rolls instead of the usual yeast rolls, and they did pair better with the steak, with a glass of milk for me and a cold beer for him. Actually, he had a couple beers, and I reckoned it had been one of those days for my uncle that called for a couple beers. I knew it wasn't the right time for me to ask Uncle Theo for a beer for myself, but someday, I would.

I went to my room after we ate and I did the dishes, with Uncle Theo remaining at the table to write his real-life Mickey Spillane, bad guys versus good guys, memoirs, I imagined. Chekhov alternated between us, lying down for a spell at Uncle Theo's feet, then wandering in to check on me. She was a smart dog and could no doubt perceive that something was up, though it didn't take much detecting to realize that. There was this awkwardness about me and Uncle Theo, this thickness, this stiltedness, each being overly mindful to keep out of the other's way.

I wanted to be alone, anyway. I was feeling anxious, questioning if I really belonged here. But if I didn't belong here, then where did I belong? I liked Uncle Theo, I liked him a lot, that was a given, and that was never going to change. And I was enjoying spending time with him, for the most part, and getting to know him better. But maybe I didn't want to get to know him too well, because who knew what else he was up to? And he sure wasn't going to tell me unless I asked him or found out about it myself, more than likely when I was doing something that Uncle Theo had told me not to do. I was in a bind, all right, and my thoughts were jumbled, and my mind was cluttered. I just lay in bed, staring up at the galaxy of star stickers on the ceiling, thinking about everything and nothing, waiting to fall asleep.

I had just begun to drift off when I heard a voice in the other room. I went to the window, my first inclination, to check if we might've had company, but there wasn't anyone out there, no more strange cars or trucks. I climbed back into bed, but I heard that voice again, so I slinked over to the wall, close to it, with my ear pressed tight. With how thin the walls were in this house, I was able to make out that it was Uncle Theo's voice and that he was talking to someone. His was the only voice I heard, and as I kept listening, I could tell that Uncle Theo was on the phone, that ancient landline of his. But who was he talking to?

I listened more intently, and if nothing else, I was developing my eavesdropping skills, not that that was necessarily something to brag about, and I surely wouldn't want Uncle Theo to know that, but it did come in handy. Uncle Theo sounded serious. I wouldn't exactly call it angry, but neither was he particularly pleased to be talking to whoever it was he was talking to. I stayed still, to hear what I could. And when he called the person he was talking to "Kitty," I had a special tingling throughout my body. Uncle Theo was talking to Mama!

"You made your point already, Kitty, okay?" I heard him say. "Now, it's time for you to let the boy come home."

And they were talking about me.

"I don't know what more I can do with him," Uncle Theo went on. "He's gotta go."

My heart sank when I heard that, it sank right to the bottom of my belly that knotted and twisted, and my legs became wobbly such that I dropped to the floor. I couldn't believe that. I couldn't believe what I had heard. It was devastating to me. It was crushing. Uncle Theo didn't want me anymore, and he was going to kick me out.

"I just don't think it's healthy for him to be here any longer," he told Mama. "A boy his age, he doesn't need to be hanging out with some old man…out in the sticks. He needs to be around other boys his age. And frankly, Kitty, I need to get on with my life as well."

Uncle Theo went silent, and it must have been Mama's turn to talk because all I heard from Uncle Theo was "uh-huh" and "I know" and "yes, Kitty, but…" Mama was a talker. She could out-talk anyone. She would talk so much around the house that sometimes I would just tune her out and not hear anything she was saying. She must've gotten the talking genes in the family, and Uncle Theo, I didn't know what kind of genes he got, silent genes if there was such a thing, and I supposed the cooking genes too, because other than her tuna mac, Mama wasn't near the cook Uncle Theo was.

I heard Uncle Theo say, and from his tone I could surmise that he was getting agitated, "I know I need to see what I caused." And he repeated, "You made your point, I already told you." I had no idea what that was about, what Uncle Theo had caused, or why he had to see it, or what Mama's point was for that matter, but Uncle Theo didn't seem to want any part of that.

They went on like this for fifteen minutes or so, back and forth, with Uncle Theo firm in his position that I needed to leave, and Mama apparently insisting that I stay. I wished I hadn't heard it, yet I couldn't stop listening. I sat there on the floor in my bedroom, ear to the wall, and eavesdropped on Uncle Theo's conversation with Mama until he concluded, hastily and as if he had had enough, "Okay, all right, fine. I'll give it a little more time." He let out an exasperated sigh. "But just a *little* more time. You need to figure this out, and sooner rather than later, because the boy can't stay here forever. That much I'm clear on."

With that, Uncle Theo hung up the phone, and he exclaimed to himself, "Gee-zus!" I heard him walk into the kitchen, his footsteps bulky—obviously frustrated with what had transpired—and yank open the refrigerator door and crack open another can of beer and take a chug, and then return to the table, the chair legs scratching against the hardwood, probably to write, maybe about that conversation with Mama, to perhaps include it as another chapter in his memoirs.

I was sick after hearing that, literally sick to my stomach, and I thought I might puke. Everything just seemed so hopeless to me all of a sudden, like I no longer belonged anywhere, with Uncle Theo wanting to kick me out and Mama not wanting to take me back. It was all I could do to drag myself into bed, where I pulled the covers over my head, curled up on my side, and silently cried myself to sleep.

CHAPTER SEVEN

It was the toughest conversation I would ever have. Although, granted, I was only fourteen, and there were sure to be other difficult conversations to come in my life, but that didn't make me feel any better for what I had to do presently, which was to march straight into that front room and tell Uncle Theo that it was time for me to go. I had to. That was the only thing I could do after overhearing his conversation with Mama last night, both of them arguing over who was going to end up getting stuck with me. I would make the decision for them, and neither would end up getting stuck with me, because my mind was made up, and I was leaving.

I had to leave. There was no choice. And I had to be a man about this and leave now, to take the initiative, to take control, to go out on my own terms and not have Uncle Theo kick me out. I couldn't suffer the indignity of that. I couldn't stand to be kicked out of another place. I had thought about it all last night, tossing and turning in bed, sweating through the sheets and the pillow case. Once I did finally manage to fall asleep, it was only to end up in another one of those weird dreams. I never had dreams like that until coming to Uncle Theo's. There was something about it here, or maybe there was something about me being here. Either way, I wasn't going to be here any longer, because I was leaving. My mind was made up.

When I got out to the front room, sure enough, there was

Uncle Theo seated at the table, a cup of coffee before him, wearing his stupid glasses, writing his memoirs maybe, who cared? I wondered if he was going to write about throwing his own flesh and blood out into the streets to fend for himself, what kind of chapter that would make for his dumb book. And if Uncle Theo wasn't going to write about it, then perhaps I would. I could write my own memoirs. I was a good enough writer, Uncle Theo said so himself. He and Mama wouldn't like what I had to write about them, but so what? I wouldn't be around anyway.

"Morning, sunshine," Uncle Theo greeted me with a smile, that smile of his I didn't think I could trust anymore, hunched over his pad of paper, pen in hand. He gave me the onceover, twice. "Rough night?"

"Huh?"

I didn't know what he was talking about, as usual.

He motioned at me with his hand that held the pen. "Your hair," he said, stifling a laugh, "sticking up every which way. Were you fighting with your pillow?"

"Huh?"

I still didn't know what he was talking about, until I put my hands to my head, and I could feel the cowlicks and thick clumps of hair poking out at odd angles, matted and messy and unkempt. And when I caught a glimpse of my reflection in the front window, I got what Uncle Theo was talking about. Even Chekhov barked like she thought it was funny. It wasn't funny to me though; nothing was funny to me at that moment.

"I can get the shears out later," Uncle Theo said, smirked, putting his pen down and taking a sip of his coffee, "the ones I use on Chekhov, if you want me to give you a trim."

"Nah." I shook my head, and if Uncle Theo was trying to distract me from what I had to say, it was working. I had to maintain my focus.

Uncle Theo waited a few seconds for me to say more, and when I didn't, because I was gathering the nerve to say more, he broke the silence. "Well now, go on," he waved toward the kitchen, "get yourself some breakfast. It's all laid out there for you on the counter." He took another sip of coffee and returned to his writing pad. "Fuel up before your bike ride. Supposed to be another nice day for that."

"I need to talk to you," I told him, staying put, staring at him, reminding myself to breathe, inhaling through my nose and exhaling through my mouth so as not to get too nervous about it, but I was already nervous about it. I had to be a man about this.

"Oh? All right." Uncle Theo's tone shifted, and so did his body as he placed both elbows on the table, his chin in his hands, to concentrate on me. "What's up?"

I knew what I wanted to say, only I didn't know how to say it, other than to just say it, to just get it out before I chickened out, and then I might never say it.

"I'm leaving today."

Uncle Theo choked out a chuckle. "You're...what? Leaving?" And he sat back. "Again with this, Rhett?"

"Yes, sir," I said.

Uncle Theo breathed like he was frustrated. "What is it this time? What's bothering you?"

"I ain't staying where I ain't wanted," I replied.

Uncle Theo squinted his eyes like he didn't understand, and like I finally had his attention. "Why do you say that?"

I shook my head and looked down.

"Cuz you said so yourself," I managed to get out, to the floor. "I heard you talking to Mama last night."

Uncle Theo let out a protracted exhale that caused me to glance up at him to see what he was about to do. He leaned back in his chair, folded his hands behind his head, and when he did, I recognized a tattoo of a squirrel under his left tricep, and it caused me to consider how many tattoos Uncle Theo had in all if I was continuing to discover new ones whenever he moved differently. But this wasn't the time for that.

"You sure are an inquisitive one," he muttered to himself.

"I apologize for eavesdropping," I told him before he could

reprimand me for it, though I suspected he might do that anyhow, "but it's just that you got a loud voice, and this house has thin walls. And besides, that seems to be how I ever find anything out around here, on account of you don't ever tell me nothing."

"Just let me explain, okay?" Uncle Theo said in a softer voice, sitting forward.

"What's to explain?" I said, and I felt my confidence and my resolve strengthen, as I was committed to going through with this, and I had to go through with this. "I done heard ya already!"

Chekhov barked at that, I guessed because she hadn't heard me raise my voice in the house. But Uncle Theo remained reticent. Speaking lower and slower, he said, "I only meant, when I told that to your mother, that I thought you needed to be back with kids your age. That's all."

"It's cuz I found out about your garden and the booby traps and your neighbors' agreement, strange fellas showing up at all hours to trade their mystery meats and whatnot for your *crop*," I emphasized. "It's on account of I know about this whole operation you're running. That's the real truth of the matter, ain't it? Why you want me out?"

Uncle Theo shook his head. "No, Rhett, it's not that. Honest." He hesitated as if contemplating. "Although," he went on, "I would've preferred that you hadn't gone snooping—"

"I wasn't snooping!" I interrupted, and I was revving up. "I have a right to know what goes on 'round here!"

"Okay, okay"—Uncle Theo put his hands up to try and calm me—"just simmer, all right, simmer. Let's discuss this."

"Nuh-uh," I said, and I was adamant. "I'm leaving. I ain't staying where I ain't wanted!" I threw my arms out. "I'll let you get back to your life. I'm sorry I disrupted it so, that I was such a burden to you."

I turned to leave.

"It has nothing to do with you," Uncle Theo said in his adult voice, and that made me know that he was taking this seriously. "It's just... It's just not a good environment for a boy, being here with me."

I flung back around at him because that struck a nerve. "That's just an excuse, and you know it! I'm tired of adults giving me excuses." I wavered, before I came out with the rest. "And I'm tired of adults kicking me out. Mr. Smitherman kicked me out of school. Mama kicked me out of our house. And now you're kicking me out of your house!"

"I told you, I'm not—"

"And Pops up and left me for no reason," I added, the words escaping on their own. I hadn't planned on saying that, it just happened. Once one thing started coming out, all the things started coming out. "I'm tired of it. I'm sick and tired of it." I took a few steps back. "It must be me. It's gotta be me. It's gotta be my fault. All of it. No one wanting to be around me. Everyone always kicking me out. And I ain't gonna let it happen no more. Because now, I'm gonna be the one who just up and leaves!"

I pivoted and plodded down the hall to my room to pack my belongings and get out of there, because I was done talking, and I was done listening, and there wasn't anything Uncle Theo could say to make me want to stay, I was convinced of that, until he hollered out to me, "Rhett, your father didn't up and leave you."

That stopped me dead in my tracks, like a blow to the back that Uncle Theo had thrown out on the off chance it would connect, and it did. It surely did connect. It liked to take my breath away. I had to process this. But how could I process this? What had I just heard? Pops didn't up and leave me? What did Uncle Theo mean? How could he even say such a thing? He wasn't there. He didn't know. What was Uncle Theo talking about?

I needed to find out more about this, of course I did, so I turned to Uncle Theo, and I just stood there without a response, because I didn't have a response. But I didn't have to tell Uncle Theo to explain this to me, because my face must've showed him that.

"Your father didn't up and leave you," Uncle Theo repeated, measured, rising from the table.

"Why do you say that?" I asked. "You don't know. How could

you know?"

"I do know, Rhett." Uncle Theo moved toward me. "I know." He paused, put his hands on his hips and stared down at the floor and got quiet, and the more he kept quiet, the more I became scared as to what might follow, before he returned to me. "I know…"—and he sighed—"because I was the one who sent him away."

"What?" I gasped and immediately became lightheaded. "What did you say?" I tried to shake myself back into consciousness. "Huh? What?"

Uncle Theo swallowed hard, then answered directly, "I sent your father away. To prison. Like I did all the bad guys." His eyes had become watery like mine, and it appeared this was as difficult for Uncle Theo to say as it was for me to hear, and it was plenty hard for me to hear. "I was just doing my job."

I was in a state of shock at that, absolute shock and surprise and astonishment. I didn't know how I was still standing. How could I still be standing after hearing that? But I was only barely still standing because I felt as if I was about to faint, the life inside of me gently fluttering out. My mouth was wide open and bone dry. The tears were flooding from my eyes and I let them, because in some odd way, it felt comforting to cry, like a relief, like a release, like this was something that had been building up for a while, and it was long overdue and just needed to happen.

"It was never my intention to hurt you," Uncle Theo explained, taking a few more steps to me. "That was the last thing I wanted, believe me. But your father, he was mixed up with some dangerous folks, and he was headed down the wrong path, doing things he shouldn't. And he was gonna hurt someone, he was gonna get himself hurt, you and your mother too. I told him that, I did, and I told your mother. I did everything I could, but…he still kept on in his ways."

"So instead, you just throw him in jail?" I yelled at Uncle Theo because I couldn't believe this was happening, almost as if it was happening to someone else and I was watching it play out before me.

Uncle Theo approached. "I tried to get off the case," he said, "to have another lawyer in my department take over for me, but the judge wouldn't allow it. And so, I did… I did…" he stammered, his eyes darting about before focusing back on me. "I did what I had to do." And more resolute, like he was trying to convince himself as much as me, he said, "I did my job."

"Calling it your job still don't make it right," I snapped, and I was angry about this and angry about everything. "And how come no one ever told me? How come I'm only learning about this now, after all this time? From you? And you weren't even gonna tell me. You just let it slip."

Uncle Theo bit his bottom lip, clearly searching for the words. "Your mother, she's protective of you. You know that. It's her nature. Right or wrong. She wanted to keep this from you for as long as she could. I didn't consider that to be such a good idea myself but…" his voice trailed off, and he shrugged and sort of mumbled, "I don't know anymore."

"This whole time, my whole life," I moved forward and got in Uncle Theo's face, as best I could, given that he towered over me, this spontaneous action, my body practically moving on its own, "I'd been thinking it was my fault, that Pops up and left because of me."

"It wasn't your fault, Rhett," Uncle Theo tried to assure me, "of course, it wasn't your fault. It was never your fault."

"How was I supposed to know that?" I questioned, and my voice cracked, but that didn't deter me. "What else was I supposed to think?"

Uncle Theo reached his large hand out and gripped my narrow shoulder. "Your father was into some serious stuff, but that had nothing to do with you. You were just a kid, what, three, four years old? Of course it wasn't your fault."

"The police, I remember that now," I told him as I was experiencing this sudden enlightenment, "taking Pops away that night. I had forgotten about it, for forever, but it's all coming back to me. Them busting in when we was watching TV, causing such a commotion, breaking everything, Mama crying. That was you? That was because of you?"

Uncle Theo didn't answer, but he didn't have to.

"That was you?" I pointed at him, accusatory. "You caused that? That's what you're telling me? And here, I thought it was my fault. I thought I was to blame. All this time, I didn't know why Pops had gone away, why he up and left. I had forgotten the real reason. My mind just wiped it away, erased everything." I felt myself slipping, losing control, yet I proceeded. "Here, I thought it was my fault, that it was always my fault." And louder, "My fault. *My* fault! I thought it was my fault. But all along it was you? You're telling me that all along it was you, that you caused this?" I pushed my hand into Uncle Theo's chest, not to move him, because he was immovable, but more for me, just to get that out of me, that rage, that frustration. "My fault. Here I was thinking all along that it was my fault, that I was to blame!"

"Relax, Rhett, just relax." Uncle Theo squeezed my shoulders harder with both hands to get me to settle.

"No, don't!" I wriggled free. "Stop it!" I demanded. "Pops up and leaving. Me getting into trouble at school. Mama being so fed up that she don't want me living with her and Ella Mae no more, sending me off to live here with you, with the man who put Pops away!" I was halted by another alarming thought. "Mama was behind this, wasn't she?" And then a revelation as I recalled what Mama had said over the phone to Uncle Theo that night when she was sending me away to live with him, and what she must've said during her conversation with him last night. "Mama wanted you to see what you had caused."

"Rhett, listen here," Uncle Theo squared with me.

"No, no!" I kept on. "I just need to get out of here!" I shoved past Uncle Theo to leave the house without any of my stuff, because I just had to get out of there right then and right there. I couldn't stand to be there, to be with him; not one second longer. But Uncle Theo was too big and too strong, and he wouldn't let me go, pulling me back.

"I'm sorry, Rhett." He bent over me, his massive torso, his thick arms, to hold me. "I'm sorry that happened. It was never your fault. You should've never had to believe it was."

"No, just let me go!" I screamed. "Let me go! I don't know what to believe anymore. Just let me go!" Uncle Theo maintained his hold on me, and it was impossible for me to break away, so I started beating him about the chest and shoulders with my hands, opened at first, and then closed into fists, just wherever my hands landed. It was nothing I would have ever considered doing, and had I considered it, I certainly wouldn't have done it, but it just happened, and I kept at it, unable to stop. "It was my fault. My fault!" I kept shouting as I continued to beat on Uncle Theo. "I thought it was all my fault!"

Uncle Theo stood there, still holding me, and he let me beat on him. Chekhov barked, but she didn't come to Uncle Theo's defense, maybe because I was family, or maybe because she could tell I wasn't making a dent, not one bit of damage, as it was impossible for me to physically hurt Uncle Theo. He just let me beat on him. And I did, I beat on him, getting it out of my system, everything, every last bit, beating on Uncle Theo until I couldn't beat on him anymore, until I wore myself out, drained of every ounce of energy. I was already exhausted from this outburst and from not sleeping last night and from just everything, and I wore myself out. "My fault. It was my fault," I said with diminishing intensity, on the verge of unconsciousness, nothing but a field of imaginary flickering stars in front of my face. "My fault...it was...my fault... I thought it was all my fault..." I was hardly able to lift my hands to pound on Uncle Theo anymore, hardly able to keep them clenched into fists, hardly able to do anything, and I just fell into him. "My fault," I exerted one final time as I collapsed onto Uncle Theo's broad chest, depleted and done for.

"It wasn't your fault, Rhett," Uncle Theo whispered into my ear, his coarse whiskers against my cheek, embracing me, holding me, keeping me on my feet. "It was never your fault."

I gave up and I gave in, too beat and too beaten. The house was spinning, and everything got hazy, and then it all went dark.

❧

I remembered when Pops up and left, that night it happened, every detail, every sensation, how it looked, how it felt, how it smelled

143

even. I had no memory of it prior, and then out of nowhere, it returned. It was like I had been sitting in an empty theater, front row and center, in darkened silence, just emptiness, before all at once, without any notice, without warning, the curtain rose, and the projector rattled to life with the flickering of light amidst the shuffling frames, and the movie began, the main feature. That was the night Pops up and left.

We were in the living room of our house, watching television, one of those black-and-white shoot-'em-up movies that Pops enjoyed so much. I was too little to understand much of it, the intrigue and the dilemmas and the plot twists, but I liked the shoot-'em-up parts, the guns exploding and the bad guys clutching their chests and toppling over. It was funny to me because it was make-believe. I would bounce up and down and clap my hands before Pops shushed me because he was trying to pay attention to the story, or Mama would carry me out, reprimanding how that wasn't something I should be watching at my age, that I shouldn't be exposed to that.

I was sitting on the floor, that ugly, coarse, brown, braided, oval rug we had, inches from the TV, this bulky wooden console that made Uncle Theo's pathetic old television seem state-of-the-art. That TV we used to have was its own piece of furniture, wide enough on the top for Mama to display framed family photos and candles she never lit and a glass candy tray of butterscotches that I didn't care for, but Grammy and Gramps ate them up like they were the best thing ever whenever they stopped by.

Mama had made popcorn on the stove top, and the entire house was filled with the lingering scent of burnt corn because she always burned a few kernels, but I didn't mind. It still tasted just fine to me, with melted butter and extra salt, the way she fixed it. Pops was stretched out in his easy chair behind me, legs splayed, his black leather wingtips flipped off, his socked feet, but otherwise still dressed in what he had worn to work, his tie loosened. It had been a long day, he complained, and he didn't feel like changing. He was drinking a beer, Pabst, his favorite, that Mama had poured into a frosty mug that she kept in the freezer, and smoking a cigarette, a Marlboro Red, eloquently as he did, with a style all his own, like a performance, a technique he must have mastered after years of smoking. Pops would inhale deeply, satisfyingly, making sure to get the tar and nicotine and whatever other chemicals into every crack and crevice of his lungs, then he pitched his head, pursed his lips, and blew the smoke high above him in a steady stream that gathered into a billowing cloud at the ceiling before gracefully dispersing. I was mesmerized by how Pops smoked cigarettes and couldn't wait until I was old enough to be able to do the same.

Mama was perched on the couch, knitting something in pink yarn, something for the baby, Ella Mae, though at the time, we didn't know it would be Ella Mae, just a baby. Mama was pregnant, her stomach so big and round and hard that it looked like she could pop at any minute. She had cooked my favorite dinner and my belly felt as stuffed as Mama's, yet I still found room for a bowl of popcorn. I sat there on the floor like that, watching Pops's movie and eating my popcorn and simply enjoying life, the three of us together, appreciating it while I could because I knew that Mama would soon send me to bed, the ticking clock on the wall counting down the time. I cherished those moments to be around Pops, which was such a treat because he was rarely home like he was on this night, always too busy, leaving the house in the morning and not returning until it was dark outside and I was already in bed. But when Pops was home, this was where I wanted to be: with him, whatever he was doing, which usually meant watching TV, one of those black-and-white shoot-'em-up movies that Pops enjoyed so much.

At some point in the evening, something caught my eye. I glanced up from the television and saw, through the living room window, red flashing lights pulsing outside. Neither Pops nor Mama seemed to notice—he was too involved with his movie and she with her knitting—but it had my attention. When it was evident that neither of them was going to do anything about it, I got up and walked to the window to investigate, my childish brain imagining all sorts of scenarios, that maybe the circus was in town, and they were parading by our house, the performers and the animals lined up in long rows. I went to the window, half-expecting to see elephants marching down the street trunk to tail or acrobats cartwheeling or clowns spraying seltzer at each other, something fun like that. It was anything but.

As soon as I got to the window and pulled the sheer curtains aside, the front door exploded open like a bomb had gone off, splinters of wood flying everywhere, and these men rushed in, a bunch of them, storming into our house, hollering and shouting and carrying on, with no regard for what they broke. This pretty vase—with painted swirls and curlicues along the side that Pops had given Mama one Valentine's Day that she kept on a narrow table in the entranceway with fresh cut flowers she got at the store on the corner—went shattering to the floor, shards of glass and a puddle of water and broken pedals of red and orange and blue scattered on the floor that the men just trampled through in their black lace-up boots.

There must have been a dozen of them, but it seemed to me that there was no end to how many were entering, one after the next. Most were dressed in police uniforms, but there were others in dark suits. The men who wore the suits held out shiny badges for us to see, and one of them had a piece of paper that he stuck in Pops's face, calling it a warrant for his arrest. Pops had this expression come over him, a sort of surprise that melted into defeat, and his face got white as a sheet. When I saw Pops looking like that, it frightened me much more than having these strange men in our house. Pops just appeared so hopeless, so helpless, so human, and seeing that caused everything inside of me to sink and drown. I didn't know what exactly was happening, who these men were or what they wanted with Pops, but I could tell it was bad and that Pops was in trouble, that we all were.

A couple of the police officers yanked Pops from his easy chair, smacking the mug of beer from his hand and stubbing out his cigarette in his ashtray that was shaped like a miniature truck tire. They spun him around and pressed him up forcefully against the back of the chair, nearly pushing him and the chair over. They snapped handcuffs over his wrists, the grating of the metal clicking closed echoing in my head. Mama was hysterical, begging the men to let Pops go, pleading that it was a mistake, that it had to be a mistake, that they must've had the wrong guy. But those men paid Mama no mind and just went about their business, some manhandling Pops, some stomping through the rest of our house and making an absolute mess, rummaging through closets and emptying drawers. There was a lady with kind eyes who had followed in after the men, and she told Mama that she needed to be still in her condition. She took her gently by the arm and ushered her back over to the couch to sit down.

Mama wasn't about to go quietly, though. She was raising all sorts of a ruckus, swinging her arms wildly and kicking her legs madly, grasping tight to her knitting needles before a burly police officer pried them from her. Pops was just the opposite. He was oddly calm and serene as if he was at peace, like this was something he had been awaiting, and now that it had come, he could relax and let go. As the police were escorting him out of the house, he called over his shoulder at Mama to "take care of the boy." Those words stuck out to me. "Take care of the boy," he said as he up and left, and I never saw him again.

I went to the window and peered out and watched as the police put Pops into the back of one of their cars. An officer placed his hand on the top of Pops's head to keep him from bumping it as they pushed him inside. The flashing red lights illuminated the entire block, and the neighbors in their housecoats and robes stepped cautiously onto their stoops and porches to find out what the commotion was about. I stood in silence and watched until each of the police cars squealed off and went speeding down the street and away. I just stood there in silence and watched. I wasn't sure what had just transpired, what I had witnessed, what any of this was, other than Pops was gone, and I doubted he was ever coming back. I stood by the window, and I watched, without saying a word, overcome by a choking dread that our lives would forever be changed and a suffocating guilt that somehow I was to blame, that this was my fault.

❧

One of the things I missed most about our house in Louisville was the brick patio out back. It wasn't much to look at: the bricks worn and discolored and chipped and cracked, some missing altogether, and stubborn crabgrass and dandelions growing up between the edges, a blanket of slippery moss covering the section in the corner that was shaded by the towering oak tree that separated our house from our neighbors. That brick patio was in one sorry state of disrepair, slowly crumbling apart under the elements. But I didn't mind, and to me, it looked just fine.

There was a folding lawn chair we kept out there, rusted through with the gray and green webbing fraying apart into stringy threads. I would sit in that chair at night after Mama and Ella Mae had gone to bed when I couldn't sleep, which was a lot of nights, my mind occupied with some thought or the other. I'd smoke one of Mama's cigarettes that I had gradually pinched from her purse and kept in a stash hidden in the bottom of my dresser drawer beneath my Bible, blowing the smoke up to the heavens in a steady stream, flicking the ashes into Pops's miniature truck tire ashtray. I would stare at the sky, at the galaxy of twinkling stars, imagining that wherever Pops was, he was staring up at those very same stars, maybe thinking about me. That made me feel closer to him as I sat out there like that, sometimes all night, sometimes dozing off and waking up at the first stray rays of sun, to then quietly sneak back into my bedroom before Mama could discover me missing.

Occasionally, I'd pretend that Pops was sitting out there next to me. We would have long and involved conversations about life and whatnot, Pops sharing his wisdom and his knowledge, tidbits of what he had learned through the years, imparting all of these lessons from his experiences. Or maybe we wouldn't talk at all, maybe some nights we wouldn't need to. It would just be enough for us to sit out there together, in the peace and the quiet, and it would be perfect. It was something that I thought of from time to time, and something that I thought of now as I lay in bed and stared up at the galaxy of star stickers on the ceiling in my bedroom at Uncle Theo's house.

I had been in bed for most of the day once Uncle Theo carried me in after my fainting spell and tucked me tight under the covers. I still wasn't ready to move. I was just lying here, thinking about everything and nothing, about how my world had suddenly been turned upside down, yet again, and how everything I thought I believed was a lie, how life could change in an instant from only a few words spoken at the spur of the moment. I didn't know who I was anymore, who anybody was, who the bad guys and the good guys were. It wasn't as simple to tell the two apart as it was in those black-and-white shoot-'em-up movies. I wondered which one I was, which one Uncle Theo was, which one was Pops. I wondered what would become of me. I had no idea, about any of it. I was just empty inside and alone. And all I wanted to do was lay in bed.

There came a knock on the bedroom door, a light knock, light enough that I couldn't rightly decide if it actually was a knock until the door cracked open, and there was Uncle Theo.

"Knock, knock," he said, as he slinked inside, carefully carrying a mug of something I could tell was hot from the steam rising off the top. "Brought you some cocoa. That always made me feel better when I was your age and I had a bad day."

Saying I'd had a bad day was the understatement of the century. But I got what Uncle Theo meant, and I guessed I appreciated it, and while I still had a ways to go to process everything and to decide whether or not I hated my uncle, I reckoned a steaming mug of cocoa wasn't a bad start.

"Thanks," I said, muted, sitting up in bed.

"Be careful," Uncle Theo warned as he handed me the mug, "I might've overheated it."

I took the mug from Uncle Theo, and he had definitely overheated it. I could barely hold onto it, cradling the mug in both hands and lifting it to my mouth to blow, and to blow some more, before I was able to take a wary sip. The melty, chocolaty deliciousness, as scorching as it was, was soothing nonetheless: liquid comfort flowing into my belly, exactly what I needed at the moment. My uncle knew me, and he knew what I needed, and maybe I didn't hate him. I didn't know who to hate.

"Left out the marshmallows, wasn't sure if you liked 'em or not," Uncle Theo said, apologetic. "Some folks do, some don't. Marshmallows can be oddly polarizing. But I can run into the kitchen and get you some if you want."

"That's all right," I told him, "it's fine like this." And it was as I took another sip.

Uncle Theo sat on the side of the bed, the springs squeaking and the mattress giving way under his weight. He watched me drink my hot chocolate, but I surmised he was watching more than that by how he was looking at me, this mix of concern and uncertainty. He released his gaze to glance about the bedroom, probing as if he'd never been in here before, which was somewhat true since, at least as far as I knew, he hadn't been in here since I moved in. Unlike I was to him, Uncle Theo was considerate about allowing me my privacy. He bent over to where I had a pile of clothes on the floor and picked up a sock.

"Remember stinky sock?" he asked, holding the sock, flopping in the air. "The game we used to play when you were young?"

"Yeah," I said, sort of sneered, "where you used to stick a dirty sock in my face."

Uncle Theo spit out a laugh. "That's the one," he said, turning to me. "You liked it."

"Mm-hmm, tons of fun," I replied, sarcastic. "Having a dirty sock in my face."

"C'mon, now." He smiled to himself, staring at the sock in his hand. "It always made you laugh."

"Yeah, it did," I acknowledged. "That game was all right." I paused, as Uncle Theo seemed to be thinking about something as he held that sock in his hand. "We ain't gonna play stinky sock now, are we?" I asked before he had a chance to stick that sock in my face, because as much fun as it might've been when I was young, I doubted it'd be as much fun now, and I certainly wasn't in the mood to play stinky sock today, and I couldn't imagine Uncle Theo was either. Still, I had to ask.

"Nah," he answered, although not entirely convincingly, and he appeared to continue to be pondering it before breaking himself free. "Maybe later," he joked, tossing the sock back on the floor, onto my pile of clothes.

There was a stilted silence, with Uncle Theo, hands on his knees, tapping his fingers to a beat I couldn't hear, surveying the room, me watching him and sipping my hot chocolate before he returned to me.

"How are you doing?" he asked, studying me for my reaction. "I mean...you know."

I shrugged. "I dunno." And I didn't. "Just feel kinda weird, not sure what to think."

"Yeah," he followed. "I should've told you sooner." He hesitated. "Well, someone should've." He focused on me. "How can I make this better for you, Rhett?"

"What was he like?" I blurted out.

"Huh?" Uncle Theo seemed surprised. "How's that?"

"Pops," I replied. "What was he like? I mean, I know you said he did stuff he shouldn't have, but was he really a bad guy? What'd he do exactly to make you go after him?"

"Oh, uh..." Uncle Theo fidgeted, visibly uncomfortable. "He, uh, like I told you: he got himself mixed up with the wrong bunch of fellas."

"But you put bad guys away," I countered, "in your job. And you put Pops away, so wouldn't that mean that Pops was a bad guy?"

"You are destined for law school, boy, I'm telling you," Uncle Theo said, before typically including, "though I wouldn't wish that on anyone." He cleared his throat. "It's, um...well, you see..." Uncle Theo fumbled. "Yeah, sure, your father broke the law, no question about that. He did some bad things. He hurt a lot of people, cheated them out of their hard-earned money. And it was my sworn duty to protect those people—*innocent* people," he stressed. "I had to prosecute your father."

"So Pops *was* a bad guy," I said, and just hearing myself say that brought a deflating disappointment over me.

"Yes, Rhett, he was," Uncle Theo replied with a sigh, and he sounded just as disappointed about it as I was. "Your father was a bad guy. But that's not to say that your father didn't love you," he was quick to clarify, "because he did. He loved you very much. Don't think for a minute that he didn't. He was only doing what he thought he had to do to support his family, you and your mother, and with a baby on the way." Uncle Theo got up off the bed and moved to the window, and I could see his reflection in the glass, his brow furled. "This was the toughest case I ever had." He lingered, then turned back around to me. "It was my last case."

That part landed with a *thud*, and I wasn't certain I had heard Uncle Theo correctly.

"How's that?" I questioned, and I somehow had a terrible feeling of what the answer might entail.

Uncle Theo breathed in heavy, and exhaled even heavier, and returned to sit on the bed, the mattress giving way, his head in his hands, rubbing his eyes.

"Those guys who shot me on the courthouse steps," he began, still with his head in his hands, before moving them through his hair, and I noticed more tattoos on the back of his arms, although nothing I could accurately discern, just random shapes and markings, some words I couldn't read, "they were your father's associates."

"Pops's buddies shot you?" I asked, incredulous, and nearly spilled what was left of my hot chocolate.

"I wouldn't exactly call them his *buddies*," Uncle Theo answered, taking the mug from me and placing it safely on the nightstand, "but yeah, those were the ones."

I sat back in the bed, and my heart was racing, could feel it beating in my temples, and my face get hot, and not just from the cocoa, as I was leveled by yet another unexpected revelation, and I wondered how many more of these Uncle Theo had, and how many more of these I could take. Before I could say anything—and I had plenty of questions, as usual—Uncle Theo held up his hand.

"Bygones, Rhett. It happened, and it's over. And now, I'm better off for it."

"How could you be better off for it?" I leaned forward, and I was frustrated that Uncle Theo wasn't angry about this, because I sure was. "You lost your job. You lost your..." I eased off and nodded to his stomach, uneasy on how to put it, about his injury and his condition. So instead, I just said, "And you nearly died." Then I added, not to be rude, but it was the truth, "And you're living out here in the sticks."

That last bit seemed to amuse Uncle Theo, how I did without even trying.

"Believe it or not, I like it out here in the sticks," he said with a grin. "I'm perfectly fine without a lot of people around me. And everything that's happened, well, I've come to terms with it. These are just the cards I've been dealt. Everyone has something, and everyone has a plan for their life. This is just my something, and my plan, part of God's plan for me." He was confident, I could tell, as he concluded, "I'm good, bud. Trust me. I'm blessed. I'm grateful for everything I have."

"Everything you have?"

"Yes, Rhett, everything I have. You might not think so, but I have a lot. I don't want for anything. It's a sin not to be grateful for what God has given you."

I was glad that Uncle Theo could feel that way, but I had trouble accepting that.

"How can this be God's plan for you?" I questioned. "This can't possibly be God's plan for you. How can you believe that, Uncle Theo?"

"That's not something I need to ask," he replied calmly, a lot calmer than me, as I still could not fathom that Pops's buddies, or whoever, whatever they were to him, were responsible for what had become of Uncle Theo, and perhaps I had found who I needed to hate.

"And it's not something you need to ask either." He waited for my response, which was nothing other than to continue staring at him in disbelief about everything. "Rhett, in my wise old age," he picked up, "I've come to understand that everything somehow works out the way it's supposed to. Might not be the way you thought or hoped or had planned for yourself, could be something you never would have imagined in your wildest dreams, but believe me when I say this, it does all work out."

I was going to speak up, but I thought better of it, even as indignant as I was, because there wasn't anything I could possibly say to match that, not only Uncle Theo's words, but his demeanor. And I reckoned that if he was okay with this, then it wasn't for me to take issue with it, and I had to be okay with this too, not that that was any easy feat, far from it, and it was going to take me a while, but I resolved that I had best try and respect Uncle Theo that way. Though I did have one burning question that couldn't wait.

"Uncle Theo, do you have any other secrets?" I asked in earnest. "Anything else you're keeping from me? Because I'm about at my limit for surprises like this."

Uncle Theo smiled, big and broad, and he reached out to try and pat down my cowlicks, but that was a lost cause.

"You hungry?" Uncle Theo replied without answering my question, blatantly changing the subject as he was so proficient at doing, and on any other occasion, I might've called him out on that, but the fact was that I was hungry, very much so, to the point of dang near starving to death, and truth be told, I wasn't in the mood to have any more secrets revealed today anyway, so I didn't push it. "We need to get you something to eat, and I can eat too. You like breakfast for dinner? I like breakfast for dinner. I think this is as fitting a day as any to have breakfast for dinner."

"Yeah," I nodded, and I managed a smile. "That sounds good, Uncle Theo." And it did sound good, and my grumbling stomach concurred.

"Breakfast for dinner it is, then," Uncle Theo confirmed with a slap on my back, and then he pushed himself off the bed. "C'mon, let's go." He rubbed his hands together and gave a clap as he strolled out of the room, his limp. I pulled myself out of bed, this leg, then that leg, and followed Uncle Theo down the hall and into the kitchen as he described what was on the menu. "I've got some eggs I can scramble, farm fresh, from one of my neighbors, and I'll fry up some skillet potatoes and onions from the garden, with sourdough toast, and jam I made from the wild blackberries that grow around here, oh…" Uncle Theo stopped suddenly, such that I nearly ran into him, and he raised a finger, enthused. "I've got a nice summer sausage that another one of my neighbors gave me. You'll like that. You'll like that a lot. You do like summer sausage, don't you? What am I saying, everyone likes summer sausage."

Uncle Theo was suddenly in a much better mood, and I was starting to get that way too, and we both deserved that.

"I like summer sausage," I said.

We got into the kitchen, where Uncle Theo moved about purposefully and with a renewed vigor, on a mission, grabbing ingredients here and there, eggs and milk and butter and cheese from the fridge, and his special spices from the cabinet, and potatoes and onions and that summer sausage from the pantry that looked to me just like a regular sausage, and he fired up the gas stove with a burst of bluish flame from beneath the burner. "Have a seat," he nodded toward the table. "I got this, bud. You want another cup of cocoa?"

"Nah, I'm good," I said, rubbing the roof of my mouth with my tongue where I had burned it on that last mug of hot chocolate and taking a seat at the front table.

Chekhov came running into the kitchen through the partially opened back door from where she had been outside and barked at Uncle Theo, and she was no doubt excited about breakfast for dinner as well, not that she might've necessarily known it was breakfast for dinner; it could've been anything, as far as she was concerned. She just got excited whenever Uncle Theo was in the kitchen, in anticipation of the table scraps she would be getting.

"That's right, Chekhov," Uncle Theo told her as he cracked the eggs with one hand into a round red bowl and tossed the shells into the trash in a single continuous motion, "breakfast for dinner. It's a real treat tonight. A real treat, for sure."

Chekhov continued barking.

"Don't you worry, girl, you'll get some. You always do. No one goes hungry in this house." Chekhov kept barking as Uncle Theo tried to cook, until Uncle Theo finally had to scold her, "Enough with your complaining, now. You hear me? You'll get yours." When that didn't seem to appease Chekhov, Uncle Theo stopped what he was doing and crouched down to Chekhov's level and examined her closely, becoming serious. "What is it, girl? What's wrong?"

Chekhov kept barking as if she was trying to tell Uncle Theo something, and without receiving the response from him that she apparently wanted, she darted to the front door just as someone knocked.

Apprehension crossed Uncle Theo's face, and his body straightened. He gestured for me to stay put as he went to answer the door. When he got there, he peered through the peephole, concentrating, to see who it was, then admonished Chekhov, who continued to bark, "Be still, Chekhov. It's just Hank. What has gotten into you?"

Uncle Theo opened the door, and Sheriff Hank rushed in with an urgency.

"Ted, we need to talk. They're back."

CHAPTER EIGHT

Sheriff Hank had come over to talk to Uncle Theo, and whatever it was, it was important enough for the sheriff to tell him in person. The air inside the house became instantly charged by the sheriff's presence, a heavy, ominous energy. There was this pronounced tension with Sheriff Hank that he didn't have the last time he was here, by the way he held himself, by the way he stood, wound up, poised to strike. Even after Uncle Theo had closed the front door behind him, the sheriff kept eyeing it like he was expecting someone to burst through at any second, his hand hovering above his holstered pistol.

It made me uncomfortable, anxiety filtering through my body. Chekhov seemed to feel the same, as she had not let up barking. Uncle Theo tried to get her to stop, reminding her that it was just Sheriff Hank, that she knew him, that she liked him, but she obviously could sense something was wrong. Among all of us, Uncle Theo was the only one who didn't appear concerned. He was more intent on placating Chekhov, getting on his knees to throw his arms around the dog to calm her, than on the purpose of Sheriff Hank's visit and whatever it was he had to say.

I didn't think I should stay, figured this had to have been adult business, yet I couldn't get myself to leave, as something told me—just a gut feeling I had, and my gut was never wrong—that this concerned me as well. So, I sat at the table and tried to blend into the background, but no such luck.

"Oh, uh, hey there, Rhett," Sheriff Hank said, noticing me, his demeanor easing slightly. He looked at my uncle. "Should the boy be around for this?"

"For what?" Uncle Theo asked him. "What is this? What's going on, Hank?"

"They're back," he responded.

"Who?" Uncle Theo stood from where he had been tending to Chekhov, where he had gotten her somewhat comforted, with her barking replaced with a dull whimper. "Who's back?"

Sheriff Hank removed his hat, scratched the top of his head. "Those two fellas who've been asking about you. One of my deputies pulled them over earlier today just outside of Cole's Landing proper."

"Oh, that." Uncle Theo's tone dropped, as he sort of dismissed it, and took a few steps farther into the front room. "Well…okay," he said with a shrug. "What'd they do?"

"Nothing," Sheriff Hank replied, before amending, "I mean, they had a taillight out. But it's not about that. It's about what my deputy noticed inside their car." Sheriff Hank got closer to Uncle Theo, lowered his voice. "They had a file on you."

"A file?" Uncle Theo questioned loudly, undermining the sheriff's attempt to be discreet. "What do you mean, a file? What kind of file?"

Sheriff Hank cast a glance in my direction, and I turned away, pretending not to be listening though that was pretty much impossible given that I was sitting right there, and of course, I was listening, and I couldn't help but to listen, which Sheriff Hank concluded as he then abandoned any further pretense to keep this from me.

"A manila folder in the backseat," Sheriff Hank went on, speaking at a normal volume. "My deputy caught a glimpse of it, a few pages slipping out. He couldn't tell exactly what all was in it. But there was a newspaper clipping…" he hesitated, "from that day, you know…at the courthouse, when…well…what happened. And a picture of you, taken relatively recent, he seemed to think: a candid shot as if they've been keeping tabs on you."

Uncle Theo didn't immediately respond. He just remained unflinching, allowing Sheriff Hank's words to sink in. Then he nodded, and turned, and made his way past me and into the kitchen.

"We're having breakfast for dinner, Hank," he said to the sheriff. "Care to join us?"

Sheriff Hank watched as Uncle Theo returned to his cooking as if nothing had changed, as if what he had just heard had no bearing on him whatsoever.

"Ted, this is serious now," Sheriff Hank warned, following after my uncle. "These fellas are getting closer. And I don't know what they want."

"I don't know what they want either," Uncle Theo acknowledged, scrambling the eggs with a whisk in the round red bowl, pouring in a dollop of milk. "Maybe they're fans of mine," he kidded. "Maybe they want an autograph." He paused. "Or maybe they want breakfast."

"I mean it, Ted," Sheriff Hank repeated, and he was getting irritated. "This is serious."

Uncle Theo stopped scrambling the eggs, turned to the sheriff, and asked him, "So did your deputy arrest them? Or question them about it even?"

Sheriff Hank wavered, shook his head, looked down. "Nah, didn't have probable cause to detain them. And they skedaddled on out before my deputy could ask them about that file."

"They skedaddled on out," Uncle Theo said mockingly.

"But we got eyes on 'em," Sheriff Hank looked back up at my uncle as if to reassure him. "Don't you worry none about that."

"Well, that's good then." Uncle Theo sounded unpersuaded as he resumed what he was doing, tossing a hunk of butter into a hot pan on the stovetop, angling the pan to cover the entire surface with melted butter, then scattering in chopped onions that steamed when they hit the heat. "We'll just keep a watch out."

"But with the boy…" Sheriff Hank gestured toward me, talking about me as if I wasn't in the room, struggling to be heard over the sound of sizzling onions. "Is there somewhere you two could go for a bit to get away until this blows over?"

"Like take a vacation?" Uncle Theo scoffed as he added thinly cut potatoes to the sautéed onions, and in another hot pan, he poured in the eggs. "Rhett, you wanna go on vacation?" he called out to me. "How about we go to my summer mansion in the Caribbean?"

I knew better than to answer that or to get involved in this business between my uncle and the sheriff any more than I already felt I was. I didn't have a chance to say anything anyway before the sheriff spoke up.

"C'mon, Ted. This is serious," Sheriff Hank kept on.

"What am I supposed to do, Hank?" Uncle Theo shot back. "Hide under the bed?" He dumped a handful of cheddar cheese onto the eggs and stirred the potatoes and onions. "We'll be fine here, don't worry. We got our trusty guard dog." Uncle Theo flung a piece of summer sausage at Chekhov, who caught it mid-air in her mouth and swallowed it down in one bite.

Sheriff Hank lingered, uncertain, watching Uncle Theo cook, but not really, more like he was trying to come up with what to say next that might convince Uncle Theo to appreciate the gravity of the situation. I could've told Sheriff Hank that it was no use, that once Uncle Theo had his mind set, there was no changing it. Clearly frustrated, Sheriff Hank gave up with a huff and a shake of his head. He turned to leave, but the partially opened kitchen door caught his attention.

"Least you can do is shut this damned door," he scolded Uncle Theo, and maybe to also save some face, pointing at the door. "And lock it." He peered about the house. "Lock both the doors for that matter, and all these windows, too, if you can. I don't know what these fellas are up to, but it's not to get your autograph…or to eat breakfast." He grew serious. "I just don't… I don't like them showing up around here, Ted. I got a bad feeling about this, I do. And why all of a sudden?

Why now?" He glimpsed over at me as he said that last part, and I recoiled.

"I don't know, Hank." Uncle Theo continued to be more interested in fixing us breakfast for dinner than discussing this, toasting bread and slicing tomatoes and tending to the pans on the stove as Sheriff Hank watched. "You sure you don't want to stay and eat? We got plenty."

"Hmm?" Sheriff Hank was engrossed by Uncle Theo's cooking skills, until he pulled himself away. "No, thanks. Looks mighty tasty though, but Linda's getting supper ready, her pot roast. Got the in-laws over tonight." He frowned. "You know how that goes."

"Not really," Uncle Theo answered, "but...all right." He interrupted his cooking just long enough to focus on the sheriff. "Thanks for stopping by, Hank. I do appreciate it." He looked over at me. "We both do."

"Yeah, of course, Ted, of course. We watch out for our own around here, you know that." Uncle Theo nodded like he knew that. "I'll keep sending a car around," Sheriff Hank added, "to check on you. Might even put in a call to KSP, see if I can't get them involved." He paused, still engrossed by Uncle Theo's cooking, before turning his full attention to me. "How have you been, young man? Are you enjoying it out here in our neck of the woods, spending time with your uncle?"

"Yes, sir, I am," I said, nervous for some reason, and I sat up in my chair.

Sheriff Hank stared at me in case I had anything else to say, and I didn't, and then he noticed my hair, still matted and cowlicked despite my futile attempts to pat it down, which caused him to chuckle. "You best cut this boy's hair," he said to my uncle, "or else they're gonna call Child Protective Services on you."

"That's the style now, Hank," Uncle Theo replied, covering for me.

Sheriff Hank laughed. "Young people these days." He winked at me, then shifted. "I'll see myself out. You two be good, and be careful." He walked to the front door, and over his shoulder, he repeated, "And keep these doors locked, you hear?"

"I hear," Uncle Theo responded, taking the food off the stove and dishing it onto our plates.

Sheriff Hank exited, pushing the button on the door knob to lock it, closing it tight behind him, then checking from the outside, rattling the knob to make certain the door had locked.

"I hope you're hungry," Uncle Theo said to me, bringing out the plates, heaping helpings of everything, placing one plate in front of me and one where he sat, and he went back into the kitchen to fetch me a glass of milk and a cold beer for himself.

"Beer with breakfast?" I teased as Uncle Theo took a sip before he even made it back to sit at the table.

"Beer with breakfast for *dinner*," he corrected me, "and anyhow, it's five o'clock somewhere." He squinted across the room at the ticking clock on the wall. "Heck, it's five o'clock here: quarter past, to be precise."

I smiled to be polite, and it still didn't strike me as the appropriate time to ask for a beer for myself, even though I sure could use one with all this stress. Instead, I just ate. We both did, making short work of that meal, heads down, no talking, barely breathing, shoveling the food into our mouths. I hadn't eaten all day, and I was famished, and I had a feeling Uncle Theo hadn't had much to eat today either. He wasn't one to show his emotions, but I suspected that this had been a difficult day for him as well.

We both eventually came up for air when Chekhov had all she could take of being patient and barked to demand her fair share of table scraps, which Uncle Theo obliged. As he hand-fed her summer sausage, I took it as my opening to try and gather some additional information from him about Sheriff Hank's visit.

"What was that about anyways, Uncle Theo?" I began. "With the sheriff? What fellas are looking for you?"

Uncle Theo brushed it off. "I don't know, Rhett. I wouldn't get too bent out of shape over it. I like Sheriff Hank. He's a good guy, and we go way back; he was the first person to welcome me here. But he possesses a flair for the dramatic. And he's prone to hyperbole."

"So, there aren't any fellas looking for you?"

Uncle Theo took another drink of beer. "I doubt it," he said, shrugged.

"And you ain't worried about it none if there are?" I followed.

Uncle Theo was deliberate in responding, clearing his plate of the last remaining scrambled eggs with the crust of his sourdough toast and finishing his beer with a fulfilling swallow.

"There's nothing to worry about, bud," he downplayed it. "Sheriff Hank, he means well, but like I told you, he has a tendency to exaggerate. And his deputy, well…who knows what he really saw in that car? A candid picture of me?" He laughed to himself. "Could've been a picture of anyone. I look like every other person in this holler."

"But the newspaper clipping," I was fast to include, "of your, um, accident. How do you explain them having that?"

Uncle Theo started to say something but stopped himself. He picked up his empty can of beer and stared into it like he was pondering, though maybe he was just wishing there was still beer in there.

"I'm gonna grab another beer," he said, hopping out of his chair and going into the kitchen, and while I impressed myself that I was perhaps getting to know Uncle Theo well enough that I was able to read his thoughts sometimes, that didn't answer my question or help to ease my mind about these supposed fellas who were apparently looking for my uncle. I waited for Uncle Theo to return to the table with a fresh cold can of beer in hand before I resumed my inquiry, and maybe Uncle Theo could read my thoughts too, for he spoke before I could.

"Listen, Rhett," he said, making a point to make eye contact, "you don't have anything to worry about. Whether there are fellas looking for me or not, you heard Sheriff Hank say that he's watching out for us. He lives for this kinda thing: to protect and serve. And besides him, everyone looks out for each other around here. So whatever it is—if it's even anything, and I doubt it is—we'll be fine. Trust me, okay? Capeesh?"

I had begun to understand that "capeesh" meant for me to trust Uncle Theo and what he said, and I did. And I wanted to believe him that there wasn't anything to worry about. It wasn't as if I didn't believe him, it was just that what I did know about my uncle, he wasn't always the most forthcoming with the truth, at least not the whole truth. I contemplated going further with my questioning, but I decided against it. I could tell that this wasn't something Uncle Theo wanted to discuss anymore. And if Uncle Theo said not to worry, then I had best try not to worry.

"Capeesh," I said, a little reluctant, but "capeesh" all the same. Uncle Theo kept eyeing me, perhaps to determine if I really meant it, and I guessed once he was satisfied that I had, he took another drink of his beer. I finished my food, pushing what was left on my plate onto my fork and shoving it into my mouth. When Uncle Theo saw me do that, he asked if I was still hungry and wanted more, but I shook my head no, and once I was able to swallow that big bite down, I said, "No, thanks."

"Good, huh?" he asked me as he took our empty plates and carried them into the kitchen to put in the sink.

"Yeah," I answered him, "real good. Breakfast for dinner. I could get used to that."

I could have actually gone for another heaping helping, maybe a couple, but I didn't want to put Uncle Theo to that trouble, and I was going to go to bed in a while, and I might have trouble sleeping with a stuffed belly, especially when I was having trouble sleeping anyway, and I really needed to sleep through the night for once. I went with Uncle Theo into the kitchen to commence with my chore of doing the dishes, but Uncle Theo stuck his arm out to stop me.

"That's okay, bud," he said. "I'll give you the night off. You go relax. Maybe see if you can get something on that TV. Watch one of your programs."

I didn't have any programs to watch, nor did I want to go

through what seemed like a monumental effort to get any kind of reception on that old thing, that television from a bygone era.

"I might just go to my room and read before bed," I told Uncle Theo. "It's been a day."

"That it has," he agreed with me.

"Good night," I said as I walked off.

I got partway down the hall when Uncle Theo hollered for me, "Hey, Rhett, you got plans for tomorrow?"

"Huh?" I turned around to him, and my only plan was to ride my mountain bike unless, considering that tomorrow was Sunday, Uncle Theo was going to force me to go to church with him. "Nuh...uh," I answered, tentative, apprehensive as to what Uncle Theo might've been getting at.

"Because I could use some help out in my garden," he continued.

"What's that?" I asked, not sure I had heard him correctly but praying that I had. "Your garden?"

"I'll tell you what," he said with a snap of his fingers, "when I get home from chapel tomorrow, why don't you help me out in my garden? This early spring's got everything in bloom sooner than I had expected. I could use a hand."

"Yeah, sure," I offered without any hesitation, and before Uncle Theo could rethink that or take it back. Then I remembered about the spikes and booby traps. "Um...which garden is that, that you need help on?"

"The vegetable garden," he answered, like he knew what I was thinking. "I'll show you where to go."

"Okay, sounds good," I said, nodding, and I tried to come across as calm on the outside, even though I was excited as all get out on the inside because Uncle Theo was finally trusting me enough to let me help him in his garden. "Thanks!"

"Thank *you*. You're doing me a great service." Uncle Theo looked on and smiled at me as I still kept standing there in the hall and smiling back at him. "Well...good night, then."

I just stared at Uncle Theo, and I couldn't get over that he was going to let me help him in his garden. "Good night, again," I said in return and kind of waved, then I beelined it to my room to try and rest and get some sleep, because it sounded like I was in for a big day tomorrow, and I couldn't wait!

It was mid-afternoon and the sun was blazing bright and burning hot, and the temperature was surely only going to keep rising with nary a cloud in the pale-blue sky. I was out back, tending to Uncle Theo's vegetable garden like I promised him yesterday I would do, and like I had been looking forward to doing, only I hadn't anticipated the sweltering heat or the amount of work this would take. I surmised that I had been at it for well over two hours, from once Uncle Theo got home from church, weeding and digging and watering and picking, and yet it seemed as if I had hardly made any headway. This garden was a fair bit bigger when standing smack dab in the center than it appeared from just creeping around the periphery.

Uncle Theo grew every kind of crop imaginable—at least that was how it seemed to me, a "big-city boy" as he called me—and luckily, he had everything marked or I wouldn't have known what all was out here. There was a burgeoning batch of tomatoes twisting around the vines—Roma and cherry and Big Beef—and willowy stalks of corn stretched up high to the heavens taller than I stood flatfooted, and bunches upon bunches of lettuce: Romaine, Boston, Bibb, and other varieties that sort of just ran together as far as I was concerned, lettuce being lettuce to me. There were green beans and wax beans and string beans, yellow potatoes and red potatoes and sweet potatoes, red onions and Vidalia onions, green and yellow and red peppers, cucumbers, rhubarb and radishes, peaches and plums and pears, and a smattering of herbs, some I recognized by their familiar aromas as what Uncle Theo used to flavor the food he cooked. The smell of that made me recollect those scrumptious meals that, in turn, caused my stomach to rumble and grumble. I was hungry anyway, having burned through the PB&J I made for lunch, but I didn't reckon I would be

166

eating any time soon, because I wasn't anywhere near to being done.

What was taking most of my effort was this wide patch of strawberries that were prime for harvesting, and if they weren't harvested soon, they would rot, or the critters would get to them more than they already were. Uncle Theo had loads more strawberries this year than he said we could eat, so he would be giving most away to his neighbors, and he had me collect them into these little cardboard containers for that. Yet, with what he did end up keeping for us, Uncle Theo promised to make strawberry ice cream to scoop over homemade strawberry shortcake. I couldn't wait for that since strawberry shortcake was my second favorite dessert after Key lime pie, and third if I considered pumpkin pie for Thanksgiving. I wished I had a piece of that strawberry shortcake now, with a mound of whipped cream, both to eat and also to cool me off. I could've used just about anything to cool me off.

Uncle Theo complained about spring coming early, but to me, it felt as if spring had come and gone and it was already summer. I couldn't recall ever having been this hot in my entire life. This was worse than August in Louisville, when I would loathe having to leave the living room of our house—the only room that really held in the air-conditioning—to step outside, which was like stepping into an oven that had been running at full blast. But today, in Uncle Theo's garden, felt way worse than that. I had sweated clear through my t-shirt and shorts, and the sweat streamed down my legs to soak my socks so that it was like I was standing in puddles. The perspiration that dripped off my forehead stung when it flittered into my eyes despite my flailing efforts to swipe it away with my damp forearm. It was a scorcher, all right, no doubting that. I had chosen the wrong day to commence to working in Uncle Theo's garden. Or, perhaps, Uncle Theo had chosen the wrong day to finally allow me to. Either way, here I was. I had finished off one bottle of Gatorade and was fixing to holler out to Uncle Theo for another, when he beat me to it with the same idea.

"What about it, Rhett," he said to me, coming around from beyond the garden where he had been tending to his marijuana field, "wanna go inside the barn and take five, get something more to drink?"

"Yes, sir," I replied without a second thought, and I couldn't drop that hoe I was holding fast enough as I hustled to catch up with Uncle Theo, who hadn't lingered for my response, probably because he knew what it would be, and he was right.

The inside of that barn was simply an oasis, like diving into a cool pool of water, with its thick, dark wood that absorbed the heat and no windows that would let the sun in. It also had an industrial-sized ceiling fan churning above us. Another bottle or two or three of Gatorade and this short respite and I would be revived enough for a couple more hours of manual labor, and gladly too, because all things considered, I felt I had a knack for gardening. Yet, first I needed that Gatorade, and Uncle Theo had me fetch him a bottle while I was at it, as he took a load off and reclined on one of his weight benches.

When I passed through that heavy fabric partition to get to the back of the barn to the supply closets, I was immediately met with line after line of long, stringy plants hanging upside down from ropes suspended from the rafters. The surprise of that took me aback. It was like vampire bats hanging upside down asleep in the middle of the day, until upon closer inspection, I recognized that these were more of Uncle Theo's marijuana plants, the same as what he had stuffed into garbage bags that I had seen him give to those two scraggly guys.

There must have been hundreds of them, shriveled and wilted and in an absolutely appalling condition. I didn't get it, didn't understand it one iota. To me, these were just a bunch of ugly, dead weeds. But I guessed it held appeal to others, so "to each his own," as Mama would say. I was too thirsty to pay this much mind, anyhow. I needed those Gatorades and pronto, so I headed on over to the far end and pulled open the door of a supply closet—but what I found in there wasn't Gatorade. I couldn't rightly ascertain what it was other than stacks of glass Mason jars crammed with a weird greenish, brownish, grassy something or other.

"Wrong supply closet," a voice, Uncle Theo's, confirmed for me, unexpressive, not sounding angry that I had stumbled upon this, whatever this was, but not altogether sounding pleased about it either, my uncle sneaking up from behind in such a stealthy manner as was his way.

"Oh, uh, sorry," I offered my standard apology for whenever I ended up somewhere around here I wasn't supposed to be, which had unfortunately become a recurring occurrence that made me consider if Uncle Theo was getting tired of hearing me say that. Even so, and also as per usual, my curiosity got the better of me, and before I could close this supply closet and move on to the other one, I was compelled to ask my uncle, "What is this?"

"You sure are an inquisitive one," Uncle Theo said, his pat response, which I thought, or more or less hoped, had become our own private inside joke, and a wry grin from him made me think that maybe it was. "I'm just curing some of my crop."

He took a Mason jar off the shelf and opened it for me to examine. I bent forward, down toward it, and the smell that wafted from that jar—a pungent earthy, musky scent, and with such a potency—caused me to jerk away, and I had to stifle a sneeze.

"Is that the same as what's on these hanging branches?" I asked Uncle Theo, motioning to the weeds all around us in a state of suspended animation. "And like what you gave to those scraggly fellas, the stuff in the garbage bags?"

"Uh-huh," Uncle Theo replied. "I dry the plants out in here." He looked about the barn, at his marijuana plants, with a certain sense of pride. "Those fellas who I gave it to in the bags, they prefer to get the whole plant so they can do with it what they want. These buds"— he nodded back down to the opened Mason jar—"that's just me tinkering. I'll pull these off the stems and store them for a time."

"What for?" I questioned, curious, as this was nothing I'd ever come across. "What's that supposed to do, drying them out and storing them like that?"

"It, um…it helps to preserve them," Uncle Theo answered, and it seemed to me that maybe he was only giving me part of the answer with how he sort of stiffened and seemed to have gotten

169

uncomfortable, like maybe I shouldn't be hearing about this, which, of course, only made me want to ask him more questions on the topic that had suddenly sprung to mind, but he promptly cut me off. "But you don't need to know about all that," he told me as he screwed the lid back on the Mason jar and returned it to its place on the shelf and shut that supply closet. "No sense in giving you a botany lesson now, on a Sunday, when you're done with your studies for the week," he included with a smile that didn't so much put me at ease as made me want to know more.

"Do you give these little dried-up pieces to your neighbors too?" I inquired as I walked with Uncle Theo over to the other supply closet.

"Occasionally," Uncle Theo answered, "although…they're mostly just for me." Before I could get another question in, Uncle Theo changed the subject. "But that's neither here nor there, now is it? Let's just get us some Gatorade, I'm as dry as a desert."

I still wasn't about to let up on my questioning. Then, Uncle Theo opened the other supply closet and revealed to me a veritable rainbow of flavors of Gatorade, the shelves stocked fuller than any grocery store, and I immediately forgot what I was going to ask. As parched as I was, that stockpile of Gatorade took precedence over any old batch of ugly, dead, dried-out weeds.

"That's a lot of Gatorade, Uncle Theo!" I exclaimed, awestruck as if this supply closet contained more gold bars than Fort Knox. "Dang!"

"I stock up because I go through it quickly," he replied matter-of-factly, like it was no big deal to him, like it wasn't the single largest collection of Gatorade ever, pulling a bottle of orange off the shelf for himself as I took a bottle of red and a bottle of blue for myself.

"On account of you working outside in the heat like this?" I said, and I twisted off the top of my bottle of red and had a huge chug, closing my eyes and relaxing my muscles and appreciating the pure, unadulterated relief of that fruit punch tapping out the fire that was raging inside of me.

"Yeah," he said as he took a chug of his Gatorade. "That, and because of my condition." Another chug and a swallow, and Uncle Theo caught my blank stare. "Missing my colon like I am," he elaborated, "I don't absorb liquids so well anymore." My continued blank stare further conveyed to my uncle that I still didn't get it. "What with the colon being primarily responsible for that sort of thing…" Uncle Theo cut himself off as if he could tell I wasn't going to get it, and I wasn't, so it wasn't worth it for him to go into it. "I just gotta make sure to stay hydrated, get my electrolytes, that's all. Anyways," he slapped me on the shoulder and ushered me out of that back room, "I don't mean to be giving you a biology lesson today either." He kind of chuckled. "No schoolwork on Sunday, am I right, bud?"

"Yes, sir," I said, and I wholeheartedly agreed with no schoolwork on Sunday, and if I had my druthers, there'd be no schoolwork on any other days either.

We ambled up to the front of the barn where Uncle Theo had his elaborate home gym. He retreated to his reclined position on the weight bench with a prolonged exhale, under the whipping breeze of the ceiling fan, to enjoy his Gatorade, while I took it upon myself to have a closer look around given that I finally had the opportunity to do so.

"You sure got some nice gym equipment," I told my uncle, admiring everything, wandering over to the multi-station weight machine and yanking down on the bar of the lat pull, or rather attempting to yank it down, because it didn't budge, not one inch, until I sheepishly removed the pin after recognizing that Uncle Theo had it set on an amount of weight I had no chance of lifting.

"I've managed to put together a decent collection" he answered, modest, flipping through a wrestling magazine he had picked up off the floor. "I've always been something of a gym rat, I suppose, always been into lifting. More so after my accident, but even when I was your age, I was slinging weights around." He smiled to himself like he was picturing something amusing. "You oughta ask your mother about the time when we were young, I was upstairs in my bedroom, had this old barbell set I would work out with, she was downstairs in the kitchen with Grammy." He snickered. "Well, I dropped that barbell, couldn't have been but thirty pounds, but it went crashing onto my bedroom floor, rocked the house such that it knocked the mirror off the dining room wall downstairs." He looked at me, paused for effect. "You could bet I caught hell from Gramps for that."

I laughed, and it was funny, but it was also reassuring to hear that Uncle Theo got into trouble when he was my age too.

"But out here…*in the sticks*," he said with emphasis, clearly for my benefit, "there aren't a whole lot of gyms around, least none within a reasonable driving distance. So, I figured I'd cobble together my own gym." He took another gulp of his Gatorade. "I don't like to go out much anyhow."

"On account of you got fellas looking for you?" I blurted without really thinking.

"On account of I prefer to keep to myself." Uncle Theo made certain to correct me, leaning up from where he sat reclined, but with another smile to let me know he wasn't completely aggravated by my questioning, though it was still difficult for me to tell at times what he was really thinking or feeling.

"So, what is it with you, Uncle Theo?" I questioned, emboldened for some reason, probably because it no longer seemed like I was going to die of a heat stroke, as the Gatorade and the industrial-sized fan were working to bring my body temperature down, and I was also becoming more comfortable around Uncle Theo, with him opening up to me like he just did.

"What do you mean, what is it with me?" he countered.

"I mean…" I walked around, inspecting his exercise equipment and checking out the wrestling posters on the walls, and with the wrestling magazine rustling as he was flipping through, I asked, "Were you wanting to be a professional wrestler when you were growing up? Or…are you wanting to be one now?"

Uncle Theo laughed heartily at that, how I was able to crack

172

him up without intending.

"Sure, Rhett," he replied. "How'd you guess? You don't think I'm too old to be a professional wrestler, do you?"

I hesitated, and I wasn't sure if that was a real question or a rhetorical one, but I answered it all the same, as tactfully as I could. "Well…I think you can do it. You're big enough, for sure, and you got that look about you…" I sort of stuttered. "Although…yeah, you are old."

That cracked up Uncle Theo even more than I would have expected, and at least he wasn't angry at me for my honesty.

"Nah," he said, composing himself enough to speak, "I never wanted to be a professional wrestler. I just enjoy it, is all. Always have. Gramps and I, we'd go down to the armory and watch it whenever the popular wrestlers of the day would swing through town." He took another swallow of his Gatorade and went on, "I've just always been a big fan…particularly as a scrawny kid. I still like it. I mean, guys settling their quarrels inside the squared circle, face-to-face, *mano a mano*, what's not to like about that?"

"Yeah, I like it all right too," I said, and I did, though not as much as Uncle Theo obviously did, but maybe that was something else we could have in common—that, and us both being scrawny kids.

"Could be you'll grow up and be a wrestler someday," Uncle Theo said with a wink, "if the mountain biking doesn't work out for you."

"Yes, sir," I said, and again, I couldn't decide if Uncle Theo was being serious or not. "Maybe that's God's plan for me."

Uncle Theo's face lit up with that.

"Hey, you never know," he said, pushing himself off the weight bench. "Who are we to say any different?"

I watched as Uncle Theo walked over to that weight machine, his limp, and inserted the pin back where it had been before I pulled it out.

"Even with how scrawny I am?" I followed.

"God works in mysterious ways, bud," he answered.

"Mysterious ways indeed."

I nodded, even while I was skeptical of that, and not just about me being a professional wrestler, though that surely seemed like a longshot, but with whatever God's plan might have been for me, because I still wasn't at the point where I could rightly see any type of plan for me coming together. But I kept quiet about it and just perused the rest of the gym equipment Uncle Theo had in here as I could feel him looking at me.

"Tell you what," he said to break the silence, "how about if you started working out in here with me?"

"For real?" I replied, and my voice cracked because that was something I hadn't thought Uncle Theo would ever offer, for a lot of reasons, but mostly because this home gym seemed to be his own personal, private space, and I couldn't see him sharing it with anyone.

"Sure, why not? I could use a spotter. And I'll give you some exercises to do." He came up to me, grabbed at my arm, his large hand fitting almost completely around. "Pump up these biceps, make it so you're not as scrawny anymore. What d'you say, you in?"

"Heck yeah, I'm in. Yes, sir!" I said, and I was in, so very much in, and I would've started working out with Uncle Theo that very second if he said so. "I would like that very much."

"All right," he said, "given that the school year's about over for you, we gotta get you something to do this summer to keep you occupied."

I froze upon hearing that, and I just stared at my uncle, because that was the first clue I'd had of what I might be doing beyond this school year. I didn't know how to react, because while I liked staying with Uncle Theo, it also made me question if I would ever see Mama and Ella Mae and my buddies again.

"I'm staying here through the summer?" I asked him weakly.

Uncle Theo hesitated, scratched his beard like he had an itch, before he sort of retracted and said, "Oh, well, I might be getting ahead of myself. Of course, I'll have to talk it over with your mother, see what she's got planned for you." Then in a lighter tone, "But we'll figure it out, the three of us." He stuck his finger in my chest, playfully but also forcefully. "In the meantime, though, we can't have you being all scrawny. No nephew of mine can be scrawny," he joked.

"I'm in, Uncle Theo," I reiterated, with increased enthusiasm. "I'm all in!"

"That's the spirit," he replied with another grab of my arm and a little shake of it. "It's a deal then." He stepped back, put his hands on his hips, took in a deep breath, squared up with me. "But first, we've got some gardening to finish. How are you coming along with those strawberries? You pick 'em all yet?"

"Um, not all of 'em," I answered, "not yet, but I'm working on it."

"Okay, well let's get back at it. Can't have strawberry ice cream with strawberry shortcake without the strawberries." Uncle Theo gulped down what was left of his bottle of Gatorade, twisted the top back on it, and tossed it effortlessly into a trash can that I hadn't even seen that was clear on the other side of the room.

"Yes, sir," I said, and I attempted to toss my empty Gatorade bottle across the room into the trash can the same way, except that I missed it, and I missed it badly.

"We'll work on your throwing arm too, maybe." Uncle Theo kidded as I ran to retrieve the bottle and place it properly into the trash.

Just then, there was a honking outside, erratic, with an insistence, piercing and extended, like somebody was really trying to get our attention. Uncle Theo was visibly concerned as the honking kept on, intermittent beeps interspersed with long, deliberate honks, accompanied by Chekhov and her mad-dog barking, the kind she reserved for when she was in full-blown guard-dog mode.

Uncle Theo sidled up to the front of the barn and peeked out through a slant in the wood. I looked on from my position several paces away, alarmed, with my pulse revving and no idea what this could be. I kept watching Uncle Theo, and even as he then seemed to relax with whatever it was he saw, I remained tense and bothered and fearful. Uncle Theo slid the barn door open, and a burst of sunlight flooded in. I shielded my eyes and saw a pickup truck parked out there with two men standing on either side of it, the one nearest to the driver's side reaching his hand in to honk the horn.

"All right, all right!" Uncle Theo shouted, signaling as he walked toward the men. "Simmer down, now. Simmer down, you two. What's with all the commotion?"

"We need to talk to you, Teddy," the man who had been honking the horn said to my uncle, approaching with the other man, the three of them meeting in the middle.

My heart was in my throat, terrified that these were the men Sheriff Hank had warned were asking about Uncle Theo, the ones who were after him for reasons no one had yet disclosed to me. I didn't know if I should stay in the barn and hide or sprint out there to fight them off. I glanced around frantically for something I could use as a weapon, perhaps some weights, or a barbell. But I was only able to pick up one ten-pound plate, and just barely at that, and once I had it, there wasn't much I could do with it. I doubted that would've been enough to fend off these guys, whoever they were, whatever they wanted.

I decided to hunker down where I was so they wouldn't spot me, to wait and see how this might play out, if for no other reason so that I'd be able to run for help if need be. But then it occurred to me that Chekhov had stopped barking, and I couldn't understand why. I strained to look out, and there she was, just standing next to Uncle Theo, tail wagging like nothing was the matter, like she knew these men, and I reckoned she did because one of them reached to pet her and she didn't rip his arm off. She even licked his hand. What was going on?

I hunched forward to get a better view, and that was when I recognized these two as the scraggly guys who had come around before. When I saw them shake hands with Uncle Theo and pat him on the back, I was able to breathe again, and my heart fluttered back into my chest. Nevertheless, I remained cautious as I gradually made my way outside to find out what was happening.

"How can I help you fellas?" Uncle Theo asked them. "Are you scheduled for a pickup today? Because if so, I apologize. Afraid I've forgotten." He went to move. "But if you give me just a minute, I can put something together. Got some fresh strawberries too."

"We ain't here for nothing from you," one of the men said, halting my uncle, who pivoted to face them. "It's what we got for you." He glanced at his buddy, then returned to Uncle Theo. "We're here to give you something."

"Come again?" Uncle Theo asked, perplexed as was I. "Give *me* something?"

"Our protection," replied the other man.

"Protection from what?" Uncle Theo questioned.

"From those two fellas who been asking around about you," the first man answered, "the ones who're looking for ya."

"Aw, hell," Uncle Theo waved them off, and he spun on his heels and noticed me standing just outside the barn. He went back to the men. "No one's looking for me."

"That ain't what the sheriff said," the second man was quick to respond, and the first man nodded in agreement.

"Oh, for Pete's sake," Uncle Theo commented with a heavy sigh.

"Now, we know how you are, Teddy," the first man picked up, holding his hands out as if that would calm my uncle. "Too proud to ask for help. Too set in your ways. Don't need no one." Uncle Theo was about to say something, but the man shushed him. "But we take care of our own around here. You know that."

Uncle Theo sighed again, although not as emphatically, and he acted as if he wanted to say something else, but instead, he just kind of shook his head.

"You been taking care of us, now it's our turn to take care of you," chimed in the other man. "Whether you like it or not."

"Well, I don't much like it," Uncle Theo said, "nor do I think it's necessary," and then softer, capitulating, "but...all right, then," as he sounded somewhat more accepting. "Though honestly, fellas, I

177

think Hank's making way too big a deal over this, as he's wont to doing."

"Hopefully that's the case," the man concurred, "and then don't none of us got anything to worry about. But if it ain't, just you know that we got your back." He waited. "And we ain't the only ones."

As the man said that, and he couldn't have timed it any more perfectly, a line of vehicles came driving up in the distance, I counted ten as they approached, cars and trucks and vans and a supercharged lemon-yellow Camaro that gunned its engine and spun its tires. They followed one another, rumbling toward us, stirring up the dust, honking their horns with the differing tones blending together like an impromptu symphony.

When they got to where we were by the barn, they fanned out into a semi-circle behind the scraggly guys' pickup and continued with their horn honking and flashing their head lights and high beams, some of them sticking their hands out their windows and pumping their fists or pounding on the sides of their doors or the tops of their roofs, letting it be known that they had arrived. It was quite the production, and some sight and sound, to behold. It got Chekhov barking along with them. And it got to me as well, motivating me such and making me emotional at once, just knowing that these people, these neighbors of Uncle Theo, were ready to fight for him, to protect him, and me too.

I choked up, and at that moment, I couldn't have been prouder of my uncle, knowing that the folks around these parts thought enough of him to rally around us like this. I walked forward and stood beside Uncle Theo, and I could have sworn I even detected a hint of emotion coming from him as well. He ran a hand over his face then subtly through his unruly hair so as to not let on that he was brushing back a tear. But he couldn't fool me. I saw what he was doing. And I didn't mind. It just made him human.

Uncle Theo acknowledged everyone with a nod and a wave, and then he put his hands up in the air, palms together, to thank them, as they kept on honking their horns and flashing their lights and pounding their fists and hooting and carrying on, this holler militia that had assembled to defend us.

CHAPTER NINE

School was finally out for the summer! Granted, it was my homeschooling with Uncle Theo, but when he gathered my textbooks and study plans and assignments and stuffed them back into that cardboard box after reviewing my last lesson and sealed it up to send off for me to receive the proper credits, it felt almost as satisfying and joyful and exhilarating as when we would all go running and yelling and roughhousing from the building in late May after Mr. Smitherman set us loose, hollering about how he didn't want to see us again until the third week of August, if then. This year was different for me, for sure, as if everything was upside down and inside out, yet I had managed to make the most of it regardless, and for that, I had fair reason to be proud.

I passed every class, earning my best grades ever, with my highest grade—a B+—coming in English Composition. That could have been from Uncle Theo and how he was always writing, which had rubbed off on me as I had begun to keep a journal, or perhaps I had inherited this from the very spirit of Anton Pavlovich Chekhov, one of the greatest writers of all time, passed on to me through the guard dog who shared his name and who had also become my best friend. She was at least my best friend out here in the sticks, yet I had a sneaking suspicion Chekhov and I would remain friends forever, even once I moved back home, and at last, I had an inkling of when that would be.

I had overheard more telephone conversations between Uncle Theo and Mama, though I didn't let on to my uncle that I had been eavesdropping. And really, as I considered it, I wasn't eavesdropping, not exactly. It wasn't my fault if I could hear Uncle Theo talking on the phone in the front room from inside my bedroom, what with how thin the walls were in this house and how Uncle Theo's voice carried and my proclivity to sit and listen on account of there wasn't much else to do at night besides reading old wrestling magazines or Mickey Spillane paperback books, and I had about gone through the entire collection of both of those. Anyhow, their conversations had become cordial for the most part, from what I could surmise, and consisted mainly of Uncle Theo providing Mama with progress reports on me, with long spells of silence in-between, which I presumed to be when Mama was doing the talking, as she was quite the talker. Uncle Theo didn't have to yell at her or stomp into the kitchen for a beer or two, which I took as a positive sign.

After their last call, it was decided that I would spend the summer with Uncle Theo and return to my house in Louisville in the fall, and hopefully to my school, as long as Mr. Smitherman and Principal Vickers and the State said it was all right, and I could think of nary a reason why they wouldn't as I had certainly proven myself while studying with Uncle Theo. I nearly jumped up and down with pure glee when I learned of that through my bedroom wall. However, I waited for Uncle Theo to break the news to me directly before I outwardly reacted so as not to let on that I was eavesdropping or overhearing or whatever. And I toned down my excitement a tad in front of Uncle Theo as well, so he wouldn't think that I wasn't appreciative of him allowing me to stay here or that I didn't enjoy being with him, because I was, and I did. It was just time for me to go home.

What good news it was, some of the best news I had had in a while, making me abundantly happy, with a lightness in my step and a smile plastered across my face. For once, I had some certainty and a plan. I had some direction, which apparently turned out to be exactly what I needed because I had been sleeping soundly ever since, no tossing and turning, and no more of those weird dreams. I was surely relieved that Mama was going to allow me to come home, and in the meantime, I was excited to be spending the next couple of months with Uncle Theo, and without having to stay put at that table learning subjects I doubted would ever serve me in real life. Now, I could get to know Uncle Theo even better, and call me crazy, but it had dawned on me that I had much in common with my uncle, such as my increasing fondness for these mystery meats he cooked.

With Uncle Theo and his gourmet meals, I was eating all sorts of interesting stuff, nothing I would have ever experienced prior, and also thanks to Uncle Theo's neighbors and what they brought over in trade for his "crop." We had rabbit and pheasant and wild duck and, of course, plenty of venison. These hills had to have been swarming with deer just ripe for the picking—or the shooting, as it were—and folks in this holler had some imaginative ideas on how to use the meat. There was deer sausage and deer bratwurst and deer bologna that, truth be told, pretty much tasted like regular sausage and bratwurst and bologna, only with something slightly off: a gamey, outdoorsy, woodsy quality. And someone gave Uncle Theo a trunk-load of Styrofoam coolers full of enough bison to feed us for weeks. Uncle Theo crumbled that bison in stews and served it as steaks and pounded it flat into hamburger patties. There were spicy bison meatballs that he mixed in with thick red marinara sauce and spooned over egg noodles. Some of the bison Uncle Theo cut up into long, thin strips and strung in the barn near his hanging dead marijuana plants to dry into meat sticks and jerky.

Once the weather broke and the creeks and lakes in these parts became fully stocked, it got to be ideal fishing conditions. People were offering us fresh-caught trout and pike and bluegill and crappie and catfish that Uncle Theo would fry or bake or blacken with paprika and cayenne pepper and toss on the grill. There was even something called mountain oysters, but after I ate those, I didn't rightly believe they had been pulled out of the waters, and while I had an unsettling notion as to what they might actually have been, with their texture and, more precisely, with what they resembled, I didn't want to ask about them, because they were tasty. Everything that Uncle Theo cooked was tasty, and I gladly ate it all up. I was eating like a king, we both were. I was frankly astonished that I hadn't gained fifty pounds, but Uncle Theo was putting me to work, so I reckoned I was burning through the calories as fast as I was consuming them.

I was outside practically from sun-up to sun-down, tending to Uncle Theo's garden, weeding and digging and watering and picking. I liked the picking the best, and especially when I could sneak a snack for myself. I had found that there was no sweeter taste on God's green earth than a plump and juicy peach plucked right off the tree, so mouthwateringly delicious and, dared I'd admit, better than candy. Uncle Theo allowed me a random peach now and again, but he admonished not to enjoy the fruits of my labor excessively, or "eat up the profits," as he put it, for there were chores to do.

Along with my gardening duties, I was also in charge of critter patrol, having to contend with the numerous animals that seemed to enjoy the vegetables and fruits—though they weren't as keen on the herbs—as much as I did. The worst of the lot were the chipmunks who, despite their cute appearance—like something drawn on a Saturday morning cartoon, and I half-expected them to talk or sing—tore up the land something awful, and there seemed to be no stopping them. No sooner would I stumble upon their holes and fill them in with whatever I could, dirt or rocks or sometimes by peeing into them—from having learned in biology class about how animals marked their territory by peeing, and after all, this garden was my territory—I'd uncover half-a-dozen other holes elsewhere in the garden. It liked to drive me nuts, but I was resolute on getting them and to tending to this garden to the highest of my abilities, because that was my life now, and I didn't mind it.

Despite putting me to work in his garden while he remained occupied with his other, and more lucrative, venture out beyond, Uncle Theo still made it a point for me to exercise daily, and not just from the performance of manual labor. Uncle Theo and his schedules. He preached about maintaining a "healthy work-life balance," which honestly I didn't entirely get since I was both working and living in the same place, which made the two kind of blend together as far as I was concerned. But I understood it enough to mean that Uncle Theo didn't want me to be constantly gardening. He urged me to get out on my mountain bike whenever I could, to explore these old coal trails while developing my cardio fitness. And, better than that, he had started letting me use his gym!

Exercising in Uncle Theo's personal and private home gym inspired me to no end. If I could have had anything in this world—and I wanted a lot—it was to be as big and strong as Uncle Theo; to get a mess of tattoos like he had was a close runner-up, but that would have to come later. At first, it was all I could do to even just budge one of Uncle Theo's weights. He had to go searching for weights I could lift, eventually finding these five-pound dumbbells that weren't so bad, except that they were bright pink and cushioned in case I dropped one on my foot, which was embarrassing, but he didn't make me feel bad about it. Uncle Theo just turned it into a goal, or a challenge, using my scrawniness and these puffy pink weights as motivation for me to get after it even harder. And he came up with a bunch of exercises for me to do that he wrote out in black marker on a piece of poster board that he tacked onto the wall of the barn, covering up his wrestling posters, so I knew he was serious about this. What with how Uncle Theo encouraged me, instilling how nothing was impossible to achieve as long as I put my mind to it, and with how persuasive he could be, it made me believe that my uncle had probably been a darned-good lawyer back in his day.

While I still sometimes longed to be hanging out with my buddies, even Timbo, I was meeting new people in Uncle Theo's neighbors from when they would come by to exchange their mystery meat or fish or whatever for what Uncle Theo had to offer, and from how they had been keeping a protective eye on us. Ever since that scare a few weeks back with those strange men spotted in Cole's Landing who had a suspicious interest in my uncle, these neighbors had been over at all hours to make certain everything was all right with us. I would spot them during the day, usually parked down by the road with their engines idling, and at night, I noticed their headlights shining outside from my bedroom window. At the outset, they were patrolling continually, in different groups, trading off shifts, and although they were adults, I got to be friendly with them. They even let me call them by their first names, and we would chitchat. Without a doubt, they were an interesting lot.

Lefty and Slim were the two fellas from that old pick-up who I first witnessed making an exchange with Uncle Theo, and those guys were a regular couple of cutups, the both of them, always making me laugh with their dirty jokes and the pranks they pulled on each other. Whenever Uncle Theo would catch wind of it, he scolded them to watch their language around me, but that didn't deter them, least not when he was out of earshot. They were funny, such jokers, although not much for personal hygiene, and they tended to smell somewhat ripe.

And there was Tasso, who ran a diner inside the gas station on Route 60, just off the four-lane, that was known for its sloppy joes. He was the one who gave Uncle Theo the recipe for the spicy bison meatballs. They said he was from the "old country," and although I didn't rightly understand what that was about—geography was never my best subject—it sounded intriguing enough, and his food sure was yummy, right up there with Uncle Theo's.

Leslie and Groggy, who I couldn't exactly determine if they were a dating couple or just close friends, actually lived in the van that they drove to our house, which I thought was neat, being able to drive your home to wherever you wanted to go, until Uncle Theo confided in me that they were only doing that because they were down on their luck after Leslie got fired from her job at the technical college in Grisham for stealing office supplies and Groggy's disability—from when a wooden beam fell on his head while he was making bourbon barrels—had run out.

Another of my favorites was PJ, who couldn't have been much older than me, with his freckles and frosted bangs and baggy shorts and sneakers. He had come into some money from his grandpa passing and put it toward the supercharged lemon-yellow Camaro that he drove. He was every bit as cool as his car. Occasionally, when Uncle Theo wasn't around, PJ would slip me a cigarette, a Marlboro Red that was a lot stronger than the cigarettes I used to swipe from Mama.

Big Ol' Tom was precisely how his nickname described him. He moved and talked slow as molasses, almost as if there was a delay for the message to get from his brain to the rest of his body. But he was an okay guy, and he crafted these awesome pieces of art, like something you'd see hanging in a shopping mall or a fancy motel, out of scrap metal he would find scouring junkyards and the dump, that he then sold at county fairs and flea markets. But what I liked most about Big Ol' Tom was his daughter, Paula, who was the single-most beautiful girl I had ever seen in the flesh. She could have been a Hollywood star or a game show model, with her silky blonde hair, luminescent in the light, and twinkling blue eyes and a flawless smile, every tooth straight and pearly. She made something inside of me stir whenever she looked at me. I wanted to get to know that girl better.

Then, there was Preacher Andy. He presided over the chapel that Uncle Theo went to on Sunday mornings. He was always trying to get me to go to church, and my reply to him was always that I would think about it, which wasn't completely a lie because I did think about it, but I always ended up deciding not to go.

There were other folks too, more than I had imagined lived in and around this holler since it appeared to be so isolated. But once I got to living here myself and fitting in, it was as if my eyes had opened to see everything I couldn't see before. I recognized that Uncle Theo's neighbors were a lot like him, preferring to be on their own and to keep to themselves. But when the situation called for it and they were needed, like when a couple of strangers showed up asking about my uncle, they came together and pitched in, doing whatever they could, whatever was needed of them. And it worked too because no one had seen hide nor hair of those fellas since. One evening, Sheriff Hank paid us a visit to tell Uncle Theo that it seemed to be that everyone's efforts had succeeded in scaring those two men away, and he called off this holler militia, although he still promised to send a squad car around every so often, and he nonetheless advised us not to let our guard down. But for now, it seemed the coast was clear.

So, that was how I was spending my summer, and I was loving every minute of it. And at this particular moment, I was speeding down toward the house on my mountain bike after exploring more of these old coal trails for much of Sunday morning while Uncle Theo was off at church. It had been a most eventful ride, and not just from the bumps and the jumps and going airborne on the uneven terrain and wiping out on a few particularly gnarly sections, yet getting right back up again. I had spotted a white squirrel in the brush beneath a grove of ash trees, leaping and bounding like it hadn't a care in the world. It startled me, the unusual sight of such a rare creature, which I initially took for a skunk or a possum or some kind of weird rat before I got closer to see that, indeed, it was a squirrel. Luckily, I didn't scare it off, and I was able to sit for a spell on a hollowed out log to watch it, the way I would watch the squirrels at the park by school whenever I ditched class.

Seeing that white squirrel like that made me appreciate the camouflage of its gray squirrel cousins, for the snowy fur caused it to stick out like a sore thumb, this glistening blaze of ivory among the plush greenery. I sure hoped that the little guy would be safe considering how the hawks in this forest were forever on the hunt. I'd spy them up high, clear above the tree line, soaring effortlessly on the mildest of breezes, wings outstretched, just barely gliding, before swooping to pounce on an unsuspecting mouse or chipmunk or squirrel, whisking their prey away, clasped tightly in their talons. Yet, if this white squirrel was fearful of that, I surely couldn't tell as it frolicked and played, scurrying up one tree and down the other, and hopping and foraging, chewing on an acorn, then tossing it aside and dashing off to somewhere else. I guessed there was something to be said for not fitting in and still being comfortable in your own skin, or fur, as it were. This spirited white squirrel was as nimble as could be, darting to and fro. I managed to capture a snippet of video of it on my phone, which was why I was racing home to show it to Uncle Theo, as church had probably let out by now, and we'd have to get back to work in the garden and beyond.

I got to the house, with Uncle Theo's truck parked outside, that old hunk of junk that tickled me so, how it looked like the slightest touch could topple it apart into a million different pieces, except for the tires, which were basically brand new. As I was leaning my bike up against a post, I noticed a car parked at the very edge of the driveway in the berm along the side of the road. I lingered and stared out to see if I could tell who it was, but I couldn't place the car, a dark four-door, as belonging to any of the neighbors. I surmised, though, that it had to have been someone Uncle Theo knew, because who else would be out this way? It could have just been somebody I hadn't met yet bringing something for my uncle in exchange for his "crop." I decided to mosey on down there to see what was what, who they were. Maybe they were trying to find where to go.

However, as I did, and I approached the car, I had a weird feeling about it—nothing I could properly explain, just this twisting and churning—as if I was somewhere I wasn't supposed to be, which wasn't an occurrence entirely out of the ordinary, as that seemed to happen to me a lot at Uncle Theo's. I also had a strange sensation of déjà vu, just something about this car, when I noticed that the windows were tinted. I couldn't make out who was inside, not until I got nearer and the person on the passenger side facing me lowered the window partway. I didn't recognize anything about this man: older and kind of rough-looking, like he had been through a lot in his life, with slicked back silver hair and pock-marked skin, in a coat and tie and wearing sunglasses, even while the sun was hidden today behind a mass of stubborn gunmetal clouds. He wasn't someone I knew, nor any of Uncle Theo's neighbors who I had seen at the house. He didn't appear like someone who much belonged out here at all.

"What's your name, son?" the man called out to me, as I had stopped short once he rolled his window down, his voice like rocks rattling around in the bottom of a rusted tin bucket.

"Sir?" I asked, more just out of a reaction because I had heard him.

"Your name," he followed. "What is it?"

"Um..." I hesitated, uncertain how to answer that, or rather, if I should, uncertain as to why he was asking my name. Then, I recalled, in that instant, everything I had been taught by Mama about not talking to strangers or going up to someone's car I didn't know, these lessons she had gone over and over with me when I was growing up until it liked to bore me to death. Still I must've retained it nonetheless: to stay away from stranger-danger. It was this alarm system ringing inside of me, warning that I had best get out of there and that I most assuredly shouldn't tell him my name, or anything, for that matter. I sort of eased back, not taking my gaze off the man. As I did, he pushed open the door and leaned to get out, placing one foot on the ground, his shoe shiny and patent leather, a diamond pattern on his sock, in dress pants.

The man repeated, in a manner that conveyed he was fast losing patience, with a scowl and stained teeth, "Your name, boy. I asked you your name."

I froze, deer in the headlights, and my mind emptied, and I doubted I could've told him my name had I wanted to, as I had momentarily forgotten it. I just went blank. Nothing. But as it turned out, I wouldn't have to tell the man anything or do anything, because right then, a blur of something flew by me like a shot and flung at the car with a wallop. I didn't know what it was, only that it was large and powerful. I focused to see that it was Chekhov, and was she ever pissed, in all-out attack mode.

The man hastily got his leg, and the rest of him, back in the car and yanked the door shut, right as Chekhov was about to take a hefty chunk of his flesh. But she didn't let up. She reared back on her hind legs and pounded against the car with her front paws, her full weight,

189

barking up a storm, a spine-tingling, bone-jarring snarling and howling that even terrified me, her saliva splattering the passenger side window. She was incensed, absolutely enraged, and she was determined to get into that car and go after whoever was inside. The driver floored the gas, and the rear tires spun helplessly, ripping out the turf in a bluster of shredded grass and dirt before gaining traction. Then, that car tore out of there, leaving two bare patches and a plume of smoke and dust in its wake. Chekhov continued barking and sprinted after them, breaking that unwritten rule not to leave the property. But she seemed hell-bent on getting at that car.

I put a hand to my chest and took a deep breath and steadied myself as I tried to comprehend what had just happened, what that was, and who that man was, and who might've been in the car with him. Once Chekhov had sufficiently accomplished chasing them away, she came trotting back to me, tongue out, tail wagging, like nothing was the matter, her job done. She was a smart dog, though, and intuitive, and she could obviously detect that I was still shaken. She pushed her oversized body against me, and when I bent over to cradle her head and rub her behind her pointy ears, she licked me on the cheek as if to tell me that it was okay. That helped to calm me somewhat, and I was somehow able to move again, but something told me that that hadn't been a chance encounter, and it probably wasn't an isolated incident either, and that it really wasn't okay. I needed to get to the house, Chekhov and I hustling back up the length of the driveway to report this to Uncle Theo.

"So what do you think?" I asked between bites of tuna mac, Mama's recipe, my contribution to the cooking, what had become our regular Sunday dinner.

I had just told Uncle Theo about that car Chekhov and I encountered earlier today. This was the first opportunity I had to discuss it with him. When I had gotten into the house right after that, Uncle Theo was already tending to his marijuana plants. I didn't want to disturb him because I knew how he was when he got to working out there: in the flow and all, his head down, back bent, toiling away. And I started to wonder, as I considered it, if maybe I had overreacted, and Chekhov too. Yet, as I worked in the garden myself and my brain replayed that episode, with me analyzing every frame of footage as if seeing it in my head, it seemed to me that it just wasn't right, what had occurred, that people, especially adults, weren't supposed to go around acting like that—and especially to young people—to be so secretive and menacing and downright creepy. And anyway, Chekhov's instincts were usually spot on, and with her being as angry at that car and at whoever was inside as she was and acting the way she did, I convinced myself that there had to have been something to it. The first opportunity I had, when we finally got some time together, I raised it with Uncle Theo.

"It's good, bud," he answered, chewing then swallowing, then following with a swallow of his beer. "Real good. You've outdone yourself with this batch. That's some outstanding tuna mac."

"No," I was quick to note and quick to correct myself. "I mean, thanks. I appreciate that. Just following Mama's recipe." And I took a swallow of tuna mac, with a swallow of my milk, and it was real good, if I could say so myself, and maybe I really had outdone myself with this batch. "But about that car and that man inside who yelled at me," I picked back up with what I had been saying, "from out on the road today."

"Oh, that," Uncle Theo replied with another swallow, before coming up for air and wiping his mouth with a napkin. "Could've just been KSP."

"Who?"

"KSP," he answered, then explained, "Kentucky State Police. Sheriff Hank said he was going to put a call in to them. Could've been one of their cars—unmarked." Uncle Theo looked at me, sucked at his front teeth with his tongue, how he did when he was eating or thinking, and he could probably tell that I wasn't getting it, how he was able to do. "Years ago, my first year out of law school when I clerked for a judge, I drove a car similar to that one you described, a Crown Vic from the State's fleet. Once a month, I took it to Frankfort to pick up files, and I would just cruise straight down and back in the left lane." He smiled to himself, like that was a pleasant memory. "People would get out of my way, thinking anyone driving that fast in such a vehicle had to have been a state trooper about to pull them over. It was nice job perk."

"Yeah, but"—I shook my head, not as convinced about it as Uncle Theo might've been—"those fellas, least the one who hollered at me, didn't look like no state trooper. He wasn't in uniform. Was wearing a businessman's suit, from what I could gather."

Uncle Theo shrugged. "I don't know. Maybe they were out of uniform. Plain clothes."

I didn't say anything, but I still wasn't buying it, and Uncle Theo could no doubt sense that as I just stared at my plate and picked at what I had left.

"Tell you what, Rhett," Uncle Theo said with a sigh, and I could feel him looking at me, which caused me to look up at him, "once we finish eating and you're doing the dishes, I'll run out there and have a look around, see for myself if I can tell anything." He paused. "How's that?"

"Okay," I told him, content with that, and I reckoned I had to be, given how that was probably the only thing that could be done for now. "But take Chekhov with you in case they show back up. She handled herself all right out there."

"Good ol' Chekhov. Where would we be without you, girl?" Uncle Theo said in a singsong voice, reaching down with a handful of tuna mac to where Chekhov was, next to him and waiting for her table scraps, and she slurped it up heartily. "If you don't like someone, they're in real trouble, huh?"

Chekhov licked around her mouth, that fat red tongue of hers, and whined at that, or maybe she was just whining for more tuna mac.

"And she sure didn't like those fellas none," I added. "She would've torn them up something awful if she had gotten to them. I ain't never seen her like that."

"Don't worry about it, bud." Uncle Theo tried to convince me with a wink. "I doubt it's anything, but Chekhov and I, we'll check it out later anyhow."

I nodded in return like I understood, and the both of us went back to eating. And I also went back to thinking. Maybe Uncle Theo was right, and it wasn't anything: that car being out there, that man asking my name. I could have still been a little on edge and somewhat paranoid with what had been transpiring these past weeks, with the holler militia patrolling, and Sheriff Hank's visits, and whoever had been going around asking about my uncle. It was nerve-racking, for sure. But I felt better knowing that Uncle Theo was going to check it out.

We switched to another topic, one more "conducive to the dinner table," as Uncle Theo said, that white squirrel I had seen in the woods this morning. I took my phone out and played the video for him. Uncle Theo was clearly impressed. He informed me, because he knew so much about everything, that coming across a white squirrel in these parts—where the odds of that, among the multitude of gray squirrels, was 1 in 100,000—was considered a sign of good fortune to come. I hoped that Uncle Theo was right about that, as I could use some good fortune to come my way. He and I both.

It struck me as kind of funny, and sort of strange, how your life could change without you really noticing. Here I was, living in Uncle Theo's house, lying in this bedroom he had put together for me as if it had always been my bedroom, staring up at the galaxy of star stickers on the ceiling, and it somehow made sense. It felt like this was where I belonged, where I had always belonged, like I had always been here. This was comfortable. This was comforting. This was home. And while it pained me in a way to think that—since Mama and Ella Mae were waiting for me in Louisville, and I still wanted to see them, of course I did, and live with them in our house there, and I would at the end of the summer—it just seemed like Uncle Theo's house was where I presently belonged.

I couldn't quite put my finger on it, how this had come to be, and so effortlessly. It must've had something to do with Uncle Theo and his routines and regimens and schedules. My uncle was smart, the smartest person I knew, and he was sneaky too, because he was a lawyer, after all, even though that wasn't his occupation anymore. But lawyers were sneaky, and that sneakiness must've stuck with him. I wouldn't put anything past Uncle Theo, and certainly not how he might've used his routines and regimens and schedules to get me used to living with him, especially when I had never been one for that sort of thing.

Up until now, before moving in with Uncle Theo, I mostly did what I pleased, whatever I wanted and whenever I wanted; no one told me otherwise, or if they did, I paid them no mind, and they eventually just let it slide. Mama tried her best with me, she really did, and I appreciated that now, but she couldn't make me do much of anything either. I just wasn't cooperative, and I wasn't easy to live with, and I pushed back at every chance. After a while, Mama just gave up, and I couldn't fault her for that, not one bit, which was why I had ended up with my uncle out here in the sticks.

As I thought about it—and I was thinking about it a lot lately with not a whole lot else to do at night but think—I never truly felt like I belonged anywhere, not once Pops up and left. I never could get settled. Then, I came to live with Uncle Theo, and with his routines and regimens and schedules, he made it so that I settled in right fast, such that, now, I couldn't imagine being anywhere different. It was sort of funny how things worked out, and kind of strange. And while I still didn't know how this would play out in the end, I wasn't particularly worried about that. Just the opposite, in fact. I was excited, and I couldn't wait to see what would become of me. I had hope. I had possibilities. I looked forward to wherever this journey would lead.

Something I was certain of was that once I did move back to my house in Louisville, I was going to get a set of star stickers and create my own galaxy on the ceiling in my bedroom there, just like what I had in here. There was just something about lying in the stillness and the silence and staring upwards in the darkness to see those stars glowing. It made me believe that someone was up there watching out for me. It was calming and reassuring, and it allowed me to relax. And it was this reminder that there was a whole world waiting to explore.

I rolled over to face the curtainless window where I could see an entire sky full of stars, the real things, shining brightly outside. Staring at the stars like that still made me think of Pops, and I reckoned there was no real way for me to ever stop thinking of Pops, not entirely. I still hadn't decided if I hated him. I wasn't sure what to make of him after getting to know Uncle Theo like I had. Yet, I still wondered about Pops, and on a night like tonight, where he might be beneath this same celestial canopy, and if he was thinking of me. I was coming to terms with his absence and starting to accept that he was gone for good, and I tried to resolve myself to never seeing him again. Although, in all honesty, I wasn't completely sold on never seeing him again. There was a feeling in my gut that told me our paths would cross again one day, and my gut was never wrong.

As I lay in bed, staring across the room out the window at all those twinkling stars, thinking about everything and nothing, I breathed out a contented sigh, and I was ready to call it a night. It had been another full day, like many of the days at Uncle Theo's, and I was tired, a satisfying tired that told me—in my sore muscles and my achy back—that I had gotten a lot done, but that now, I needed to sleep. I steadily drifted off, to begin the day anew tomorrow, when a light flashed in from outside, streaked across the bedroom wall, and then disappeared, accompanied by the sound of car tires crunching the rocks in the crushed-limestone driveway.

That struck me as peculiar, given that folks didn't usually stop by at this late hour to meet up with Uncle Theo, and the neighbors had ceased their patrolling. Perhaps though, Uncle Theo had called some of them over after my experience with that man in that car today. Uncle Theo never did report back to me as to what he might have seen when he went out there after dinner to look around or what he thought about the whole thing. But it could've been that something else might have gotten his attention, and he hadn't had a chance yet to tell me, so I didn't make much of it. And besides, if the holler militia had returned to keep an eye on us, it made me feel safe enough, as I fell asleep.

❧

"Rhett, wake up."

I faintly heard that voice in my dream, or what I thought was a dream until it repeated, with an increased intensity, and a firm pressure on my shoulder. I opened my eyes to see Uncle Theo standing over me, shaking me awake but being muted about it.

"Come on, bud. We gotta go," he whispered, his sizeable silhouette casting a shadow over my bed.

I paused to acclimate, to get an understanding of where I was and what was happening, as I must've been in a deep slumber. I had no idea how long I had been out. I reached for my phone from the nightstand to see what time it was.

"Three in the morning?" I said to myself, to my phone. Then, louder to Uncle Theo, "What is it? What's happening?"

Uncle Theo shushed me and took his other large hand and placed it over my mouth and applied more pressure to my shoulder to sort of restrain me. "It's okay," he said, "you just need to get up. We gotta go."

"Where?" I asked, when he took his hand away, lowering my voice into a whisper like him. "What's happening? Where are we going?"

"Just...just out of here," Uncle Theo stammered, and I could detect his adult voice, which made me pay attention. "Get dressed, put your shoes on. Let's go." He moved away so that I could get out of bed, and as I did, this leg, then that leg, he diverted me from the window. "And stay away from the window."

On instinct, as soon as Uncle Theo said that, I looked out the window. I saw a car that I immediately identified as that car from today—or I guessed now technically it had been yesterday—parked beside the house. That sent a shiver of fear and a pulse of panic throughout my body. Uncle Theo pulled me past the window, and he waited as I threw on a pair of shorts and a t-shirt and stepped into my sneakers, clumsily tying the laces. When I was ready, Uncle Theo cracked open the bedroom door, peeked down the hallway, and then watchfully walked out, gesturing for me to follow him and cautioning to "be quiet."

I tiptoed closely behind Uncle Theo, not yet fully awake but recognizing the gravity of this situation all the same. The house was dark where Uncle Theo normally kept the stove light on in the kitchen and the lamp on where he sat at the table at night to write. I thought maybe the power had gone out, as I kept on closely behind Uncle Theo. He pointed for me to go into the kitchen, which I did, and then I turned and watched him slink toward the front of the house and take the shotgun down from where it hung above the mantel. That made me tense up, and I swallowed hard. I had assumed that gun was just for show, a decoration, like the framed painting of the beach over the sofa, even while Uncle Theo had always warned me to keep my hands off of it. I thought he was only saying that because he didn't want me to mess with it, to break it or whatever. But now I understood that that must've been because the shotgun was real, and what was happening, whatever was happening, must have been real too.

"Where are we going?" I said to Uncle Theo as he joined me in the kitchen.

"Out to the barn," he replied. "Walk fast, no running, but move swiftly...and stay down."

"Stay down?" I questioned. "What? Why stay down?"

"Don't worry about it," he said abruptly, and then pulled back some as if to console me. "It'll be all right."

I was now fully awake—and also fully scared—and Uncle Theo didn't sound at all confident when he told me that it would be all right, which made it difficult for me to believe him.

"What'll be all right?" I asked him. "Why are we going out to the barn?"

Uncle Theo didn't respond right away, and I could tell he was concerned by how stiffly he held himself, and by his lack of expression, and by not getting on me for being "an inquisitive one" with all of my questions.

"It's just safer there."

"Safer from what?"

Uncle Theo hesitated like he didn't want to say it, and maybe I didn't want to hear it, but I had to hear it. And I felt we were wasting time with him not saying anything about what we were doing and us just standing in the kitchen like that, and I reckoned Uncle Theo felt the same, so he came out with it. "Those guys are here."

"Those guys?" I said it like it was a question, but unfortunately, I had a clear idea of what the answer was.

"The ones I think who've been looking for me," he replied, and before I could get out another question—and I had so many questions—he cut me off. "Now is not the time for this, Rhett," he snapped. "We just gotta go. Come on."

Uncle Theo opened the kitchen door, just wide enough for us to squeeze through. He gave a cautious glance around outside before nudging me in front of him and directing me to "go ahead, straight to the barn. I got your back."

I nodded like I understood, but I surely didn't. I glimpsed over my shoulder and saw that Uncle Theo was angling his shotgun as if he was fixing to use it on whoever or whatever might've been lying in wait.

"I got you, bud," he told me, his hand on my shoulder, with a squeeze and a pat, which I took as his attempt, although not the best, at being reassuring. "Promise."

I just stood there, unwilling to move, or, more likely, unable. It was like when I was a kid atop the high dive at the public swimming pool, summoning the courage to step off and take the leap, but temporarily paralyzed under the consuming fear of what could happen, a multitude of scenarios flicking through my head, all of them ending badly. I didn't want to go. I was afraid to go.

"Where's Chekhov?" I asked him, partly because I wanted to know and mostly to stall.

"She'll come around," he said, with an insistence, and he prodded me forward. "Now, move. Let's go."

I considered resisting but that was futile. With no alternative, no way to put this off any longer without irritating Uncle Theo and placing us further in jeopardy, I took a deep inhale, and I took the leap, out the kitchen door and onto the stoop, those three concrete block steps that seemed as intimidating to me in my uncertainty as any high dive. I went boldly into this night, walking fast and staying down, as I had been instructed. My objective, the barn, was visible straight ahead, about the length of a football field away, but it might as well had been to the end of the earth for how anxious I felt. There was nothing between here and there to cover me, except for Uncle Theo, who promised that he had my back, and his shotgun that he held cocked and loaded and pointed into the yard.

CHAPTER TEN

One time, when I was a kid, Pops took me to the circus, just me and him, a "real guys' day" he called it. It wasn't one of those fancy circuses, not the kind that sold out the fairgrounds for two straight weeks each spring or that would arrive on a train to much hoopla and fanfare and parade through town, elephants marching down the street, trunk to tail. This was a small, local, modest circus that performed every so often at the high school gymnasium, usually on a Sunday afternoon when there wasn't anything going on, that advertised with paper flyers tacked to telephone poles that just read: CIRCUS THIS SUNDAY! Even so, I would beg Pops to take me, promising that I would never ask him for anything else for as long as I lived. But he was always too busy with work or whatnot, and he kept putting it off, said we would go the next time, and the next time after that, and then the next time after that, and so on and so forth, until this one time—and maybe I had finally worn him down, and perhaps Mama had gotten involved too, as she could be rather persuasive—when we went to the circus one Sunday afternoon.

There weren't any lions or tigers or bears or elephants, no high wire walkers or trapeze artists or aerialists, nobody getting shot out of a cannon or throwing knives or swallowing swords, nothing that extravagant. But there were clowns and tumblers, and trained poodles in frilly skirts that jumped through hoops, and a guy who juggled bowling pins without dropping many of them. And there was a ringmaster, this boisterous gentleman with a waxed handlebar mustache, who wore a shiny, red suit trimmed in sparkling rhinestones and a top hat that reached to the sky. He had a bold manner about him and a presence that commanded your attention. Through his giant megaphone, he would announce each act in a booming voice and provide a running commentary, hollering out stuff like, "Well folks, won't you just look at all them clowns getting out of that teeny-tiny car," or "How 'bout them tumblers and their flippity-flops?" or "It ain't easy juggling twenty-pound bowling pins, take it from me, y'all." He was funny, and it was fun, and this circus was okay enough. I liked it just fine. And Pops bought me a tub of popcorn and an extra-large soda and a blue cotton candy, so I was happy.

Toward the end of the show, to set up the grand finale, the gymnasium went pitch dark, and a lone spotlight shone on this fella who came marching from behind the curtain, all businesslike, a mountain of a man who must've weighed well over three hundred pounds, dressed in a leopard-printed single-strapped singlet, with a leather belt and leather wrist cuffs and matching leather boots. It was the strongman, and as he entered, he was pulling this steel cage mounted on a cart with thick, rumbling wooden wheels. Inside this cage was a real live gorilla with a massive body, broad shoulders like a football player, and bulging hairy arms and legs as sturdy as tree trunks. As big as the strongman was, this gorilla dwarfed him. And the gorilla appeared none too happy to be confined in that cage. In fact, he was downright spitting mad about it, lashing out with its meaty fists and yanking at the bars and howling something awful, exposing his razor-sharp teeth.

An anxious hush fell over the audience as everyone stiffened to attention and grew silent, the air thick with anticipation, nobody knowing what exactly this strongman was intending to do with this angry gorilla in a cage. The ringmaster informed us, in a solemn, foreboding manner, that the gorilla had only recently been captured from the wilds of the jungle and brought all the way here to Louisville in the cargo hold of a container ship that had traveled for days and days down the Ohio River from New York City. I wasn't much for geography, had nary a clue if one could properly sail from New York City to Louisville down the Ohio River, but it sounded plausible enough to me, and I reckoned that—if it was true—a lengthy, uncomfortable, cramped trip like that would've made anyone ornery, especially a gorilla that had only recently been captured from the wilds of the jungle. Yet, it was what the ringmaster said next that seemed truly unbelievable. He said that the strongman was going to wrestle this gorilla!

There were scattered murmurings and whisperings among the audience, blank stares and shrugs, mouths agape. Surely, as we all thought, that had to have been a joke, and we waited in earnest for the ringmaster to offer some indication of that: a subtle grin, a mischievous wink, if not just coming straight out with it and admitting, through his megaphone, "Nah, folks, I'm just kiddin'." But no, nothing like that, and instead, the ringmaster assured us that this was "certainly no joke, folks," resulting in further scattered murmurings and whisperings, blank stares and shrugs, mouths agape. I sat perched on the edge of my seat—everyone did—to see how in the world this was going to transpire, especially given that there was no wrestling ring and, moreover—and more importantly, as far as I was concerned—no ropes or partitions or any type of barriers to prevent the gorilla from escaping into the stands. I glanced over at Pops, but he didn't seem to be concerned. He just looked on with this vague smile on his face and a faraway gaze as he drank his beer out of a paper cup.

I took a deep breath and steadied myself and watched as the strongman pulled the cage into the center of the gymnasium floor, with the gorilla continuing to carry on as if it wanted nothing more than to get at this strongman, probably to take out all of its pent-up aggression from being captured and then sent on a slow boat down the Ohio River. And sure enough, that gorilla got its chance, because no sooner had the strongman opened the cage when the gorilla leaped at him as if it had been launched from a catapult. The crowd let out a collective "ooh," followed by a collective "aah" as the strongman and the gorilla proceeded to flat-out brawl, wrestling each other with a ferocity like two mortal enemies. The ringmaster provided a play-by-play that nobody was really paying much mind to, as we were all too focused on the fighting.

It was quite the spectacle, and a surprisingly even bout. The strongman would be on top for a spell, and then they would flip over, and the gorilla would be on top, and vice versa. It went back and forth like that, the two of them rolling about on the gymnasium floor with neither appearing to gain any competitive advantage nor getting the better of the other. I couldn't believe what I was witnessing, had never seen anything like this, not on TV or in the movies and certainly not in the flesh: a man wrestling an ape. People cheered and shouted, although it wasn't entirely clear who everyone was rooting for. I wasn't for certain who to root for myself since, after all, that gorilla had been uprooted from its home and brought to be in a circus in Louisville, so it had every right to be perturbed, but I also didn't want to see this strongman get hurt. It was thrilling regardless of picking a side, the most exciting event I had ever been a part of, and I couldn't wait to get home to tell Mama everything about it.

This clash went on for a while, certainly longer than I had anticipated, and it seemed to be moving toward a draw, when the gorilla, with a precipitous burst of energy, got its second wind and hauled back and then rushed at the strongman with everything it had, driving its humongous shoulder into the strongman's chest and knocking him up into the air and onto the ground with a wallop that echoed off the gymnasium walls. There was a thunderous roar that arose from the crowd at the apparent victory of the gorilla, with high-fives and pats on the back and acknowledgments of "way to go!" and "you did it, buddy!" to the gorilla. But the gorilla wasn't interested in anyone's adulation or in basking in this victory, and it also didn't seem content with merely besting the strongman. Indeed, the gorilla wasn't yet done and began stomping on the strongman as he lay flat on his back, out cold and completely helpless, its gigantic feet throttling this poor man, the gorilla's arms raised high above its head in triumph.

The crowd was once more silenced at this unexpected turn, this horrific spectacle, with the audience members clearly concerned for the wellbeing of the strongman, as it appeared the gorilla might stomp him clear to death. People yelled for the ringmaster to do something about it, to put an end to this carnage, some pleading, impassioned, others furious and demanding immediate attention. But the ringmaster, for all of his previous bluster and exuberance, looked to be as frightened and worried as everyone else. Furthermore, since he was down there on the gymnasium floor in the midst of the action and well within striking distance of the gorilla, he did what I supposed most folks would've done in his circumstance, though for those of us in the audience, it came as quite a bombshell. The ringmaster simply turned tail, and he ran, scurrying off so fast that his top hat went flying and he threw a shoe. He just skedaddled away from there as swiftly as he could. With no one now in charge, the crowd was flung into a panic, me included. But I glanced over at Pops, and he was still just looking on, smiling and enjoying his beer.

After a fleeting few minutes of this uncertainty, which nonetheless felt like an eternity, the gorilla finally ceased its assault on the unconscious strongman and eased away. The crowd let out a shared sigh of relief, but it was short-lived upon the realization that there was still a wild—and very much agitated—gorilla on the loose in the high school gymnasium. And sadly, the gorilla didn't seem to want to call it a day, as it slowly turned its attention to the stands. I then watched in absolute horror as the gorilla began to make its way toward the audience. Everything downshifted into slow motion for me as people screamed and squealed and shoved each other aside with no regard for one another, tossing their popcorn and sodas and cotton candy, scrambling for safety as the gorilla tramped and trudged and lumbered up the rows of metal bleachers. And to my utter dismay, it was headed directly to where Pops and I were seated!

I was momentarily frozen by that but managed to break myself away enough from that petrifying scene to turn to Pops, and he still didn't seem concerned, not in the slightest, and I simply could not fathom how he could remain so calm and collected. I guessed that maybe he had drunk too much beer—as he was apt to do—to be in any actual fear. But he needed to be afraid, and he needed to get out of there. We both did. I grabbed at Pops and tugged on his shirt sleeve, and I exclaimed, hysterical and terror-stricken, "Pops, let's go, let's go! We gotta leave! Let's go! That gorilla's coming into the stands. That gorilla's coming at us!"

Pops didn't react, other than to keep smiling and drinking his beer. I had spilled my soda and dropped my popcorn and cotton candy like everyone else, and I was fixing to run like the rest of them too, my body jittering, my heart thumping, wide-eyed and frantically searching for an escape route. All the while, that gorilla was steadily approaching, as pissed off as it had ever been, snarling and bellowing, those razor-sharp teeth. I was convinced that the gorilla was coming for me, that that was my destiny, just the unfortunate hand I had been dealt: to be attacked by a gorilla at some local circus in the high school gymnasium on a Sunday afternoon. There was nobody else around, everyone but me and Pops had up and left, and Pops didn't seem to care. I was smack dab in the path of this enraged beast that had already beaten a strongman into submission, so what chance did I have, just some kid?

"Pops, come on, Pops! Let's go!" I yelled, my voice cracking, tears streaming down my face, but Pops just smiled and sat back in his chair and crossed his legs and drank his beer from a paper cup. "Pops, come on, we have to leave! We have to! Let's go!"

I was jumping up and down, and grabbing and tugging at Pops, begging for him to do something, anything, to get us out of there, whatever I could do to get his attention so that he would understand the seriousness of this, screeching and shrieking with hardly any voice left, imploring Pops to take me away from there, to please just take me away. And I kept on like that, and on like that as the gorilla drew closer and closer, and Pops still did nothing about it. I couldn't understand this, and I couldn't believe this, and I knew that this couldn't be happening to me, and still, it was.

The gorilla was right there, squared up in front of me, so close that I could reach out and touch its tangled and matted fur. All I could do was close my eyes and pray for this to be over and that it wouldn't hurt too badly, that hopefully I wouldn't know what hit me, like that strongman who had been left for dead. I waited for whatever it was that the gorilla was going to do, and I accepted my fate. I was sorrowful that I might never see Mama again, or any of my buddies, but I was plumb out of options at that point. So I waited. And I waited. But nothing. There was nothing from the gorilla. I cautiously opened my eyes, squinting through one eye, and then both, and saw the gorilla standing before me, staring at me, a scowl, and those razor-sharp teeth, but otherwise, its expression was oddly fixed. I couldn't figure it out, had no idea what this gorilla was up to. Then, it did something I would have never expected. The gorilla put both of its catcher's-mitt sized hands against its ears and kind of shook and twisted, and it pulled off its head!

Underneath the gorilla's head was a man's head. As it turned out, it wasn't a wild gorilla captured in the jungle after all, but a man in a gorilla suit, a sweaty and red-faced and portly man, with a ruddy complexion and long stray strands of wet hair in his face that he pushed back over his bald spot with his bulky gorilla glove. It had been a man in a gorilla suit the whole while, and when he saw me, how I was in shock and disarray and disbelief and still altogether fearful—as well as a bunch of other emotions, none of them pleasant emotions—he doubled over and started laughing like it was the funniest thing ever. And everyone around us, as people returned to their seats and also saw that it was only a man in a gorilla suit, started laughing, with the loudest laughter coming from Pops as he pointed at me and finished his beer with a chug, then wadded up the paper cup in his fist and tossed it to the floor.

The ringmaster came back as well and shook hands with the strongman, who had bounded up off the gymnasium floor to take a bow, with the both of them laughing. The ringmaster announced through his megaphone about how they liked to end the show with a joke, and he said some other stuff too, but I wasn't listening after that. And I wasn't laughing, either, because I didn't see the joke. I didn't think that was funny at all. I exhaled heavy, and looked down and noticed that I had peed myself, the front of my shorts with a wide wet spot that I coyly attempted to cover with my hands. I just looked down and wished for this moment to pass as my heart resumed its normal beating, and I wiped the tears and snot from my face, and I swallowed hard to try and dislodge a lump that was stuck in my throat. I just looked down until this was over, until Pops got me out of there and took me home. We didn't talk in the car, and I didn't say anything about it to Mama. I didn't say anything about it to anyone. I just tried as best I could to forget about it, to bury it deep in the farthest corner of my mind and never think of it again, that one time when Pops took me to the circus, and it was the most scared I had ever been in my life.

Uncle Theo and I were hiding in the barn. We had made it safely from the house without being detected—as far as I knew—and had been lying low for forty minutes or so in the pitch dark, with just the stray slivers of light from an exceptionally bright full moon streaking through the cracks and slants between the wood, and the only sound was that of the monotonous, synchronized chirping of the cicadas that had risen from the dead after seventeen years and taken up residence in the trees in and among this holler. It was every horror movie I'd ever seen, and I was scared, the most scared I had ever been in my life. Yet, I couldn't let on to Uncle Theo that I was scared. I needed to put on a brave face for him because he would expect that from me. And I had to be here for him the way he had been here for me. If only I knew what this was all about, or better yet, if only this would pass and be nothing, but I doubted that would happen, because things rarely worked like that. I just had to wait this out with my uncle.

"How you holding up, bud?" Uncle Theo asked me from where he was leaned up against the front of the barn, peering through a tiny knothole in the door.

"I'm okay," I replied, lied, faintly from where I was cowering behind a rack of weights toward the back. "You seein' anything?"

Uncle Theo shook his head, remained focused straight ahead. "Nuh-uh," he said, "but that doesn't mean they're not out there."

"What are we gonna do?" I questioned. "We can't hide here forever."

"Won't be long before the sun comes up. That'll flush them out, and then we'll see what's what."

I didn't say anything to that, didn't have anything to say to that, but that didn't sound like much of a plan. Although, I didn't have a plan of my own, so I guessed that plan was as good as any. I had to trust that Uncle Theo knew what he was doing, like I always trusted him. It was only that, sometimes, that was easier to do than others, and this was one of those others. I sighed and shifted position, with my legs tingling and going numb with how they were bent at an odd angle the way I was crouched to stay hidden. I glanced around, but I couldn't make out much of anything. I wondered where Chekhov was. Not having her here only added to the tension. She was our guard dog, for Pete's sake. It wasn't like her to just disappear and leave us hanging, and when we needed her most. This wasn't right. None of this was right. But I didn't know what to do other than to stay put where I was and to pray.

I might not have been one for going to church, never had been. It didn't hold my attention—like most things—and I didn't like to be told what to do, or when to do it. But that didn't mean I wasn't religious or that I didn't still pray. I prayed constantly, without ceasing, as the Bible said to do—and I read the Bible too. I just didn't feel the need to advertise it because it wasn't anyone's business but my own. Yet, I talked to God all the time, about whatever, or maybe about nothing in particular, least not in the grand scheme of everything God had to do. There were even times—and I wasn't particularly proud of this—when I yelled at God, when I was angry at him, like when Pops up and left and never came back, no matter how much I prayed that he would. I did feel bad afterwards for yelling at God, because I guessed God had his reasons, and in hindsight, I reckoned that he did, at least with Pops not coming back.

God and I would make up eventually, and he seemed to understand, though he never told me as such. I just sensed that God seemed to understand. And I kept going back to God for help. It was like what Mama would say: if you had a problem too big to handle by yourself, then that was when you had to turn that problem over to God. I did that a lot, turning my problems over to God, since I had plenty of problems. And that was what I did now. This was, without a doubt, a problem too big for me to handle on my own, hiding out with my uncle in this rickety old barn from a couple of strangers with bad intentions, and I dared to say—and as much as I admired and respected him—it was a problem too big for Uncle Theo to handle too.

I folded my hands in front of my face and closed my eyes and bowed my head where I was, behind that rack of weights, and I silently prayed. I prayed for God to rescue me and Uncle Theo from this mess and to send those bad guys away. I didn't pray for God to hurt them, because I didn't think that was appropriate to pray for, but just for God to make them disappear. I also prayed for the strength and the courage to get through this ordeal, and the same for Uncle Theo. And most importantly, I prayed to be able to see Mama and Ella Mae again, because at the moment, that didn't seem very likely, and I was rightly sorrowful that I might never see them, or my buddies, even Timbo. I prayed exceptionally hard, squeezing my fingers together and squinting my eyes tight. I ended my prayer how I normally did, by thanking God in advance because God always answered my prayers, maybe not precisely how I might have wanted or expected, but God always answered my prayers, that much I was certain of. Whenever I turned my problems over to God, I was confident they would be handled, even if I wasn't sure exactly how—or when.

Just then, as if a switch had been flipped, a powerful light shone from outside and flooded through every split and crevice of the barn. The shock of that nearly knocked Uncle Theo backwards, and me too, and we had to cover our eyes. It sent a couple field mice that were apparently hiding out with us scattering, yet it didn't do anything to silence the cicadas and, if anything, it caused the cicadas to chirp even louder. A jolt of adrenaline rushed through my veins, and my heartbeat upshifted into overdrive. Whatever this was, whatever we were waiting for, was about to happen.

"Send the boy out," a voice called out.

I recognized that voice, like rocks rattling around in the bottom of a rusted tin bucket. I feared that voice. That was the voice of that man from that car. He had returned. And he wanted me?

"You hear?" he repeated. "Send the boy out, and no one gets hurt."

"Get the hell off my property!" Uncle Theo shouted back.

"We're not here for you," the man replied. "You got yours already. We saw to that. Now all we want is the boy."

"You're not getting the boy!" Uncle Theo was adamant, and justifiably pissed, as he doublechecked to make sure his shotgun was loaded, breaking it open and confirming a shell in each chamber, and then closing the gun back up with a slap and a solemn, foreboding click.

"That's not for you to say," the man outside was just as adamant and seemed just as pissed. "His daddy wants him."

When I heard that, it nearly caused my body to buckle. "Pops?" I said, a spontaneous response, and I rose from my hiding position. "Is Pops out there?"

"Your father's not out there, Rhett," Uncle Theo answered, his back to me, still focused to the front. "It's a trick. Now just stay put."

"But—"

"I mean it!" Uncle Theo whipped around, casting me a glower that warned me not to dare challenge him on this. "Stay put, I said."

There was a momentary lull before the man outside continued. "How about your doggie? You want your doggie?" he asked in a mocking manner.

That got Uncle Theo's attention straight away, and he turned to the front. He propped his gun against the wall and placed both hands around his face to stare closely through the knothole.

"Come on out here, and get your doggie," the man said.

Uncle Theo wavered, like he was weighing his choices, before gesturing for me to get down. Then, he picked up his shotgun and slowly slid the barn door open.

"Don't you try anything funny," Uncle Theo cautioned the man, poising his shotgun across his body.

The opened barn door revealed two men outside, standing in front of their car, that black sedan, with the high beams on such that I couldn't make out much else about them, just two silhouettes, except that one of the men was struggling to subdue Chekhov—who had a muzzle strapped over her snout—as she violently shook her head to rid herself of it.

"The boy for the dog," the man offered as his partner fought to get Chekhov under control. "One mutt for the other."

"I'll go," I said, rushing up beside Uncle Theo. "I don't mind. You can trade me for Chekhov. I owe you that."

"I told you to stay put," Uncle Theo scolded, but even as he did, I could recognize how worried he was, and that made me more scared.

"Ah...there he is," the man said upon seeing me, taking a step forward and grinning, not a happy grin, but a sinister grin. "We've had eyes on you, boy, ever since you boarded that bus in Louisville to come to this godforsaken place." He waved me over. "Come on," he said, "your daddy's looking forward to seeing you. You two have got a lot of catching up to do."

"Is Pops with you?" I asked, instinctively moving toward the man before Uncle Theo threw his hefty arm out against my chest to keep me from going any farther.

"You're not getting the boy," Uncle Theo told the man. "Now give me my dog." And then he called to Chekhov, "Chekhov! Here, girl."

Chekhov fought even harder to get loose, and that man was scarcely able to contain her.

"Shut up!" the man who was doing all the talking hollered at my uncle. "This isn't how that works. You're not a prosecutor anymore. You're not calling the shots. You're not making the deals. I am." He took a few more steps closer, and he reached into his suit jacket and pulled out a shiny handgun that he pointed in our direction, the rays from the moon catching the metal to make it sparkle. "This is the last time I'm gonna say this…" He breathed in deep as if Uncle Theo had gotten on his last nerve, and he commanded, his voice stern, menacing, "Give me the damn boy!"

At that instant, Chekhov broke free and shook off the muzzle and leaped at the man who had been holding her. He screamed for help, a disturbing shriek, as Chekhov proceeded to maul him something brutal, this unbridled, ruthless onslaught. She had devolved into a wild animal, this enraged beast, and there was no question that she was going to kill this man, to tear every strip of flesh from his bone. The other man pivoted from where he had his gun trained on us and fired a shot, point-blank, that dropped Chekhov in a heavy heap with a yelp and a heartbreaking whimper, and then, her movement ceased.

"No!" Uncle Theo exclaimed and discharged both barrels of his shotgun with an explosion that reverberated inside the barn, rattling the walls. It propelled me sideways, causing me to lose my balance. Disoriented and confused, with a single high-pitched ringing in my ears—no other noise, not even the cicadas, just that single high-pitched ringing—I stumbled to stay upright. I couldn't tell who Uncle Theo had shot, if he had shot one man, both of the men, or what. I couldn't believe he had shot that gun. This was too much for me to take in, and for a fleeting instant, it was as if I had left my body and was watching this safely from the rafters. But I was snapped back with a harsh tug on the collar of my t-shirt, Uncle Theo grabbing me and dragging me through the barn and out the back door.

I staggered to my feet and steadied myself, and Uncle Theo and I tore off out of there, out of the barn and across the yard, not knowing who or what or if anyone was chasing after us. We just ran, Uncle Theo clutching at my arm with one hand and at his shotgun with the other, a trail of smoke streaming from the barrel. We just ran across the yard and disappeared into the garden, not caring where we went in there or what we stepped on, trampling through the neatly arranged rows of lettuce and carrots and all those strawberries, charging through the winding vines of tomatoes, mowing over the stalks of corn. We just ran—without looking behind—as fast as we could, or as fast as I could, as Uncle Theo urged me to keep up with him and I wasn't as physically fit as he was. For a person his age, and with what he had been through, he was in a lot better shape than me.

I was huffing and puffing and choking in air, my legs wobbly and my arms flailing, trying not to trip and fall. It had to have been the ugliest run ever; no style points, for sure. But I was giving it my all to maintain this pace that Uncle Theo was setting. We just ran like that, with no regard for anything that stood in our way, squashing over and upturning everything that I had been dutifully tending to in this garden, as if none of it mattered anymore, and maybe it no longer did, just as long as Uncle Theo and I could get away. I didn't know what we were doing or where we were going or what the plan was, if there even was a plan at this point, and I didn't care. I just ran with Uncle Theo, treading through the garden, crushing and mashing over everything until we got to the other side. And that was where Uncle Theo slammed on the brakes, stopping us both. We had arrived to the edge of his part of the yard, where he spent his days cultivating his "crop." We were standing at the outskirts of his marijuana field.

"Okay," he said to me, breathing heavy, but not as heavy as I was. "We need to be careful here. *Very* careful, all right?" Uncle Theo emphasized. "You gotta follow me, *step-by-step*. Wherever you see me put my foot, that's where I want you to put your foot. The same exact. You got that? Capeesh?"

"Capeesh" in that instance meant that Uncle Theo didn't want me to wander onto one of his spear-tipped booby traps, and I surely didn't want that either. I nodded, and I understood, as I was regaining my hearing, though I hadn't yet caught my breath, and in my head, I was still trying to come to terms with what this was. "Capeesh," I repeated, winded.

Uncle Theo lingered on me for a few seconds to ascertain if I did get that, if it was "capeesh" for me, until he said, sounding only marginally convinced, "Okay, then," and he moved in front. "Remember, every step I take, you take. The same exact."

"Uh-huh, the same exact," I confirmed, concentrating on where Uncle Theo was walking, stooped forward to pay close attention to his feet.

Avoiding Uncle Theo's booby traps was difficult enough, but it proved to be an even greater challenge under these trying conditions, and with the height of these tall weeds blocking out the moonlight, forcing us to go at it blindly. Uncle Theo took it gradually, conscious with his pace, which helped. I centered myself in each of his steps, picking out the subtle indentation in the grass damp with dew, and I stuck my foot in the same exact spot, feeling even smaller and weaker than my uncle, as his footprints dwarfed mine. Still, I kept at it, determined, shoving aside the marijuana plants as we tramped and trudged and lumbered into the middle of the field. While I had caught my breath, I hardly breathed, too stressed, too nervous, too afraid to wind up on the wrong side of one of those spears, noticing a cluster of them peeking up out of the ground as I persevered, step by agonizing step, behind Uncle Theo.

I had to give my uncle credit: he must have had a mind like a steel trap to recall where each of his booby traps were to be able to navigate this course, which wasn't straight in the slightest but meandered about like a twisted river. There was neither rhyme nor reason to the zigzag path we were taking, but then again, I reckoned that was the point. With Uncle Theo's objective to keep poachers out, it was no doubt necessary to scatter the booby traps every which way, and he had done an exceptional job at that. There was no chance I could've figured this out on my own, and with the ground covering fresh and new this time of year and springing back to its original form nearly as soon as we passed over, there was no chance I would be able to find my way out of here on my own either. I just had to continue to trust Uncle Theo.

"Okay, here we are," he announced, as we eventually arrived into somewhat of a clearing, an empty pocket in the midst of these towering, wavering plants as if Uncle Theo had planned it like that, as if he had carved out this little safety zone in case he would ever need to flee to it, for an occasion such as this, as if this was something he had been anticipating. "Just be still," he told me. And when I didn't say anything, too overwhelmed to say anything or to even think of anything to say for once—and what was there for me to say anyway?—he asked, "You still doing okay?"

I nodded, and more or less lied, and replied, "Yep."

Uncle Theo turned to gaze out onto the area we had just come from, the barn outlined beyond the garden by the glimmering high beams of that car. He took out two more shotgun shells from the side pocket of his shorts and reloaded the gun. I watched him as he did this. He was so detached and unaffected that it was apparent he had done this before, and I realized there was still a lot I didn't know about my uncle. I wondered how often he had done this before and if he had ever shot anyone else, but then again, maybe I didn't want to know that, and I didn't. I settled in and considered our surroundings as we were concealed beneath the high weeds waiting for something to happen, with me hoping and praying that nothing would happen or, if it did, that nothing *bad* would happen.

To calm myself—and did I ever need to calm myself—I lifted my head and looked to the sky, staring up at the thousands of twinkling stars in the galaxies above. As I did, I once more pondered my life, how it could change in an instant, often in ways I would have never imagined. I surely would have never imagined being in this situation, standing in the middle of Uncle Theo's marijuana field, in the middle of the night, in the middle of nowhere, on the run from a couple of mean men who meant us harm. And yet, here I was. And oddly enough, this, too, made sense to me, for reasons I couldn't properly discern. It just seemed that, right now, this was where I needed to be.

It was reassuring in a way, to know that despite how wide the world was, I always ended up where I needed to be. And as preposterous as this chain of events might have seemed a year ago—or even just last week, or last night, or, really, presently—and as outrageous a scenario as this was, I still believed that everything was happening the way it was supposed to, some plan that I didn't have a hand in but that I was party to nonetheless. Just thinking that, and accepting it, helped me to relax somewhat, and that was all I could ask for at this moment: to just relax.

I stood out there, among the chorus of cicadas behaving as disconcerted as I felt, like a one-note, ominous concert, and the anonymous rustlings and scamperings of whatever other critters were milling about in the brush, remaining vigilant for anyone who might be coming up on us, uncertain if those men were still alive after Uncle Theo's shotgun blast or what kind of condition they were in. I thought about Mama and Ella Mae and my buddies. I tried to picture what they might be doing right now, probably tucked away safely in their beds and sound asleep, except for possibly Timbo, who might've been going through his old man's dresser. And if Pops really was out of prison, like that man seemed to say, and he was somewhere wanting to see me, then it could've been that he was staring up at these same galaxies of stars too, and maybe thinking of me. I had a bunch of emotions wrapped around the possibility of seeing Pops, shock and disarray and disbelief and still altogether fearful being at the forefront. And I still couldn't completely decide if I hated him or not. But if that was my fate, to meet up with Pops, then I would have to accept that as well.

I stood out there like that, thinking like that, about everything and nothing, until Uncle Theo interrupted my train of thought.

"Shush!" he said harshly, even though I wasn't talking or making noise nor had any intention to. "Someone's coming."

I looked in the direction that Uncle Theo was looking and noticed a light emerging from the barn, faint and weak in comparison to the high beams that were still glaring, but direct and distinct, hovering as if floating in the air, and moving toward us.

"Who is that?" I asked, which was a dumb question as I asked it, because how was Uncle Theo to know, other than it was one or

216

both of those men, but I asked it all the same.

Uncle Theo didn't respond. He just raised his shotgun, pointed it toward that light, and watched—we both did—as the light got brighter and closer.

"Olly olly oxen free!" a voice cried out after a couple minutes of us watching that light, that same voice, that same man Uncle Theo had shot at, and my heart sank, and my body tightened. "Come out, come out, wherever you are!"

Uncle Theo put a finger to his lips to signal for me to be quiet, which I already was and planned on being, with my eyes on the light, as the shape of that man in the distance grew nearer and came into focus. I saw that he was holding up his cell phone to use it to guide him.

"The reception out here in the sticks is for shit," the man complained, laboring and limping, and it was evident that Uncle Theo had shot him somewhere, though not enough to put him down, just enough to make him angry, angrier than he had been. "I said," he repeated louder, more rocks rattling around in the bottom of that rusted tin bucket, and he was definitely angrier than he had been, "come out, come out, wherever you are—the game's over!" As he spoke, as he walked, he angled the light back and forth to hunt for us in the darkness. "Nice garden you got here," he remarked as he appeared to be taking great pleasure in kicking over plants and stomping on our harvest. "What a shame to have to lose it all."

Watching that man go out of his way to destroy our garden was making me angry, though I didn't act on it, just hunched behind Uncle Theo, who was ready, with his shotgun aimed forward. I had my hands up around my ears, which were still ringing from the last shot, in case I would need to cover them should Uncle Theo fire again. I watched, uneasy and replete with apprehension, as the man, with his cell phone shining to find us, made his way through, and through, and then out of the garden.

"And what do we have here?" he said, sarcastic, pulling up. "Is this the famous marijuana field I've heard so much about?" He laughed, taunting. "You sure have come full circle, barrister: from putting away the drug dealers to becoming one yourself. Though"—he hesitated as he assessed the area—"not much of one, but still."

Uncle Theo was bristling, I could tell, every muscle on him taut and strained, but he remained reticent.

"The thing about these homegrown marijuana fields," the man went on, "is that very often, they'll be booby-trapped, usually with some sort of crude, makeshift device: sharpened sticks or strung up piano wire or the like, could even be bear traps." He stayed put and waved his light about, like he was contemplating his next move, and exhaled as if he was disappointed in something. "Well, I'm not gonna chance that, and I'm certainly not going to give you the satisfaction. I'm not some drunken rube who's going to stupidly fall for your shenanigans. Nope, nope, I think, what I'm going to do"—he held up his gun—"is to count to three, and if you don't send the boy out, then I'm just gonna start shooting into this field." He paused. "In which case, counselor, you better hope I shoot you first, because if you cause me to shoot the boy, his daddy'll do something worse to you than any bullet."

I could make out the glistening pistol in the man's hand, aimed in the general vicinity where we were, although it didn't seem like he had exactly located us. Uncle Theo reached his arm back around and pushed me farther behind him to use his own body to shield me. Then, he redirected his shotgun at the man.

"You understand, Rhett?" the man said, and it made me shutter to hear him call me by my name. "You got three seconds to come out, or I start shooting."

I glanced up at Uncle Theo, but he was unyielding, still concentrating ahead.

"One..." the man began, and waited for effect, and then, "Two..."

I huddled down while keeping a wary eye out. Uncle Theo's bicep flexed as he clutched the shotgun, pressed firmly against his shoulder.

After another few seconds, the man resumed his count. "And..." he said, stretching the word to build the anticipation. I braced myself, and I silently prayed as hard as I could for God to do something about this, for God to save us, because it seemed like Uncle Theo and I were plumb out of options.

But before the man could get to "three," he was aggressively struck from behind by something, some solid mass that had surged forth from the emptiness and upended him. The impact rocked the man such that he jerked awkwardly and landed forward with a wallop to the ground and a force that caused his whole body to convulse. Then, there was nothing, nothing from the man, nothing from anything, nothing at all, until, after a short interlude of stunned silence, a dog barked.

"Chekhov!" Uncle Theo yelled, and he received another bark in reply. "It's her," he told me excitedly, and he grasped my hand to lead me through the maze of booby traps, taking another circuitous path, different from how we had gone in. "Your footsteps in mine," he reminded me.

I nodded, and of course I remembered. I focused on the ground ahead, my modest footsteps in Uncle Theo's king-sized ones. We weaved our way in and around the marijuana plants and out of the field, to find Chekhov lying on her side, next to the body of that man who was face down with a bloodied stake protruding through his back, right between his shoulder blades. I gagged and it sickened me, and I spun away to see the condition Chekhov was in, her fur tangled and matted and splattered deep crimson, panting uncontrollably, her eyes closed.

"Oh no—Chekhov!" Uncle Theo rushed to her. "Rhett, we've got to get her to the house."

Uncle Theo set his gun aside as if it was useless to him now, and with any luck, it was. Then, he gingerly grabbed Chekhov by the front, and I took her by her back, and together, we hoisted her up: no easy feat, as she was a weighty dog. Moving in tandem, Uncle Theo and I hurried through the garden and around the barn and across the backyard into the house, through the kitchen door. Once inside, we gently set Chekhov down on the kitchen floor.

"Get the first aid kit from the bathroom," Uncle Theo directed as he ran the hot water in the sink and got several towels wet.

I went to do just as my uncle said, darting into the front room and down the hallway, when I was immediately halted by the smell of cigarette smoke. I whirled and saw somebody, a man, seated on the sofa, legs casually crossed, arms folded, with the rest of him obscured by a jagged shadow. The man pitched his head, pursed his lips, and blew the smoke high above him in a steady stream that gathered into a billowing cloud at the ceiling before gracefully dispersing. I had known a man who smoked his cigarettes just like that. And when he leaned into the light, I saw that it was Pops!

I couldn't move. I couldn't speak. I couldn't think. I couldn't do anything other than stare at him. It was Pops.

"Rhett, hurry! I need that first aid kit," Uncle Theo called out from the kitchen, but he might as well have been calling out into the night, because I couldn't respond, and what he was saying wasn't registering. "Rhett, what's going on?" he queried, curious, as there was still no response from me, walking into the front room, a wet towel in his hands, to find me confronted by Pops.

"Hello, Theodore." Pops greeted Uncle Theo with a disarming congeniality. "You're looking well. Very fit, all…buff. Those arms and, my God, all those tattoos. Subtle." He winked. "You could use a shave and a haircut, though."

Uncle Theo appeared stunned to see Pops, as stunned as I was. He turned to me, concerned. "You okay, Rhett?"

"I'm not here to give you any trouble," Pops said, dropping his cigarette with a sizzle into a partially empty can of one of Uncle Theo's beers on the coffee table, and then standing deliberately. "I only want my son, that's all. It's my right as a father."

"You lost your rights when I put you away," Uncle Theo countered. "What are you doing out, anyway?"

Pops smirked. "I was a model inmate. They let me out for good behavior."

"Unlikely," Uncle Theo muttered as he squared with Pops, hands on hips, taking him in, sizing him up, and I would've sworn that Uncle Theo was about to fight him. But then, he ran a hand through his messy hair, scratched the top of his head, and retracted. "I'm calling the sheriff," he said as he went over to his ancient landline and picked up the receiver.

"Nuh, uh, uh," Pops replied, coaxing Uncle Theo not to go any farther, slyly producing a handgun of his own—not as shiny as that other man's but certain to be just as lethal—and directing it at my uncle. "You just leave the sheriff be. This here's between me and my boy."

When Uncle Theo saw the gun, he sort of shrunk, more vexed than anything, and, resigned, he hung up the receiver. I caught him glancing over at the mantel, where the shotgun normally hung, except he had left it in the garden, and it was as if I could see that registering for Uncle Theo with a disappointment draping over him.

"Now, look here—" Uncle Theo started, undaunted.

"No, you look here," Pops interrupted and jabbed the gun at him. "This is none of your business. You've done enough as it is to cause all of this. Now, I'm taking my boy, and I'm leaving, and that's the end of it." Pops turned to me, with the gun still trained on Uncle Theo, and smiled as if that was going to make everything better. "Rhett, gather your belongings, and let's go. Just me and you, son. A real guys' day."

I just continued looking at Pops, not believing that I was looking at Pops, in front of me, in the flesh. And as much as I was looking at him, maybe I wasn't looking at him either, because he wasn't really Pops, at least not the Pops I knew when I was four or so and he was everything to me: the Pops who would let me stay up late and watch black-and-white shoot-'em-up movies with him, or who took me to the circus, or who would wrestle with me some evenings after dinner when he wasn't too tired from work, scooting the furniture out of the way in the living room to make space so that we could really go at it, as much as a little kid like me could go at it with a man of Pops's size—not as big as Uncle Theo but he was a giant to me then—with him letting me pin him for the count every time. This man, older, wrinkled, gray, and pudgy around the middle, might have technically been Pops, but he wasn't my Pops, not the Pops I would picture sitting quietly and gazing up at the same stars at night as I did. And it went beyond just the physical. It was intangible. It was something about him on the inside. This man was different. This man had changed. I had no idea who this man was. And while it pained me to my core to arrive at this conclusion, I acknowledged—and I accepted—that this man wasn't my Pops anymore. And I didn't much care for him.

"C'mon, now," he said, motioning me to go with a flick of his hand that held the pistol, while still keeping Uncle Theo at bay. "Hurry up and pack a bag. Time's a wasting. We got places to go, things to do. We got a lot of catching up, me and you."

I remained there and just stared at him because I didn't know what else to do. I didn't feel I was capable of doing anything else until I recovered enough from where I had been immobilized at the initial sight of him. My eyes were teary, and I got choked up as I told Pops, "No."

"No?" Pops clearly wasn't expecting that, nor did he appreciate it, twisting his face and angling his head. "What do you mean, 'no'?"

"I mean"—and I swallowed hard—"I can't go with you, Pops." And I couldn't go with Pops. It didn't seem right, because Pops didn't seem right, none of this did. And then, I said something that I never would have thought I'd ever say to Pops, all those times after he had up and left when I longed for nothing more than for him to come back, "I think it's best if you just up and leave."

Pops's eyes widened, and his jaw dropped, and he became irate as he admonished me, "You don't talk to your daddy that way." He lowered his gun and bent forward at me. "What's gotten into you?" He swung back toward Uncle Theo, the gun raised at him. "What have you done to my boy, you shyster? You turn him against me, like you turned everyone else against me? It wasn't bad enough you had to take my freedom, break up my family? Now, you gotta take my son?"

"Uncle Theo didn't do nothing," I spoke up without planning on it, and it just came out, with this powerful need to rise to my uncle's defense. "This here's my decision, and mine alone. And I ain't going with you. I can't. I won't. I ain't! I don't even know you no more." I stomped with both feet and emphatically pointed to the floorboards beneath me. "This here is where I belong. With Uncle Theo."

"Ha!" Pops laughed, only it wasn't a laugh, it was spiteful. "With this loser?" Spittle spewed from Pops he was so upset, glaring at me but continuing to direct his gun—and stab it in the air with his words—at Uncle Theo. "This is where you want to be? With this has-been, this never-was, this coward who ran off to these hills when the real world got too tough for him? Your uncle is nothing but some low-level, two-bit pot dealer, with *no guts*," which he stressed with a snicker for Uncle Theo, and followed with, "literally."

I found that to be flat-out mean and wholly uncalled for and not one bit fair to Uncle Theo, not fair to him at all, what with Pops being responsible for that. It made me feel bad for Uncle Theo, and it just had me convinced that this wasn't Pops, and I was right in my decision to not want to go with him. Not only that, but I was quickly resenting Pops for being here in the first place, showing up like this out of the blue and thinking he could just strut on in and steal me away from the one place I belonged. For all of the people and all the situations I had been rejected from in my life, now it was finally my turn to do the rejecting. I could feel my temperature rising, and my cheeks got hot, and my pulse skipped and revved. I had this hatred that was bubbling to the surface and an all-encompassing desire to hurt Pops the way that he had hurt me and *my* family.

Without giving it any more thought, nary a thought at all, I dove at Pops, and perhaps my exercising in Uncle Theo's home gym was paying off because I felt strong and invincible, and I wasn't afraid. I felt nothing but this impulse to go after Pops. I grabbed at his gun with both of my hands to wrench it upward and away from how he had it aimed at Uncle Theo. As I did, it went off with a blast, jostling the both of us, with an instantaneous and penetrating burning to my hands and through my fingers like they were on fire.

"Freeze!"

The front door exploded open like a bomb had gone off, splinters of wood flying everywhere, and these men rushed in, several of them, storming into Uncle Theo's house, hollering and shouting and carrying on. It was Sheriff Hank, with his deputies who promptly tackled Pops. It happened so fast, I couldn't react, but once I understood what was going on, I noticed that I had blood on my hands.

"I got you, bud," Uncle Theo said as he swooped to my side and wrapped my hands in the towel.

"You okay, Rhett?" Sheriff Hank squatted beside me.

"Mm-hmm," was all I could muster as I watched the deputies wrestle Pops into submission.

"Had a report that Rhett's daddy skipped out on his parole," Sheriff Hank said to Uncle Theo, "and his mama tipped off KSP that he might be headed this way. Reckon she was right."

"Mama," I said, although in the state I was in, I couldn't be positive if I had said it or if I might've just thought it, but either way, it was comforting, just knowing that Mama was watching out for me.

"Your mother doesn't take shit from anyone, Rhett," Uncle Theo said. "You and I both know that."

"Yes, sir," I replied with something of a laugh, and I was already feeling better, even while the towel was becoming soaked with my blood.

"We need to have someone look at that," Sheriff Hank told me, taking his radio out.

"And Chekhov's down, in the kitchen," Uncle Theo added. "She's in bad shape. She needs help." And then, as almost an afterthought, "Oh, and you'll find a couple of his henchmen"—Uncle Theo nodded toward Pops—"out back. But no rush on them."

"I leave my post out here for one minute…" Sheriff Hank got up, acting like he was annoyed, and proceeded to take charge. "We got it covered."

Sheriff Hank called for an ambulance, then instructed one of his deputies to tend to Chekhov, while he stood guard over Pops as the other deputies pulled him to his feet. Pops had stopped struggling, admitting defeat. While he was being escorted out, his hands cuffed behind his back, Pops hesitated at the doorway, and he glanced over at me, his demeanor drastically softened.

"I never intended it to be like this, Rhett," Pops said, contrite, and he seemed to mean it, and for a split-second, I spotted the Pops I remembered. "I wanted to take care of you. I love you, son. I always have."

Before I could respond, the deputies yanked Pops from the house and to the awaiting squad car out front, the flashing red lights illuminating the entire yard. Uncle Theo led me to the couch and kept hold of the towel on my hands until the paramedics arrived. He sat by me the whole time as they cleaned and dressed my wounds, rubbing me on the back and telling me that everything would be all right. I was getting faint, clinging to consciousness, but I fixed on Uncle Theo and what he was saying, those words and how he said them, over and over. He just kept telling me that everything would be all right. And I believed him, because I trusted my uncle, and I always would.

EPILOGUE

Uncle Theo and I were seated at the table having dinner, something called a grouse, which resembled a skinny chicken you would find wandering out in the woods, which was basically everything that Uncle Theo cooked: something that someone found wandering out in the woods. Gus and Lucretia, some of Uncle Theo's other neighbors, had gotten this on a hunt to exchange for my uncle's "crop." It was tasty enough, especially how Uncle Theo fixed it, with his gourmet chef skills. My uncle could probably make an old leather shoe appetizing. He had roasted this grouse sprinkled with various herbs and spices—I couldn't pronounce the names of half of them— and served it over a bed of wild rice, with mushrooms he had foraged and butternut squash from the garden, something new he was trying to grow, and he was doing a fine job of it, like most of what he grew. Uncle Theo was drinking a beer as usual and also, as usual, and I was none too happy about it still, I was drinking milk. I had had about enough of drinking milk and I decided right then and there that it was high time I had a beer. After all, I deserved it.

"Hey, Uncle Theo," I started, not entirely sure how I was going to go about this, and then just winging it, figuring that the direct approach would be best, "how 'bout you let me drink a beer with dinner for once?"

Uncle Theo finished chewing, and he swallowed, and he wiped

his mouth with his napkin, and then he looked up at me from his plate.

"Sure," he said without hesitating, and shifted as if he was going to get up and go to the kitchen to fetch me a cold one, which nearly bowled me over, for while that was certainly the answer I was hoping for, it wasn't what I expected, and it made me question why I hadn't asked him for a beer sooner. But right as he was about to rise from his chair, he held off. "Oh," Uncle Theo added, a quizzical expression, "you are twenty-one, aren't you?"

I had a chuckle at that, not necessarily because I thought it was funny, but because I thought Uncle Theo was joking. But when he didn't crack, I realized, sadly, that he was being serious.

"Well, um…no," I answered, sheepish. "You know I ain't."

"Yeah, I didn't think you were," he said as he got comfortable in his chair and picked up his fork and knife to resume eating. "But could've been we'd had a time jump and you were twenty-one all of a sudden, because things like that can occur. I've read about them."

I watched as Uncle Theo returned to his grouse, delicately slicing a piece and running it through the wild rice with his fork, to get a mouthful of grouse and wild rice together in one bite, indicating to me that that was that, and the end of the discussion—not that there had been much of a discussion—and I wouldn't be getting a beer for dinner, not this evening anyway, and it seemed not until I turned twenty-one, which was disappointing, to say the least.

"My goodness," I said as I went back to eating and pretending to be bothered by that, "just one little beer won't hurt nothing."

"When the State says you can have a beer, then I'll be more than happy to drink a beer with you, Rhett. In fact,"—Uncle Theo raised his glass for emphasis, or just to rub it in, and took a long, slow, satisfying swig—"I can't wait to share a beer with you. But until that day, you won't be engaging in any underage drinking, not on my watch, not when you're in my charge."

I shrugged and kind of smiled, and I got it as we ate the rest of our dinner without much more talking, like we did, just utensils clinking against plates, chews and swallows, Chekhov begging for table scraps as she always did, only she wasn't allowed to be doing that anymore. Uncle Theo needed to be careful with what food he gave her after that bad man shot her; got her right in the belly. It was touch and go there for a while, and they had to send her off to some fancy animal hospital in Ashland. We weren't sure if Chekhov was going to make it. Uncle Theo was really torn up over that, we both were. But she pulled through. She was one tough dog, our guard dog, and our best friend. Chekhov had to be on a special diet from now on, and she hadn't yet come to accept that.

I still carried the scars on the inside of my hands from where the bullet from Pops's gun nicked me and I got burned by the flash. But I didn't mind it. I recalled once, Timbo came to school with a scab on his elbow he claimed he got from skateboarding and boasted about how he couldn't wait for it to scar over because he said that "chicks dig scars." I wasn't rightly aware of that being true, hadn't had the opportunity to test that theory out for myself, but maybe someday I would, perhaps whenever Big Ol' Tom's daughter, Paula, came back around and I didn't get so tongue-tied and twisted in her presence. Lefty and Slim thought it was cool, though, and Sheriff Hank called me a "real trooper," and PJ let me sit in the driver's seat of his Camaro and gun the engine while it was parked in the driveway, so I reckoned, for now, that would have to do. I was just grateful that that was the extent of my injuries from that scary night that now seemed so long ago.

It was already September—and Uncle Theo was right when he would complain about time just flying by—and a new school year had gotten underway. I was continuing my lessons with Uncle Theo. I had done so well on my grades last semester that Mama agreed to let him continue homeschooling me as long as he didn't mind, and he said he didn't. Uncle Theo told Mama he could use the help around here anyway, out in the garden and whatnot, and I wholeheartedly agreed. I had a sneaking suspicion that Uncle Theo needed me about as much as I needed him, only he wasn't one to admit something like that, and I wasn't about to press him on it. But I could just sort of tell.

I was going to see Mama and Ella Mae before long, as they were planning on coming up for Thanksgiving. Mama said she would "reassess the situation" then, and I didn't fully understand what that meant other than I would get to live with Uncle Theo a bit longer, at least through the fall semester, and I was excited. He already promised to take me turkey hunting. It would be good to see Mama and Ella Mae, and I definitely still missed them, no question, but when I was packing my belongings at the end of the summer, thinking I would have to leave Uncle Theo, I had a sinking feeling, a melancholy I hadn't known since maybe when Pops up and left, that I might miss my uncle more. And, of course, Chekhov too.

Pops was locked up for violating his parole, and a bunch of other charges they tacked on resulting from all that went on with him and his goons. He was housed at the penitentiary in West Liberty, not that far from here, and the closest we had lived to one another in a while, but it seemed like a world away. He had reached out, called the landline once, but Uncle Theo didn't put the call through, wouldn't accept the charges, and Pops had sent me a letter that I hadn't read. I saw the return address and just stuffed it away in the bottom of my dresser drawer, under my Bible. I wasn't ready to read that letter. Maybe I would at some point, or maybe I wouldn't. But I couldn't presently say. Pops had a lot of sorting out to do with his life, and so did I with mine.

It struck me as kind of funny, and sort of strange, how things turned out. One moment, you were comfortable one place, and the next, you were comfortable someplace else, someplace entirely different, someplace you hadn't even thought of before, with people you hadn't really known. I hardly knew my uncle before I got here, only from his cards and gifts over the years and what little I had remembered about him when I was just a kid. He kept to himself, some would say he was a recluse, and by all accounts, that was how he preferred it—but I knew him better than that. He couldn't fool me.

For extra credit in my English Composition class, I had commenced to writing my own memoirs, and I did so nightly, and routinely, in my bedroom while Uncle Theo continued to work on his out at the front table. As I considered the events of this past year, it occurred to me that with our resilience and our self-reliance and our sense of gratitude—not to mention our love of gardening—the thing about my uncle was that we had an awful lot in common, and I hoped to be just like him one day.

ACKNOWLEDGMENTS

Many thanks to…

Joni and Vern, and everyone else at BHC Press, for their hard work and support in the publication of the First Edition of *The Thing About My Uncle*—and wishing you all the best in your future endeavors!

Isabelle, my editor, for her attention to detail (I never knew that cicadas didn't chirp at night unless the moon was "exceptionally bright").

And, of course, my wife, Christine, for encouraging me to pursue my passion for writing.

ABOUT THE AUTHOR

Peter J. Stavros is a writer and attorney. His work has been featured in anthologies, newspapers, and magazines, including *The Saturday Evening Post*, *The Boston Globe Magazine* and *Chicken Soup for the Soul*. He is also the author of three short story collections and a novella. *The Thing About My Uncle* is his debut novel. Originally from Queens, New York, he now lives in Louisville, Kentucky with his wife and their cheese-stealing rescue Golden Retriever, Molly. You can find out more about Peter at www.peterjstavros.com and follow on X/Twitter and Instagram @peterjstavros.

ALSO BY THE AUTHOR

Three in the Morning and You Don't Smoke Anymore

(Mostly) True Tales From Birchmont Village

Tryouts

All The Things She Says

EPILOGUE 2

I was careening down Route 60 on my bike, speeding on the berm, hugging the guardrail—even though Uncle Theo had warned me against doing that in case a coal truck came rumbling through and might sideswipe me. But there weren't many trucks out on the road at this time of day, early afternoon, and I thought it best to chance it because this was the quickest way to the house and I had some precious cargo stashed in my backpack: a sack of sloppy joes. I was returning from that diner out at the gas station, having dropped off something from Uncle Theo, a package wrapped in plastic and brown paper. Uncle Theo told me not to open it, something about "plausible deniability." I had nary a clue what that meant, but when I questioned him, Uncle Theo said I would learn about it at law school, along with his usual caveat that he wouldn't wish law school on anyone. I gathered that it was just some of Uncle Theo's "crop," though which particular kind of crop apparently wasn't something my uncle wanted me to know, plausible deniability or whatever, or "capeesh" as I had told him. In exchange for that delivery, I was given enough sloppy joes to feed us for a week, which I was intending to eat just as soon as I could— my mouth watering just at the mere thought of that—to maybe sneak a couple before Uncle Theo even realized I was home.

However, as I was riding, I spotted something in the distance. When I got closer, I saw that it was a car that had pulled over, something expensive, like a BMW, and there was a person standing outside of it. I slowed, not knowing what I was coming upon. At first, with the way the man was dressed, not in jeans and flannel and a ball cap like most of the men around these parts but in pleated slacks and a starched button-down, kind of like what Mama used to make me wear whenever she would drag me to church, only a lot nicer, definitely not Walmart, I feared it could have been another one of Pops' goons. To the best of my knowledge, Sheriff Hank and his deputies had rounded up all of those hooligans, but they were a crafty lot so who knew. Yet when I got nearer, he didn't seem like one of those hardened criminals; he was more just like some businessman, middle-aged with graying and thinning hair, and pudgy. But what really struck me about the man was that he appeared to be in some serious distress.

This man was leaned up against the Cole's Landing exit sign, bent over, throwing up, puking a storm, really blowing chunks— coughing and spitting and convulsing. I ceased proceeding any further so that none of that noxious spittle wafted onto me from the breeze of the passing cars. I wasn't sure what was wrong with this man, but I reckoned I had better find out in case he required assistance, since that was how I had been raised.

"You okay, Mister?" I asked him, as I dismounted my bike and cautiously walked over, though still not too close.

The man stiffened, caught off guard, like he hadn't expected anyone else to be out here. He tried to compose himself, hastily wiping his mouth with the back of his hand and then pushing his hair, which was either sweaty or just greasy from styling gel, out of his face.

"I'm, um ... uh," he kind of mumbled, giving me the onceover. "Yeah, I'm, uh ... okay. Just an upset stomach or something. I dunno . . ." his voice trailed off.

"You need something to drink?" I asked, pulling the plastic water bottle off my bike and offering it to him. "It's Gatorade—the blue flavor."

The man glanced down at my water bottle, as if contemplating whether or not to take it, before declining with a wave and telling me,

"That's okay, I got water in the car."

"Where you headed?" I asked him, not intending to pry but I figured that a businessman with such a fancy car might be going someplace intriguing.

"Cole's Landing," he answered.

"Cole's Landing?" I repeated, surprised, nearly floored by that response, which the man could obviously tell.

"Yeah," he said, defensive. "Why?"

"Oh, no reason," I said, more measured. "It's just that most folks seem to be wanting to get out of Cole's Landing. Ain't never come upon a person trying to get in."

"Well," he said, almost apologizing, "I've got family there. I'm just going to ... recharge and refresh." He swallowed hard. "Just to get away from everything for a while."

"Cole's Landing is definitely the place to go to get away from everything," I told him, "really anywhere in these sticks."

"Are you from here?" he asked me.

"Kinda," I answered. "My uncle lives down one of these hollers. And I've been staying with him. He's schooling me, and I'm helping him with his gardening."

"Ah, I see," the man said, although to me it didn't seem like he did, about much of anything. And he still looked in distress, although he had stopped puking, but he just looked a bit off kilter. I didn't say anything about that to him, though, because it wouldn't have been polite.

We stood there for a few seconds, each of us sort of sizing the other up, with not really much else to say after that.

"Okay, then," I spoke up. "Maybe, I'll see ya around. My uncle and I go into Cole's Landing every so often, the town ain't that big. I heard they just got some state-of-the-art gym. Are you fixin' to move there?"

"Gosh, no," the man was swift to reply, "just visiting for a few days." And again, he told me, with another hard swallow. "Recharge and refresh."

"Well, good luck that with," I said, and I meant it because it just seemed to me like that man could use all the luck he could get.

"You too," he said, which didn't quite make sense to me in that context, but he must've had other things on his mind.

I mounted my bike, checked to make sure my backpack was securely strapped on, and headed toward Uncle Theo's as fast as I could before the coal trucks started clogging up the road on their overnight routes and also so that I could commence to dining on some delicious sloppy joes. But on that whole ride, I just kept thinking about that man, curious as to what was really going on with him, and hoping that he would be all right, that whatever it was, he would figure it out.

www.ingramcontent.com/pod-product-compliance
Lightning Source LLC
Chambersburg PA
CBHW051945220626
47052CB00004B/803